INAGEHI

Jack Cady

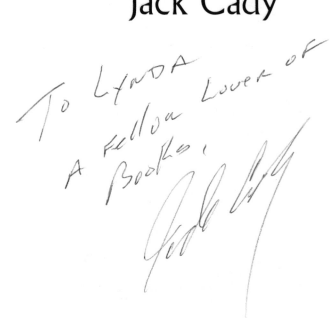

To Lynda
A fellow Lover of
Books,

Broken Moon Press · Seattle

Printed in the United States of America.

10 9 8 7 6 5 4 3 2 1

ISBN 0-913089-50-8
Library of Congress Catalog Card Number 93-71564

Author photo copyright © 1992 by Ken Dunmire. Used by permission.

Project editor: Lesley Link
Copy editor: Paula Ladenburg
Text preparation
and proofreading by: Melissa Shaw and Brandy K. Denisco

Broken Moon Press
Post Office Box 24585
Seattle, Washington 98124-0585 USA

For Carol,
who has walked with me in sacred places

He hath showed thee, O man,
what *is* good; and what doth the
Lord require of thee, but to do
justly, and to love mercy, and to
walk humbly with thy God?

Micah 6:8

Author's Note

Spoken Cherokee is a warm and musical language containing soft gutterals. The traditional language probably formed when people still wore lip pendants, because Cherokee is largely spoken without closing the lips. It's possible to get some hint of the sound by pronouncing a few Cherokee words open-mouthed:

INAGEHI (In *naw* geh hee) A person who lives alone in the wilderness.

NUNNEHI (*Nun* neh hee) A tribe living near the Cherokee, and believed by some to be mythical.

GIGA (*Gee* gaw) Red.

SIKONEGA GISQWA (See *cone* ee kaw *geese* quaw) Bluebird.

OOJO-NIDA (Oh ho *neee* da) Rattlesnake.

MOLLA Cherokee name. In English it would be Mary or Molly. It is pronounced as much with an "O" or "W" sound as with an "M."

As you can see, pronunciations are approximate. It is quite difficult to bring sounds of one language into sounds of another.

The small tale in Chapter 22 is taken complete from *Nineteenth Annual Report to the Director of the Bureau of American Ethnology, 1900*, by James Mooney.

Chapter 1

FAITH was the thunder, Hope was the wind, and Charity the bright robes of lightning that thunder wore. Currents of all three raged as Harriette peered through a second-floor window of Winston's YWCA. Brick streets ran dark with storm. Her hands beckoned to the approach of high-striding lightning, and her eyes cared only for rain.

Harriette, or Named By Thunder, or Tree's Friend—depending, she thought, on the heart of storms or on what name you signed on the YWCA register—heard running feet of teenage girls in the hallway. The girls hollered, laughed, but stayed where no windows could shatter from the storm. They seemed like voices of spirits subdued by thunder—thunder—thunder—boom and shock.

The lords of Winston-Salem, she thought, the fine white folk with fine Moravian eyes, were taking a shake along those storm-beaten streets. Houses trembled as shocks of broken air battered trees and buildings, while electricity and ozone blew brilliance and scent across the stenchy towns. Back of town, negroes watched roofs of shacks leak, peel, sail away in the wind. The storm swept like the rush of a flooded stream. A cleaning job went on out there, a purification, and the lords of Winston-Salem were not going to like that a bit.

The streets lighted in a great sheet of white and electric blue. Immediate thunder shook the old brick building, while wind bowed the glass inward. It seemed the window would have to shatter. Debris of paper and leaves blew above the storm-black streets like butterflies tossed by an enormous fan.

The next lightning came rolling on a whickering of other lightnings: like a quick-stepping ladder of light. The small room turned sheer with brilliance. Lightning and thunder were one, the door rattled, furniture shook, and she felt pinioned in a great dimension of light. She felt two-dimensional, like photo film etched by blue and white flashes, but three-dimensional if the storm was going to kill her. The building shook, seemed to be cracking. Earthquakes must be this way. Wagnerian music tried to explain this. In the halls childish voices stopped with fear. Those children out there were children of North Carolina, children accustomed to storms; but no storm was supposed to be this way.

When the next lightning flashed, the crack of thunder had moved one second away, the illumination interpenetrating with the approaching bulk of dark rain; and rain arrived in a flood.

Gutters instantly overran; water rose in black streets, rushing beneath blue and white flashes. Harriette turned from the window, muttering, the voice of a dead mother in her thoughts, her dead mother's Bible in her mind.

"And when they say unto you, Seek unto them that have familiar spirits, and unto wizards that peep, and that mutter; should not a people seek unto their God?"

Thunder, shock, but moving away now as rain obscured the window.

"I'll take the familiar spirits. I'll take the wizards," she told herself in trembling tones. "What I'd actually take is a fresh cup of coffee."

From the hallway the girls resumed their roistering as the storm moved toward the outskirts of town. Those kids had been here for two days now. They had not come on a school outing, because school would not start for a few more days. She knew, because she taught in the schools. Not this fall, though, she told herself. She had already announced to the schools that she would not work this fall.

For herself, she had stayed in this small room for five days, walking with as much dignity as possible each time she passed the woman at the front desk. The YWCA could not refuse to room you if your skin was a bit bright, your nose a little hooked; but they could let you know that the only good Indian was a dead one. In the stores, when clerks assumed their nigger attitudes, you asked for the manager and demanded an apology.

It was, all in all, a pain in the neck. The pain and trouble in the heart were something else.

Her mother, this day, was one month dead; and her mother's house stood silent back in the North Carolina hills.

Her mother with a failed heart, and age sixty did not seem a reasonable time for an otherwise healthy woman to suffer two days in a country hospital, then die.

Her father, this year, was seven years dead.

Her grandmother, this year, was twenty-four years dead.

She, although she did not think of it, was thirty years old and ridden by more mysteries than a detective might see in a lifetime.

The rain slacked after the initial flood. She looked into misty, smoking streets which had lain so sun-brightened and hot before the storm. Mist rose like spirits, and her frustration seemed nebulous as the mist. In another day, possibly two, she would leave this place.

She had come to see an attorney concerning her mother's will. She would leave here, returning to the hills with dark knowledge that she, as yet, could not comprehend belonged to her.

Always, she had been told, her father died in a logging accident.

Now, returning to those hills, she returned with the knowledge that he had been murdered. Her mother lived and died holding that secret. She, Harriette, was powerless.

Chapter 2

WHEN it comes to telling stories, the Apostle Luke is my favorite. He starts his Bible-book by saying he has "perfect understanding" and I like that in a story-teller—so I, Janet Scott, will start the same. I do it because, in these North Carolina hills, there are Cherokee tales immemorial; and, since Indians have the same respect for facts as everybody else, a good ninety percent range between flim-flam and chipmunk chatter.

Some of the nearly true stories are about a woman walking naked through a storm while carrying lightning in her fingers. Those stories almost get it right. The stories rise from a time when these mountains were alive with both loveliness and murder; a time when the Cherokee code of vengeance seemed to stalk the valleys. People were angry with a young woman named Harriette. They were afraid of an old woman named Molla. I was only a girl at the time, but a smart one. I had good child-sense and a tape-recorder memory.

Even as a girl I knew a lot about Indian ways to power. I knew how to be straight-forward, and knew a lot about storms. Then, growing up and sometimes getting ambushed by life, I learned how pain can destroy all power when someone you love gets killed; and, since there is a part of me in the drama that follows, I'll tell a little about that now.

Young girls grow up. Some learn about faithfulness and trust, some even get to go to college, and some get married. I did all of those while loving the boy/man who would become my husband. Davey was a child, and then a man, of both the times and North Carolina. We were both raised in this Cherokee world where the work of men and women has always been less separated than in the larger world. The ideas of "think like a woman" or "think like a man" are white ideas.

Davey and I just thought like ourselves. I have studied the way we thought, because for all our lives the subjects of history and religion would not leave us alone. Only pieces of those subjects came from the Cherokee. A lot of them came from the times, and from North Carolina.

Davey died young, in a war. I don't talk about it much because the pain caused by his death is too pure, even now, and deserves its privacy. After he died I spent time wandering in classrooms and libraries. Then I wandered the streets and neighborhoods of cities. Then I came back home to wander the trails of these harmed but perpetual forests.

Harriette was following her own trail, and sometimes we met at branchings. After our separate excursions into pain, then into silence, Harriette's trail, and mine, gradually came together. We now live in a cabin in the high forest, and we have not sought power, but we have it. That is how our story ends.

But its beginning is different. At the beginning of the story our North Carolina world was a world of small farms and subsistence economy. Men ran that world and women sometimes ran the men. The great social movements of the 1960s and '70s were still in the future. Girls might be star-struck by movie actresses, but they did not hear of female executives because, for all intents and purposes, there were none. It was a different time, and we behaved in different ways; and from what I've seen lately, some of those ways were maybe not so bad.

And in the beginning we had no idea that Harriette would even have a story. She was pretty timid as a young woman, and only gradually gathered strength and enormous power. We had even less an idea that she would be unable to tell her story; so this is where I am needed. Harriette's story is not the melodrama of film or the bathos of television. She was witness to a tragedy as authentic as ancient Greece, and as dark as an Elizabethan play. Like all great tragedies, it requires a chorus.

I am the chorus. I introduce the drama and take a small part—occasionally I will appear and you will recognize me—but this is Harriette's story. And I will close the drama because that is what the chorus does in tragedy.

My main explanation is that Harriette cannot tell the story because some of her experiences cannot be put into words. The history of mysticism teaches that big experiences must be explained by the way a person lives. Thus, Harriette explains by living, and I explain with words.

Before coming to this cabin Harriette lived in a house built by her father before he was killed. Then her mother died, and that is really what caused Harriette's story to begin. The story starts at the YWCA in Winston-Salem, in the middle of a thunder storm. At the time, August, 1957, she is not prepared to like anything or anybody. The Apostle Luke would likely understand.

Chapter 3

S HE, Harriette, stood in that YWCA listening to the diminishing storm and unable to comprehend murder. She would soon learn more about that murder. For the moment, though, I think of her as she must have been in those days.

She was romantic, although her way would lead toward the shadowed side of romance. At that time, confronting a fresh death, a past that spelled a cold-blooded murder, and a future bound to contain struggle, she still wore conventional dreams.

There is genuine innocence in a diary she kept.

One entry goes this way:

I dreamed I was a young girl standing in a sunlit street. There were store fronts and reflecting concrete pavement. A lovely boy stood beside me, and as I embraced him he ran his hand through my hair. I held him and did not hold him, searching for touch in sunlight and radiance, but he turned and hurried through a nearby doorway, smiling and looking back. A sign read Youth Group Meets Tonight, and, entering the darkness because suddenly it was night, I walked an unlit hall filled with blues music from a sax, entering finally an equally long room full of bright electric light. The room filled with shadows like people, and the shadows played at games. Across the room was the boy, playing table tennis with a shadow of himself, laughing as the small white ball bounced back and forth across the green table beneath lights, sometimes getting away and passing through one of the other shadows, pinging and ponging carelessly across the room.

As I started toward him a shadow hesitated before me, seriously stopping in the middle of all the sporting and cavorting to ask, "Girl, excuse you, girl, but have you maybe come in the wrong door?," and I excused myself while despising both myself and the shadow, and admitted I probably had.

Her names were a problem for her. Her Christian name followed a small history of the Cherokee, being the same as a famous woman, Harriette Gold, New England Puritan, loved wife of Elias Boudinot.

Boudinot's Cherokee name was The Buck. He was full-blood, an Indian lad transshipped through the Foreign Mission school at Cornwall, Connecticut, from which he returned to become a leader of his people. This occurred in the late eighteenth century, and in the nineteenth he would die on June 22, 1839, from a single stab in the back, and seven hatchet wounds in the head.

Boudinot was considered by some to have been a traitor. A group of full-bloods invoked the ancient Cherokee laws of vengeance and killed Boudinot with a knife and hatchets.

Harriette Johnson held the Cherokee name of Named By Thunder, for Harriette was born during an August storm. This also followed an old Cherokee custom. Female babies often held names carrying the shape of violence—Came With Thunder, Came With War, War Girl, and so forth.

Her true name as she discovered it was Tree's Friend, of which more later, since it was as Harriette Johnson that she had, for the second time, visited the attorney Alan in Winston-Salem.

Clear skies and fantastic summer-city heat had surrounded her as she walked a single flight of stairs to the law offices of Judge Alan. She had walked these steps with her mother, but that was years ago. Judge Alan had been her father's friend, her mother's friend, and there seemed no other reason except friendship for her parents to drive to Winston-Salem for legal matters. Asheville was much closer to their home.

Alan was tall, gray-haired, and perhaps one-eighth blood, which in his case made his face look like a face she would be unsurprised to find carved on a mountain. Heavy brows rode above eyes surrounded by a cross-hatching of wrinkles, the eyes as clear as a child's. He stood when she entered.

"Difficult times."

"Surprising times," she said, "and awfully difficult. I cry a lot."

"So did I when I heard. At my age you don't have that many tears left." He said it softly, and for the first time since her mother's death she felt a little bit safe.

"What it is," she said, "is that you get to feeling trapped in the present. History shortens up. The house is empty. Old voices are gone."

"Trapped in the present." He paused, perhaps remembering faces of the dead. "When my own father died the entire nineteenth century seemed to go with him." He indicated a chair, oak, solid and old. It occurred to her that nothing in this office betrayed the fact that this was the twentieth century, although from the front office came the rapid beat of a modern typewriter.

"The last Victorian, my father," said Alan. "How gently he loved us." He paused. "At least that was true when we were children."

There was, after all, something in the office from the twentieth century. An electric fan purred like a cat getting its brisket rubbed. Through the open window a voice rose in a gabble of words riding high and Almighty amid heavenly hosts. Alan chuckled.

"That's old Charlie," he said, "and drinking again. And early again because today is only Friday."

"It happens on Saturday most usually," she said, "but I'm not much acquainted with drinking street preachers." People came to town on Saturday. Saturday was a day of panting street preachers.

"He never gets so loaded that he drops the good book."

Alan sat behind his desk, oak, solid, old. "You are sole surviving heir to this estate. I am executor. There is a will. Your people were careful."

The high-riding voice of the street preacher rolled like muted thunder in the clear air. It was a spell-binder's voice, a deep one that could even give authority to hysteria.

"My people were always careful."

"Except for once," he told her. "Dan, your father, had no earthly business being in those woods. He might be alive today."

"Men cut firewood."

He looked puzzled. "These are approximately the assets."

It seemed she owned the farm which, of course, she knew about, and seven hundred acres more or less of timberland she had not known about. The assets were a little appalling. There was money in the bank, some nine thousand dollars, and a ten thousand dollar insurance policy. That was more money than she could make in six years. There was a tobacco allotment and eighty acres with a tenant house not far from Winston-Salem. She knew that her mother kept accounts on the place, but that had never seemed important. It occurred to her that there was a lot she had not known; a person who lived beside a mother for so many years should know of these things. She did not believe she liked this business of owning property.

"I am afraid of this." She could not identify the reasons, but something was wrong, wrong, wrong. It was like opening a door in a familiar house, and entering an alien and tainted room. Her people had never acted poor, but they lived simply. "What should I do?"

"Sell that damned forest land," he said. His response was so quick it surprised him. How could you be an attorney with his reputation and still get trapped by an automatic response?

"I have better answers," he told her. "You have to make decisions. As your representative I can offer options, but decisions belong to you." He spoke formally. That was awful. The feeling of wrongness, of something alien and unwanted pressed at her. For a moment she nearly hated him.

"We were such friends just now." She felt stupid, somehow, or tricked.

"We still are." He moved his chair from behind the desk and sat beside her. "That land is a sore point. I just knocked myself out of the saddle because of it. Let's start over."

She really was afraid. This was going to be bad. Bad.

"I did not know about the land," she told him. "I didn't know much about the place outside of town or the tobacco. If we start over can we start with that forest?"

"Your father was killed there."

"The forest is not responsible."

"It is. Indirectly. Men have murdered for less." In the fan-purring room he was distinctly unsweaty, but distinctly uncomfortable. "That land is a dark place for your family. It is evil." He paused. His eyes, so clear and friendly, seemed not so friendly now. "My maternal grandmother," he said, "was one-half blood. My father was one-eighth. I am a lawyer, but I'm talking about things that are not law, just lawful."

She could not understand why, on a brilliant day, with the deep-voiced song of a street preacher rising above the sounds of traffic; why she should feel close to horror. "Murder," she said. "Was someone murdered?"

"You do not know? You really do not know?"

"I really don't."

"Sweet, sweet Jesus."

He told the story, and because she was rapidly becoming desperate, she believed him without question.

Her father, Dan Johnson, who had been such a quiet man, was discharged from the infantry in early '46. He was forty-eight years old, a sergeant with combat experience, although he spent some of his time in a field headquarters. Had World War II not been of such a desperate nature he would never have been in the Army in the first place. A nation fighting a global war on two fronts was not particular about age or disabilities.

"A friend of mine," Alan told her, "had lost hearing in one ear and half of his right hand in a mining accident. The Air Corps accepted him and he became a bombardier."

"I was a girl, little more than a child."

"Ours was a frightened nation." Alan tapped his fingers on the arm of his chair, seemed disinclined to speak, chose to wrap the facts in the best light possible. "Ours was also a cynical nation. A lot of people made a lot of money. Black market, padded industrial accounts, and counterfeit ration coupons. Your father made some money."

She expected some awful story of black marketeering, or of military supplies diverted and sold. The tale, as Alan told it, seemed nearly anticlimactic.

• • •

On a gray evening of snow and ice in Belgium, her father, the sergeant, found himself outside a village in company with eight surviving men. A couple of houses still stood beside a broken railway station. It was December. In the near distance artillery lit the sky. The sergeant did not know that the Battle of the Bulge had just gotten a good start. All he knew was that the military situation had gone to hell and taken the whole war with it. All patterns were broken. He had one man wounded, and if there were other survivors of his company he did not know about them. He figured he was surrounded. Since he was both realistic and cynical, he probably told himself he had expected something like this all along.

He made a decision to survive. Nine men, and one of them with a smashed shoulder, and the lot of them carrying nothing but rifles, were going to make no difference in whatever was going on out there. His men were not even a squad. They were a group of privates and noncoms who fled to the Belgian countryside when shells began to rain on their headquarters. The sergeant unofficially resigned from the war.

The railway station stood dark and torn by shellfire. It looked abandoned, but he guessed it was not. He had no maps because HQ's maps were scattered over half of Belgium. He knew he was about twenty miles north and slightly east of St. Vith.

His company had been encamped when the storm of artillery broke. It was everyone pulling his own red wagon, and the first place to pull it was out of that encampment. For eighteen hours he and his men walked and hid. If they did not soon find food and shelter they were dead.

The railway station was their best option. When they came fading in with an infantryman's caution, and under cover of dark, it seemed the dust of the exploded building still mixed with falling snow, and the sharp smell of high explosive. Snow filled the tracks of tanks. A shattered British truck sat burned beside a shattered building. German infantry had to be in the area.

Inside the station two British soldiers lay dead amid a litter of papers. This had been a command post. The same thing that happened to his outfit had happened here. No one had yet raided this place. There was food. There was even a stove.

While his men took care of the wounded man, and while they opened cans of food, the sergeant went scavenging. In thirty paces he became rich, or at least with more money than he ever expected to see in one pile. In a side room shattered by a direct shell hit, a corpse lay virtually blown to pieces. Remnants of clothing showed the man dressed as a peasant. A package had been tucked into the peasant blouse, and now it lay partly exposed against the bloody chest. Inside the package were ten thousand British pounds, although the sergeant was in no position to start counting. He concealed the money, returned to the main room and made arrangements to survive. He was lucky and smart. There was a sub-cellar. He had a place to hide. All nine of them lived.

"The money," Alan said, "who knows? It may have been profiteer money, but that is not likely since it was in pounds. More likely the British were out to buy something. Information, perhaps."

"My father stole money."

"It is called the fortunes of war," Alan said. "The Allies lost seventy-seven thousand men in that battle. He brought himself and eight other men out with him, so perhaps he earned it."

"Was he murdered for the money?"

"No," said Alan. "With the money, and it took some time to convert it to U.S., he bought those properties. He bought the forest land from a man named Peter Lee who is another client of mine. Peter Lee is full blood, related to both you and me, but distantly. He may be your grand uncle, figuring by white ways.

"Figuring by Indian ways he is no relation at all." Alan's voice carried the slightest hint of distaste, but Harriette was not sure whether he thought of the land or of Peter Lee or her father. "In a sense Dan stole that land," Alan said, "but that land has been stolen so many times that one more theft makes little difference."

"If I sell it," Harriette told him, "that would be sort of like stealing."

"I did not mean that. I am neither displeased nor pleased with Dan's actions, with myself, with my memories. It is simply that anyone who has ever owned that land has suffered. Perhaps because it has been stolen so often, it is cursed."

Chapter 4

"AND in the synagogue there was a man, which had a spirit of an unclean devil, and cried out with a loud voice...." The street preacher's voice rolled, was textured, beating above the hot summer streets with loving hatred.

But her father never cried with a loud voice. Her father was quiet, a man given to disappearing into the forest. He cared for them, for her grandmother, her mother and her. In those very years when he engaged in exchanging money and buying land he sent her through college. She had been in college, in music school, when he was killed. At the funeral the casket was not opened.

Nothing she knew of her father matched the story she heard. Seven years ago, at the time her father was murdered, she had been twenty-three. Surely there were newspaper stories, an investigation, questions asked. Why had she not heard?

"Because your mother chose to conceal it," Alan said. "I thought after this many years you would know. Still, you live among those hills. You know about conspiracies of silence that are tenuous, and yet binding. You are, I have no doubt, a part of more than one of those conspiracies."

She was. On a farm, when you mostly kept to yourself, little was known except what you chose to tell. At the same time, among the farms and small towns, a good deal was known and not discussed. She knew, for instance, of children in two separate families who were not being told who their true fathers were. People made mistakes. She did not approve of deceiving children, but she would be the last ever to say anything. Yes, a conspiracy of silence; and even the bigoted, the hate mongers, did not break the silence. Some gossip was not repeated because those who were mean enough to talk were also smart enough to know that, if they did, they would not be welcome even in their own homes.

But a murder. A murder was a public matter.

"How many people do you actually know?" Alan asked her. "How many of the strangers you meet know who you are? How many people were at the funeral? If your mother asked them not to make a fuss over you, how many would have given the matter a second thought? Did you read any newspapers?"

He had a case. She had returned from college for the funeral. Alan and a few other men were present. She sat startled, unable to think of any Indians who had been there. Only a few whites. She stayed with her mother for a week, and then returned to college. The next spring she graduated and returned home. She stayed at home for two years. Then for two years she taught music in the public schools of Charlotte. Then she once more returned home.

She was content to live on the farm, not in idleness, but without much contact with anyone. She gave music lessons. She directed the choir at her mother's church. The farm was being worked on shares. It took part of her time and her mother's time to manage the farm. She, Harriette, had been reclusive. It occurred to her that while her mother concealed her father's murder, it was not the only concealment. There were reasons for her reclusiveness, but none she had been willing to tell her mother.

The purring fan was joined by the distant purr of a small plane somewhere in the intense blue sky. From the next room the sound of the typewriter stopped, and she realized for a minute, or several, that the street preacher's voice no longer knitted words into the air. It seemed a moment of near silence in the city, although of course people still walked about, talking, and buying things.

Part of her reclusiveness was natural inclination. Part came from long ago, in the days of her grandmother, and most—she had to admit—came from a confused and confusing love affair.

Murder. People walking and talking and buying things.

Money. Land and tenants on the land. Stolen forest. The fan purred, Alan waited.

"I see it is possible for concealment to have worked, although I'm not proud of it. Please tell me about the murder."

"It was never solved."

"Why?"

"No motive. Not a clue pointed to anyone."

"There will be newspaper accounts. I can look at those accounts."

"You may not want that. It was ugly. It was done with knives. More than one man was involved."

"Why?"

"If I knew why," Alan told her gently, "I would know my own heart. Dan timbered that land and he was ferocious. Where he moved his equipment not a stick stood, not a shrub, not a runner of blackberry. He was like a man obsessed. He even had a bulldozer tearing at the brush, tearing up the land."

No man, at least no Cherokee. . . . Her thoughts rushed, swirled, and it was not that she comprehended too little but too much.

"It was as though he hated the land," Alan said. "As though he engaged in retaliation or revenge."

"And someone stopped him."

"Two or three people stopped him," Alan said. "Brutally. Quick. Not much was destroyed, except a man's life."

She could tell that he knew better, but was not saying what she had to say to herself. What had been destroyed was a man's soul, and that must have happened long before the murder.

Why had her father, a Cherokee, turned in vengeance against the land?

"So it was not really murder?"

"It was an execution. The only possible motive."

She did not understand this strange world into which his words had thrown her. "I believe," she said quietly, "I've had about as much as I can take in one day."

"There will be other days," he said quietly. "Will you be in town for very long?"

"I don't want to go home. Not yet."

He wrote an address and a phone number on a yellow pad.

"If you need to call when this office is not open." It was obviously his home address and phone. "I think there is nothing more to tell, but you will want to discuss options on the property."

"Thank you," she said. As she left the office she wondered why in the world she had thanked him.

Chapter 5

S HE moved slowly through the sunlit Moravian streets, the Presbyterian streets, the hell-howling Baptist streets where words
like revenge and execution seemed to her right in line with the
current panoply of worshipped Gods. Her head bowed. She saw little
and looked for less. Some men turned to watch her tall and fluidly
moving figure. A man physically attracted by her slender body and
narrow, high-cheeked face might have been even more attracted by
her grace. She wore a simple summer dress cut just below the knee,
and it made her seem like a young girl in town for a movie or for
shopping.

She thought of the land, that same land where she would someday
come to power. She knew something of land since she had been raised
on a farm, but she suspected little of the forces which she would soon
encounter, and they are powerful forces.

They are forces of the land. You learn them by living with them:

Because it is this way to live in a clearing in the forest, sleeping one sleep after another, cycling the conquests of day and night, the great and slowly moving circle of the seasons and the years; the day which divides not by minutes,
but is undivided, and appears and fades. And there is night: its particular
voices, subdued clouds that grow and also fade, uncounted by voices of night
birds, or seconds, or any measure.

Living in a clearing in the forest, sleeping one sleep after another, there are
things obvious, things subtle; all profound as the sun.

The grass varies, and ten species may be present, and there is the soil. There
are untamed plants, of which at least fifty thousand flowering varieties exist

on the North American continent, wildflowers, trees, thistles and vines.

But figures are a generalization. Living in a clearing among flowering plants one learns that each is particular.

While superstitious people remark a four-leaved clover, the dweller in a clearing learns to remark tonal variations.

Nor is there needed description for rocks that abut from the earth with iceberg mysteriousness, bases anchored and invisible; nor of rocks in the stream, nor the changing nature of the stream—for all exists, and is—lives rolling on the wheel of light and dark and season, the rolling of mist and cloud and snow and wind.

There is all of life; mice, chipmunks, squirrels, the many animals. Insects; the hum and buzz and whir and hop.

There is soundlessness sometimes. Sometimes there is a great exclamation of silence.

And above it all stands the mountain; and it, round-shouldered, ancient, mist-capped and haunted, is the focal point of the sun; the hill that, not existing, would make the sun lose some of its bright meaning.

She thought dully, as she walked in Winston, that if she were going to stay in Winston for awhile she should move to a hotel. Then, every bit as dully, she understood she would not.

It meant more aggravation, more people whose actions would require curtness, more stares, more aversion. She was a beautiful young woman, and beautiful young women could get by with a lot—even black and beautiful young women could get by with a lot—but the price was loneliness. The more flim-flam you engaged in, the more lonely it got.

She returned to the YWCA and sat on the edge of the single bed. In the room was a small mirror, a writing table, a three-drawer chest, a chair; plus an ugly floral picture. Except for the picture the room was monastic.

She removed the picture from the wall and hid it behind the small chest.

Okay, she told herself, her mother was dead. Her grandmother existed only as a childhood memory. Her father was a thief. Her father somehow lost his soul or had it stolen. She faced these things and her hands were fists, her body rigid; angry, terribly afraid, explosive with tears until finally the explosion came. She wept from anguish to desolation, and then she slept in the little room with the North Carolina sun like a searchlight at the window.

Chapter 6

S ATURDAY was good, became bad, became better than she might
have hoped because she met her last Moravian, her last Edwardian, in the form of a brave old man.

About ten in the morning street preachers gathered in front of the
post office to lay out gospel, rejoicing in the text of the morning; and
just about any text they chose she could complete from memory.
There had been too many texts delivered over too many years; texts
by quiet preachers, or by hell-sniffing preachers. She directed the
choir at her mother's church only because she loved her mother and
loved music.

Town came alive on Saturday mornings, pretty girls chattering,
young men walking, watching, loitering; old men before the pool hall
with its beer smell sour, but somehow staid and comforting—the
click of pool balls—it would be nice to be a man standing at the old
bar swilling beer and telling stories about how great you were while
spitting expertly into copper spittoons. Even negro men, probably,
got to do that. Or maybe they just stood around knifing each other.
She did not know much about negroes.

The Cherokee Indian—which she was, even if some full-bloods
sneered at mixed-bloods—was the most over-documented, over-
interviewed, over-catechized people in the world. The Cherokee had
suffered more exploratory operations by preachers and sociologists
than any society could rightly bear. Only one mystery remained
about the Cherokee. The mystery was why, after so much documen-
tation and research, no one yet knew a farthing worth knowing.

One reason, and she was sure of it, was that so far the English language hadn't been wide enough to fully understand the mind and heart of the Cherokee, and that wouldn't do. It would not do. It simply would not. But, on the other hand, if the Cherokee were so piddling smart, would not the Cherokee know how to arrange the words? If they were, she had never heard the words.

Walking in sunshine, wanting to stand at a bar and spit in spittoons, she realized she suffered an absolutely foul mood.

As she crossed a street, which she was perfectly entitled to cross because the traffic light showed green and she paid her taxes, a couple of white boys in a brand new purple car made comments, the boys awfully young, pretending experience as men of the world.

"Is that a chest or is it an ironing board?"

"Good legs."

"Nope, too old."

"Touch of the paint brush is good for you."

The old sickness, the rage, the feeling of being little and insignificant—impotent—chastised—filled with shame—tainted—painted—came over her. If she could turn around and slap them, it would do them no good or her, either.

She felt herself slumping, drawing inward, slouching toward the safety of the far sidewalk. From behind her came the boys' loud, frightened voices. A ringing of metal. She turned.

The boys shouted with indignation that held more than a hint of terror. An old, old man, and a white man at that, slowly struck the hood of the car with a walking stick. He struck in a deliberate and unhurried manner, made a quiet comment, struck the hood, made another comment. The walking stick flashed yellowly in the sun, descending, metrical, like a conductor's baton measuring the slow beat of a Bach chorale. The light changed.

The golden baton above the purple car made her think of high school marching colors. The two boys sat blinking. Then one began to open the car door. He hesitated. The old man's voice sounded clear, making a point about behavior that constituted a gentleman and behavior that constituted scum. Another slow-ringing and resonant smack. A chip of purple paint hopped like a flea, tumbling, dancing, on the sun-hot steel hood.

Behind the car another car honked. A crowd gathered, a bigger crowd than any street preacher could attract.

The driver, tow-headed and skinny and perhaps seventeen, carried the desperate look of someone about to be tortured. He pulled away as the light once more changed red and there was no accident because even drivers at the other stoplights were more interested in the show than they were interested in going anywhere. The other boy, also tow-headed but chubby, turned around and leaned over the car seat looking backward at the scene of desolation. His mouth hung open. It appeared he might begin to drool.

It was beautiful. Beautiful. Sin and rapid retribution.

It was just lovely. Of course, it was also embarrassing. She watched the old man examine dents on his walking stick, like maybe, she thought, a knight errant examining chips taken out of his sword. Another old man, but not as old as the first old man, walked up and shook hands with the knight—her knight. Then a young business-type man shook hands with her knight. Someone started to laugh. Then the whole crowd was laughing. A policeman walked up. He was laughing. For some reason the people of Winston-Salem were having a right wonderful time. She envied them. Then she realized that she was having a right wonderful time.

Living alone, thinking solitary thoughts, was a way of getting warped. You forgot in your bigotry that other human creatures were, after all, human. She paused, asking herself if she was wrong about the white man. Was she being insulted again? He looked honest. He sounded honest.

She would have to thank the man even if it was embarrassing. A matter of honor. A matter also of not slinking away before public attention, or failing responsibility because of the insults from a couple of white children who were going through an extremely liquid time of life. She moved her mouth, was pleased to find she could actually smile. She recrossed the street.

He did not dress in southern white linen, or in southern gray linen. He did not look like Thomas Jefferson. He did not even vaguely resemble Robert E. Lee. He wore a short-sleeved ready-made shirt, old work pants, scuffed shoes. His remaining hair fluffed thin and white. It seemed a nest for the old fishing hat. He stood tall, thin, and up close he was not as frail as he seemed from a distance. Blue, nearly gray-blue eyes were serene in spite of the incident, and in spite of the fact that wrinkles on cheeks, even forehead, seemed trying to overcome them. She approached timidly. The crowd lingered, waiting for the show to continue.

"Thank you," she said, and in spite of her own entertainment her voice seemed to be quavering.

"Absolutely ridiculous display," he said. "Although under the circumstances not totally ignoble." His eyes were amused, his mouth wrinkled. "A circus, and like any good circus it certainly was fun." He looked at her. "You are trembling."

"I seem to be."

"Then walk with me. We will proceed slowly." His voice expressed every confidence she would do as he said. As he held his arm to her, she found herself doing it. She placed her hand on his arm. Theirs seemed a small promenade through the busy streets.

"Mark Warwick," he said. "The first name Biblical, the second a genealogical never-never land." He carried his walking stick in his left hand, the stick necessary and not an affectation. "I am the last Moravian," he said, "at least the last one worth hanging. Also, perhaps, the last Edwardian."

Only yesterday the attorney Alan had called his own father the last Victorian. It seemed to her that a lot of last people inhabited this city.

"Harriette Johnson...." she said, and searched for further identity. "...I teach music...from over near Asheville," she said. "In town on business."

"Tedious business." His reply was a statement of the obvious.

"How?" How did he know?

"You do not seem a slumping sort of person," he said, "yet even before the incident you slumped. Also, murmuring to yourself."

They arrived at a corner intersecting a tree-lined street of old brick houses. The trees were like great canopies under which sunlight and shadow mixed in a faint breeze. The trees stood like proofs against thunder, shock and storm.

"A lemonade sort of day, but I prefer a virulent brand of coffee. However, we will find lemonade if you wish." He guided her. They turned through an iron gate and into one of the old houses.

The house, which she thought should seem musty, felt strangely unmusty and fresh as they stepped into the living room.

Screened windows opened to every breeze. Edwardian furniture—or at least old furniture—glowed with light polish. An upright Baldwin piano rested comfortably among the old furniture. The fireplace was swept-stone, colored by fires of many years.

Through one doorway books walled a room. Books sat stacked on the floor, on a table, on a desk. It looked untidy, and that was comforting.

"A teacher?" she asked.

"A student," he told her. "Emeritus. Awfully happy to be emeritus. A student of history. Coffee or lemonade?"

"Virulent coffee."

He disappeared toward the kitchen. Methodical sounds of a man engaged in a small important task. The slow grate of a coffee grinder. In a few minutes he placed a tray before her, poured, took a chair opposite. He looked for all the world like a figure in porcelain as he smiled. "My wife died eleven years ago. You are the first beautiful woman to grace this house since then."

"That is a wonderful compliment."

"Had you known my wife you would know how wonderful." He paused, perhaps remembering. "Of course, how can a wife be unbeautiful?"

Then he chuckled. "That was not a very modern thing to say." Then he sighed. "Sometimes I am tempted," he said, "as was the late and lamented Erasmus Darwin, to write the natural history of everything."

Chapter 7

"I T seems," said Warwick, "you are presented with a variety of
mysteries. Historians enjoy mysteries. They would not be historians did they not."

She did not mean, coming here, to unburden herself. She only
meant to be courteous to an old gentleman who had been kind to her.
Somehow, though, it happened. Warwick proved a wonderful lis-
tener who posed surprising and difficult questions. Partly, she
thought, it was his manner. If he should ask something as simple as
her opinion of the weather she would feel obliged to give a thoughtful
answer. He must have been a wonderful teacher.

Later she would discover he was something more than a wonderful
teacher. In libraries, she would find him acknowledged as a leading
historian whose main contributions concerned changing theologies
of the western world.

But that was later. At present she sat feeling like a schoolgirl who
has taken her problems to her teacher. Perhaps it was the comfort of
the clean-lined and sunlit room with its bulky furniture.

"The most fascinating of the mysteries," said Warwick, "is the one
which asks why your father behaved as he did. Your father, I take it,
was Indian?"

"He was full-blood. My mother was one-quarter, but there is a difference." She paused. She did not know how much she wanted to say
about this. "My father was raised Cherokee and my mother was
raised Presbyterian." She saw Warwick's amusement, but amusement
touched with kindliness. "Not southern Presbyterian," she said.
"Northern."

"You state a huge difference," he said. "Do you know the difference?"

"The northern is quiet."

"And exact," he said. "There is a great history there, but I do not think we will ever get to talk about that history. Meanwhile, we speak of an Indian who was ambitious, who bought land, and began to ravage the land. That is not as untypical as it seems."

"My father would not do such a thing."

"But apparently did."

"Yes."

"Another mystery," said Warwick, "asks who murdered him. We have a possible motive."

She had not thought of the murderers. Maybe the murder was not really a murder. Maybe it really was an execution. Maybe it was revenge, in which case it was not exactly a murder; but there was no possible way of explaining that to Warwick. He would not understand the Cherokee history of revenge. How could he? She did not understand it herself.

"A third mystery," said Warwick, "and one that is perhaps a key to solution of the others, is the land. You have not seen the land. Or, if you have, you have only seen it from afar and without knowledge of its importance."

The land. Of course.

Outside there, beyond this quiet room, an entire civilization seemed hell bent on destroying itself; a civilization finding Communists under every bed. A civilization that wanged and banged around in purple painted cars. A civilization depending on enormous bombs, on banks and lawyers like Alan, although most of them were probably not as nice as Alan. All of that going on out there, and here Warwick talked about the land. He brought her smack down in what was important about the present. The land.

"My attorney says the land is evil. Everyone who has owned the land has been harmed."

Warwick chuckled. "I don't think there is time to mull over the nature of evil," he said. "In addition," and he chuckled again, "the human race has spent sufficient time on the issue. There is some reason to think of elemental forces."

He talked beyond her. Was he a mystic, a fanatic? No, he could not be that. "I really do not understand," she told him.

"It's only conjecture," Warwick said, "but you may discover some deep sacredness in that land." He rubbed a wrinkled cheek. He seemed more frail, more like porcelain. "Bag of bones," he said. "This old skin tires more easily. I must rest soon." Then his composure returned.

"There are two other mysteries. First, why was this concealed from you? Second, why does concealment continue?"

"I must be going," she said.

He smiled. "Thank you for the courtesy, but we are defining the problem. We can do that in a short time."

"There is no concealment."

"Your attorney either lies or withholds information. You will want to find out which."

She could not believe it. Alan would surely not lie.

"How did the pounds get exchanged for dollars? Not by some Indian walking into a bank. Why does your attorney counsel getting rid of the land? Why, if they were such great friends, does your attorney not have some knowledge of what your father thought? What history of the land has branded it evil?"

This old, old man who described himself as a bag of bones was brilliantly laying out an entire problem that it might have taken her years to fully appreciate. Of course, she told herself, she was in the center of the problem. A person did not have much perspective.

Warwick looked amused with himself.

"We will close with a lecture," he said. "It is your penance for consorting with pedants.

"Civilizations die for a number of reasons and one of those reasons was responsible for the destruction of the American Indian, not just the Cherokee. When a people takes over the responsibilities that it once assigned to its Gods—and being inept abrogates those responsibilities—then that people is doomed."

She did not understand, and knew her confusion showed.

"Take our own civilization...," he paused, saw her hesitation,

"...yes, our civilization. You may think of yourself as Cherokee, may wish to be, but you are also white." He motioned toward the quiet, tree-lined street.

"Our own God," he said, "used to perform miracles. He healed the blind. Now our physicians transplant lenses and restore sight. Our Jehovic God once held the power of total destruction, but we undertake that power with the release of the atom. Our Gods used to see all and know all, and we now build the largest and most intricate communications system in history.

"The society usurps the powers of its Gods." He smiled. "This is a normal course which progresses in western lands.

"The Chinese, on the other hand," he said, "ridicule their Gods when their Gods fail. It gets the Gods' attention.

"The American Indian, with new ideas from the whites, new technology and new hopes, proved not so wise. Instead of ridiculing, and thus seeking safety in religion, the Indian began to hate his Gods. The Indian has been very like the white man.

"Because," he said, "our white society is failing, in decline. We have taken power, but we have no new divine powers. We are at play with the universe, fumbling our great power as an idiot child might fumble with matches as he stood in a field of dry grass. The same thing happened to the Cherokee."

Chapter 8

WALKING, walking; quiet streets giving over to quiet streets. She walked in hot midday past big houses, then smaller houses and finally past shanties on the edge of town, Harriette—Named By Thunder—Tree's Friend—found her mind trying to push aside silent but growing horror.

Sooner or later she must return to the farm. Sooner or later old voices and forms and shapes of remembered customs would assail her. She must enter the empty farmhouse where her mother's Bible even now lay on a bedside table. Her mother's quiet voice would still seem present. Her grandmother's voice would whisper in the winds. Her father's voice, quiet, patient, must surely approach, and it would ride the night like the silent wings of owls.

More terrifying even, she would have to walk that land. She might walk unknowing across the very piece of earth that once soaked her father's blood.

Sidewalks gave way to a path worn in dry clay, the path holding the dull sheen of pottery. She crossed a railroad track, looked down the grade, then looked in ditches where thistles and weeds grew covered with dust.

She told herself that she had other memories, memories that made her strong. She might fear land that held her father's blood, might fear nights that held the dark spirits of religions; but she also had strength to oppose those fears. Not all memories threatened. As she walked she thought of the memory more precious to her than anything else except, maybe, music.

When she was eight she saved the spirit of a tree. At least once in her life the luminous self and the world self melded.

It was a fine old chestnut and it held her swing. When her father said the tree must come down because it was getting sick, she thought it more than she could bear. She was only eight, had by then already lost her grandmother, felt thus uninstructed, and now was about to lose the tree.

It is not easy to save a spirit. Many ways may be tried, but only some of those ways work; and only then if the person is truthful.

You must be careful; chestnut to chestnut, spruce to spruce. The wispy spirit of a mimosa would be no companion for a chestnut. Were you to help a chestnut into a mimosa both would be unhappy.

Prayer is necessary. She did not know if she was doing anything correctly. In the mornings when she woke she would wash herself and go into the yard. Sometimes the household would be waking, but on one morning she rose in the dark and the house lay still. When she stepped into the morning the two farm dogs came sniffing. She walked between them and went to the tree. She placed her hand against the bark.

Morning air moved but it was not quite a breeze. A twig fell close to her on the south side of the tree.

One of the dogs raised his leg to the tree, made water, then whined. Then the dog walked south and so did she, reaching to flop his ears and pull at the thick hair on his back.

The woods were south but there were other trees before them. They rose in shadowed forms that changed with angle and closeness. She hoped one would do. She did not believe she could carry a spirit very far. She turned to the movement of air touching her face like a whisper, and made a prayer. The prayer said her heart was good; that a thing must be done to aid a brother and another brother. She came to an oak.

She felt it, then sat beneath it. Dawn found her by a tree which she did not know well. Smoke came from the chimney of the house. She knew she must return. Soon she would be called.

She walked around the oak and then moved away a dozen yards. The oak seemed strong and permanent. It was well formed but younger than the chestnut. She worried because it was not a chestnut and hoped all would be well. She turned to the house.

That day she saved the spirit, although she was not sure that what she did had worked. She first tried to carry the spirit in her hand, but felt that nothing happened. Then she took bark from the chestnut and placed it in a branching of the oak. She thought that did not work, either. In evening, as the sun was a glow in back of the mountain, and the sky a red-yellow, a light breeze lifted. It blew on a line between the two trees.

Everything else had failed. She became stern with the chestnut and told him it was time to go, that now he really must go, tomorrow was too late. She did her best and hoped she had done well.

The next day the chestnut came down with a dull thud, lifeless, dead-rustling. She kept watch on the oak all winter.

In spring a new branch rose and grew too quickly for a regular branch. She knew she had succeeded. . . .

Further up the track an old negro man walked, following the tracks to town. He was still at a great distance, but coming toward her. She turned off the grade and started following clay paths which returned her to sidewalks and to town. Negroes frightened her because she did not know anything about them.

Of course, if you were part Cherokee there was a good chance you had some negro blood.

Of course, if your family was four generations southern there would be negro blood in the line somewhere, whether the family was Indian or not. She paused, startled. She had never thought of herself as southern before.

Southerners were people who lived in awful places like Arkansas, or horsey places like Virginia.

Her lover, her white lover, had thought of her as southern, but it was not because she was southern that he went a different way. It was because, with the reality of approaching college graduation, with the reality of an approaching career, he figured an Indian wife was not going to help a career.

She paused. That was being unfair. Maybe. Maybe his father made the decision for him. Maybe she made the decision.

She had not wanted to be a business wife who traveled to places like India; and those kinds of places were where young businessmen traveled these days. In fact, she did not want to be a business wife at all. She did not yet know what she wanted to do with and for music, but you could not do it as a business wife.

You had to go to parties and give parties. For a moment she remembered him, tall, brush-cropped hair, aggressive but gentle at least with her. Even now, after seven years of solitude, there were times when she missed him.

It would not have worked out. Would not. Better to miss him than have to give parties.

Her mind hurried and scurried about, doing everything it could to avoid thinking about murder.

"Murder," she said to the quiet street. "Murder, murder, murder."

And there were all kinds of murder. Her mother's body was barely cold before the tenant for the farm came by wanting to buy the fields where her father once worked. Her mother's body was hardly cold when the new preacher of the congregation came by caring only about what was in the will. . . . "Murder," she said, "murder, murder, murder."

She could call Alan, but that was not a good idea if she was going to confront him. If he lied, or held back information, then best have it out in a formal setting. Nothing was going to happen with Alan until at least Monday.

She could not solve her father's murder—she paused—but she could read about it. Surely the library kept newspaper files. She walked with direction and purpose, headed for the library.

Warwick said that when a people usurp the power of their Gods, then those people are doomed. She nearly understood.

Before whites arrived the Cherokee practiced rituals. Some of those rituals, like hunting rituals, must have rapidly seemed valueless in the face of steel blades and gunpowder. For a while, back then, hunting must have become awfully easy. Until the game ran out.

The Cherokee acted a pattern that was acted elsewhere.

Plains Indians drove herds of buffalo over cliffs. On the west coast tribes decimated the sea otter, and the otter was one of their great totems. Eskimos no longer tried to take a walrus. They went in motor boats with rifles and shot every walrus in sight, collecting the few that did not sink.

On the face of it, the noble savage did not look very noble.

The library stood nearly abandoned on this sunny Saturday afternoon. A girl of eleven or twelve engaged in serious conversation with the librarian. The girl wore a light summer dress. Her shoes were polished. She had a longish, country sort of face. It was clear that her whole family had come to town this Saturday. The librarian looked about forty, and school-teacherly. She showed complete attention to the young girl. It was obvious she was having a good time.

This morning, Harriette told herself, she had wanted to stand around bars and spit in spittoons. Now she found herself wanting to stand in libraries and help children learn things.

She inquired about the newspapers and got them. It was so easy. Somehow she supposed they would be in the basement under dusty boxes of discarded books.

The papers did not give her much. Her father was found lying near his truck which was parked on the logging job. There were two stab wounds, and the sheriff guessed two knives were used. One wound was much bigger and deeper than the other. One wound was in the side, one in the chest.

Her father had dismissed his logging crew early that day, although the men did not know why. The body was discovered when one of the crew passed along the road and saw the truck still sitting on the job. The sheriff investigated. His name was Daryl Blaine.

She sat thinking. That sheriff must be an extremely unemotional man. He made no comment about the ugliness of the murder. If he had, the paper would have printed it. Papers liked that sort of thing.

Maybe the murder of an Indian in the North Carolina hills was uninteresting. The newspaper had not wasted any of its front page on the story.

The sheriff was investigating. She wondered if he really had, or if he pretty much ignored the whole matter. Alan had said that the case was never solved. Maybe it had not been solved because no one cared to solve it. She returned the papers to the desk. This whole affair kept making bigger and bigger demands. The next thing was to talk to that sheriff.

Chapter 9

I N that August when Harriette was thirty, and I was fourteen, the old woman Molla had lived in a clearing on that forest land for many years; and it is now that Harriette's story needs to pick up a stitch. Or, more likely, turns must be made, like a hound curling around itself for a nap in the sun. We will leave Harriette who faces a tedious weekend in Winston's YWCA. She cannot see Judge Alan until Monday, and she cannot see Sheriff Blaine. We leave, because, to know Harriette's heart, we must glimpse two other women.

The forest land that so dismayed Judge Alan had, for the best part of a century, held a clearing and a solid, two-room cabin where Molla had lived for many years. Above the clearing, in rolling blue mists, lay what in North Carolina is known as a bald. A bald is a place on a mountain where no trees grow. There are grass balds and rhododendron balds, depending on the acidity of the soil. This mountain is different.

Were you to approach in an airplane at ten thousand feet, the waves of green hills would be interrupted by the black and red summit which stretches like an abandoned monument erected by forgotten giants. Or, if you viewed the mountain from the crest of a neighboring mountain, the ridge would rise above your gaze and march into the mist; black marked with red, as if some pagan pottery maker used hugely sweeping hands to form original creation.

Deposits of iron ore lie on that mountaintop. The ore is like a magnet for lightning. In summer storms, lightning walks across that ridge like the legs of Gods. It is hugely flashing, tall and omnipotent. The ridge holds sacredness of place and power. The name of the ridge holds that same sacredness. In English we may speak of it as Lightning Ridge, or—because of the thunders in the Cherokee mythology—Thunder Ridge.

The old woman, Molla, lived on the mountain, and perhaps she was wise and perhaps she was silly. In the story lore of white America there are numbers of tales in which a young white meets a wise old Indian, and that meeting changes his life forever. Those stories are often touched with hysteria, for white America has enough trouble understanding the wisdom of its own thinkers, leave alone the wisdom of an Indian.

Where she lived, at the downside of the clearing, a persimmon, a female tree, stood heavy with fruit that after first frost would bring foxes and possums. The animals would come in gathering darkness, the seeds of sticktights and yellow clover carried by their fur to be broadcast across the hills.

They would nuzzle the acrid, dry-puffing and astringent fruit, eat, then fade into the dark forest.

To the observer the woman's life might seem but rudimentary movement about a clearing that by mid-summer stood overgrown with tall grasses and weeds. Trilliums and gromwells grew, with selfheal beyond the border of the clearing. The plants have their nature, and to men that nature is most often friendly. In Cherokee mythology the plants, in man's great war with the animals, came to man's aid. Plants supplied healing and color, medicine and dyes. If Molla knew the story it is possible she understood it—and in a white sense, even a white can understand it. Life on this planet gathered through aeons of life begetting life, and the plants made this possible. Without flowers there could not have been insects. Flowers stand at the base of the evolutionary chain, at the base of all human creation.

Molla ate little, although she had visitors who always brought food. Color disappeared from her face as age groped after her spirit. Her face became a dried-paper face, resembling mummified remains sometimes discovered in graves throughout our American Southwest. Her visitors came believing that, in North Carolina, amid mountains worn by time and rain—those elements even more perpetual than legend—Molla could direct them to ways of knowledge and power. Thus she lived among the forms of creation, and, perhaps, she was wise.

• • •

The hound now takes another turn, settles its long spine into a curl of sun-warmed dust, and dreams hound dreams, or dozes with hound memories. Harriette, who remains woeful and indignant in Winston-Salem, will soon meet Molla. Perhaps only then will Harriette realize that she has already known one great Indian.

Until Harriette was six her grandmother lived at the farm. Her grandmother was good to her and filled Harriette's childhood with stories and instruction.

They went to meet the plants and trees. They lingered with mountain laurel and the light green of new holly. They talked across running brambles of wild blackberry, and plunged their hands into cold-rushing streams. In Harriette's memory it was a vague and luminous time. Another dark-skinned girl in North Carolina, even a glow-skinned girl, might mean nothing much. The meaning came because her grandmother acted the part of a grandmother.

"Step gentle," her grandmother said. "E-ni-da. He is your friend. Oojo-nida, he will have respect. Rattlesnake."

Or, meeting the rattlesnake. "Tell him this. Let us not see each other again this summer."

In the mornings movement always started early and increased with the light so that just after dawn the forest became a frenzy of excitement and food-getting. Sometimes her grandmother forgot to speak clearly.

Kneeling by the stream bank for a feather. "Here. Trap."

"A cat?"

"Wild."

"The cat from the farm killed the jay?"

"Sikonega gisqwa he. Bluebird."

At home her grandmother said little. She occasionally spoke to Harriette's father in a curious mixture of languages.

Harriette's mother and grandmother always spoke in English. The two women lived contentedly, and worked the same way. On a farm there was always plenty of work. After the grandmother died, Harriette's mother always spoke of her with respect.

"She had a difficult life in her early years. She was born around 1853. She lost her husband to disease, but I don't know which. She lost one child to scarlet fever, another to influenza. Your grandmother knew people who escaped the removal. Your great-grandfather was one of them. He was a child at the time."

"She never talked about it."

"Nor did your father. I can't truthfully say that Dan even wanted to think about it."

"Giga," her grandmother once told her. "Red for the east."

And again, "See. See now his trouble. Young, he. Fast. Fast." And they watched from the safe distance of a hillside as the young bear slapped futilely at pool-trapped trout. They laughed when the bear lost his footing and fell with a splash.

In the fall they sang as leaves fell about them, speckling streams now slowed in their rush along the watershed.

During the winter her grandmother did not often go outside. In the evenings, she spoke of old tales: the making of the mountains, the war with the animals, and how a man and a pine and a star were all the same.

Harriette's mother would listen in silence. The fireplace glowed red and yellow, like burning, exploding clay. Wind poured through the valley, rushing about house and trees so it was no trouble to hear spirits speaking from the night. Harriette's mother did not interrupt the stories, although her religion held a different view.

To Harriette the stories were true and perfect. Later, in Sunday school, the olive and the pine and the bear, the man and the cross and the star, would get all mixed in her mind.

In the spring of her fifth year they returned to the forest and lived a part of most days speaking to the birds.

Autumn came and went, changing again to winter. The following spring, when Harriette was six, urgency entered her grandmother's voice.

"You will remember this. There. He goes. He lives in moist places.

Chipmunk. He is one of your great friends. Now approach him, slow, more slow, move shoulders slow—he goes, you were too quick."

The summer over, her grandmother was dead in the waking hours of morning.

"An old woman," her father said, and he performed the burial on a hillside at the farm. Then he disappeared into the forest for three or four days.

Chapter 10

ON Monday Alan's secretary said that Alan would be in court during the morning. Harriette made an appointment for early afternoon.

It was her birthday and she was thirty, but she did not think of it at the time. She thought of Sheriff Daryl Blaine who lived beyond Asheville. It took a lot of quarters in the pay phone at the Y before she finally tracked him down. He was retired. When she rang his number she found she had made a silly mistake. She had forgotten to prepare her questions.

"You are Dan Johnson's daughter." His voice sounded husky, and comfortable with authority. "I met you once when you were little."

"You were a friend of my father?"

"We drowned a few fishworms through the years. Your dad liked lake fishing."

Across the YWCA lobby a young woman sat behind the desk. Usually a cranky older woman sat there. The young woman watched Harriette, but her manner seemed friendly and not nosy.

"This will seem foolish," Harriette said to Blaine. "Only last Friday I learned of the murder."

There was a pause at the other end. "It had to happen sometime," Blaine said. "I opposed concealment from the first."

"You knew my mother?"

"I knew everybody in my county."

That was promising. Even if he had not solved the murder he might know something about her father's motives.

"Your parents were good people," Blaine said. "As you dig into this mess I want you to remember." His voice did not exactly lecture. It sounded genuinely concerned. "Don't forget. Your parents were good people."

"My father did something strange."

"He was clearcutting. It is not good forest practice. Erosion."

If he had been her father's friend then he concealed something by talking about good forest practice. She felt the frustration and stupidity of trying to handle this over the phone. She should have exercised patience. She should have gone to visit him. In fact, that was his next suggestion.

"When you get home, come for a visit."

"Yes," she said. "Yes, of course..." and paused. "Did you ever have any indication of who killed him?"

"Two Indians," Blaine said. "The question is which two Indians."

"You are certain?"

"When you visit you will agree. You'll see only one possible motive, saving the land. Thus, two Indians." His voice sounded kind, but the authority in his voice told her nothing more would come from a phone conversation. "When you return home call me."

"Of course. Yes..."

"Also," he said, "see Johnny Whitcomb. He was on Dan's logging crew. For a while I suspected him. I must hang up now."

She reached in her purse for more quarters. Paid the operator. Turned from the phone.

Johnny Whitcomb was a neighbor. Rather, he lived in an old bus parked on the two or three acres Johnny owned. He lived about three miles from the farm. At least she could find him. She did not know what Johnny was; Portuguese and maybe just about every other thing except Irish.

The young woman at the desk watched Harriette's confusion. She smiled in a sympathetic way. "Problems?"

"I would not know where to start."

"Sandy," the young woman said. "Sandra Smith. A real eye catcher of a name." She wrinkled her nose, then grinned. "If I ever do get married it'll probably be some guy named Jones."

"The other lady is usually here. I've not seen you before."

"The old bat is at home, making her family miserable instead of us.

Summer flu."

"Harriette Johnson," said Harriette. "I thought it was just me the lady didn't like."

"Don't go to thinking you're special. That old bitch has buried three husbands."

Sandy was the athletic type, big boned and a little ungainly looking in a light summer dress. She would look just fine in track clothes, or dressed for swimming laps, or riding a horse. Her hair was shorter than the current styles asked, her face broad and happy. Smiling brown eyes.

"Uh, uh," she said to Harriette as she saw Harriette glance at her hair. "I had me a man once, and I'm gonna get another. Maybe I'll get a whole chicken coop full."

Harriette knew she looked confused.

"Who do you think stays at YWCA's," Sandy said. "Dykes, retired ladies, neurotics, suicides and junior high school kids, that's who."

"Doesn't leave me much to choose from." Harriette could not keep from smiling. Sandy was not much more than a girl, maybe twenty-three. It was impossible not to be attracted to her.

"You don't count," Sandy said. "You're one of them who are just passing through."

"Maybe too quickly. I'll be leaving in a day or two, and I have a business appointment soon." Then she had a thought. "Maybe to-morrow we could have lunch."

"Twelve-thirty," Sandy said. "Nothing too wholesome. I love ham-burgers."

Harriette turned to go.

"Watch it," Sandy said. "Storm later on."

How did she know?

"Old negro lady in the laundry," Sandy said. "She says storm, we have storm. Negroes got rain in their bones."

At least, Harriette wryly told herself as she left, she had learned something about negroes.

She walked without sign of storm. Streets filled with sun. Cars overheated. A young negro man stood in an alleyway. She wondered if he had rain in his bones. No clouds. No wind. Of course, if storm came it would come up fast. It would happen in late afternoon when all those temperatures up there started changing.

So the sheriff held something back. The same sheriff who said he had not approved of the murder being concealed from her. A lot of people who claimed they wanted to help were not helping much.

She arrived early for the appointment with Alan and sat in the quiet waiting room. Harriette leafed through a *LIFE* magazine. An excited article discussed medical possibilities of some new drugs called hallucinogens. An old farmer came from Alan's office. He wore a rigid and satisfied smile. Maybe he had changed his will and left his money to a home for orphan goats or something. She caught herself. There was no earthly sense to head into a confrontation in a bad mood.

Alan was as comfortable in her presence as he had been during the first appointment.

"I have some questions..." she began, then paused. "I've been thinking. A few things have come up."

"Bound to happen."

"Why did my mother conceal this?"

"I'll wait for the other questions," Alan told her openly. "Answers to the other questions are probably going to answer that one."

"How did the British money get exchanged for American?"

"I exchanged it. No great problem." He did not like the question. "As an attorney I will say I did not know the source of the money at the time of the exchange."

"You and my father must have been awfully good friends."

That question Alan did not mind. He sat comfortably behind his old desk. The fan purred. No street preacher hollered. "We were second cousins," Alan told her. "He was like a younger brother. We were sometimes raised together."

She had not known that. If she were really any kind of Indian she might have had thoughts about family.

"Then we are related. When you talked about that man Peter Lee I should have asked better questions."

"This is North Carolina," Alan said. "We are probably related to more than half the people in that county." He paused, maybe considering the ethics of what he was about to say. "Being related to Peter Lee is not likely to make anyone happy. He is an old and bitter man."

"If," she said, and wondered if she sounded like a prosecuting attorney, "you were so close to my father, how can you not have known the state of his mind?"

"This will take awhile," Alan said, "so I might as well get comfortable." He removed his light summer jacket, loosened his tie, rolled his cuffs. He was really a very attractive older man. "You have never killed anyone?"

"Of course not."

"Dan did. During the war he killed at least five men. Those are the five he actually saw die."

She sat stunned. Of course, men did that in war. Her quiet father. Her father who fished with friends, who sometimes disappeared into the forest for two or three days. Her gentle father. She listened to the purr of the fan. It would almost be comforting if a street preacher started to howl.

"If that were all," Alan said, "he could probably have lived with it. A lot of other men live with similar matters."

That was not all? What could be worse?

"He suffered two miracles," Alan said. "Some call them the fortunes of war." Alan leaned on his elbows, a man pondering miracles. "There is no reason why your father should have survived. This is what happened..."

Dan Johnson's first combat assignment was mickey mouse and he knew it. The company commander was a kid second lieutenant who led an eighteenth-century charge against seven well-placed machine guns. Johnson knew it was insane. As he stood to move forward he yelled No, No, No, but he obeyed orders.

He was the only one who survived. They were enfiladed.

He lay in a field of tall grass, calling softly; and he lay among dead men. The reserve squad could do nothing. Three times during the day he tried to inch backward, and all three times machine guns opened up at movement in the grass. Through the long day, and without water because his canteen was punctured, he lay motionless. At nightfall he pulled out, got back to his lines, was assigned to another company.

Later he understood he was deranged, but he thought he used good sense at the time. His squad caught a patrol the next morning. The company commander sent for him. Four men stood in the street in the middle of a captured village. The company commander, two sergeants, and Dan.

The company commander told Dan to take it easy for a couple of days. Dan said the hell with that, if his squad had a patrol he would pull the patrol. He spoke like a crazy man.

Then, making his point like a crazy man, he walked away in defiance. When he was twenty yards away a random shell came in and killed the company commander and the two sergeants.

"Miracles," Alan said. "The problem is that Dan was Indian. He could believe in luck, but not in miracles."

"I don't understand."

"That is something we share," Alan said, "because I've never killed a man either, and because I can almost believe in miracles."

"You've thought about it?"

"I assure you," Alan said, "had you dealt on behalf of as many returning soldiers as I have, you would have thought about it. These days my soldier clients return from Korea." He looked at his watch. "Another client in a little while, but we have some time."

He looked at her, and his eyes held both sadness and affection. "What happens to a man," he said, "when that man is relieved of his Gods; and then, a white God passes miracles? Your father was an extremely complex and intelligent man." Alan stood. He walked to the window which overlooked the street. He looked into the street as if searching for someone.

"Three days before the murder," he said, and turned back to her, "Dan came in here. His sole purpose was to make certain his affairs were in order."

"He knew he would die?"

"He was scarcely beside himself," Alan told her. "I think he knew he was at some risk, but was strangely optimistic about the risk. If I had to choose one word I would call him serene. If two words, then serene and happy."

"How could that be? Had he changed into a white man?"

Alan looked with disapproval at her words. "If you wish to understand this, you'll have to think more carefully." He continued. "I told him that even if what he was doing was correct, he still went about it incorrectly. The economics were against what he did. Selective cutting would have been more profitable. He replied that he was doing it the only way it could be done."

"Then you really do not know the state of his mind?" She accepted his honesty. She really felt the truth of his words. "Why do you counsel selling that land?"

He returned to the window, staring into the street. She thought he might be hiding his emotions. Finally he turned.

"When I was a young prosecuting attorney, I was to try an old man. He came from the reservation, but had taken a deer illegally. His sole defense was: 'I cannot recognize your right to indict me, because I cannot recognize your right to be here in the first place.' He was fined and released."

"I have no right to own that land."

"Legally you do."

"I understand. Who has that right?"

"Legally, anyone who pays for it. Otherwise, no one."

"Not even the Cherokee nation?"

"Especially, perhaps, not the Cherokee nation." Alan rolled his cuffs down and buttoned them. He adjusted his tie.

"If you do not understand, then you will understand after you think about it for a while. Governments, even tribal governments, have a record of wrecking people."

"What does this have to do with selling the land?"

"Sell it to a corporation," he said. "If you sell it to an individual . . ." He broke off. "This sounds both silly and unprofessional," he said. "I think it is unproductive land. Much of the timber is so old it is unmarketable. At the risk of seeming unprofessional I believe the land is evil."

"And my mother? Why did she conceal all of this from me?"

"You have not guessed?"

"I would not ask if I had."

"To protect you," Alan said. "Your mother, for all she was Christian, was also Indian. In addition, I remind you that her religion has just as many so-called 'superstitions' as the religion of any Indian. Someone, in fact two men, were out there and capable of murder. Your mother believed that if you knew nothing of the matter you would not become a victim." He slipped his jacket back on, and was once more the formal-appearing man of law.

"Also," he said, "she could not possibly understand why Dan behaved as he did, and Dan did not tell her. It may be she tried to save you from a religious form of shame. The Presbyterians call it sin." He moved again toward the window, and this time looked into the sky. "It will storm within the hour," he said.

Chapter 11

THE storm strode across Winston-Salem striking with electric fingers, with boomings and cracks as the hot stench of ozone preceded rain. Storm walked across the central North Carolina flatlands. It beat on carefully tended tobacco, on scrub pine, on gray graveled roads and on main highways. The storm was focal, and for something so huge it was not ponderous.

It blazed quick, agile; and, like the concentrated fire from gun turrets aboard capital ships it sailed the sky with its bombardment. An old tree, straight and ancient as an ancestral monument, split, the sound like shrieking. A small barn exploded, and a dazed man staggered into wind to save his mules as the barn burned. Vibration rolled through streets, currents of shock; and a plate glass store window buckled as wind poured across pastel summer frocks, across summer suits, across the hurried rag-tag of small items. A power station flared, took the overload, and kicked off the line. The storm commanded the world until, as if satisfied, it faded its winds, tucked in its lightnings, and departed in the soft echo of rain.

Harriette—Named By Thunder—Tree's Friend—stood in that YWCA room listening to the returning, playing voices of children. Soon it would be time to plan, time to move according to new information. For the moment, though, she stood in complete awe of the storm. In her memory nothing loomed so huge, not even the mountains themselves. If there were spirits walking out there, Cherokee spirits remembering ancient ceremonies, ancient fires, then surely they cried as one voice in the voices of that storm.

The sky began to lighten. It would be exciting to walk out there after a storm. Leaves and twigs and branches would clog streets. Damage would lie across the face of civilization, and men would climb power poles or work with chainsaws to repair it or hide it away. Streets would be washed, the faces of buildings, washed.

Her breasts, which two teenagers had agreed were too little, felt heavy, the way they always did just before her period. She would have to take care of that. It would not be appropriate to bleed on the YWCA's sheets. It would shock the laundry, except maybe, the old negro lady who knew about storms.

She left the room and went to the showers, washed, returned to the room, dressed thinking of going into the streets.

Then she thought of a solitary dinner and a return to the solitary room.

Warwick had been so kind. It would be bold to ask him to dinner. There were limits. At the same time Warwick was an old, old man. People would think she took her grandfather to dinner. Warwick did not seem the type of man who would be insulted by an invitation. She checked the phone book.

He was not insulted. In fact, on the phone he sounded delighted. "I know just the place," he told her. "We will not even need a car. I will make the reservation for you, and shall be ready to greet you at seven."

When she turned from the phone another young girl sat at the desk. A clock read four-thirty, and the calendar informed her that today was her birthday. That was a shock. How did anybody forget her thirtieth birthday?

She stepped into wet and steaming streets. The storm had lowered temperatures, but now late afternoon heat was returning.

Were birthdays a time for remembering? It appeared this one was, and as she walked she remembered her father.

"Mumps," he once reported when he returned from town. "The whole school. Cheeks puffed out like chipmunks." She remembered him, tall and as narrow for a man as she was for a woman. Wearing brilliantly colored plaid shirts year round because poachers roamed the forests and he did not want to be mistaken for a target. A lot of men worked their fields in colorless work clothing. Of course, her father had been in a war and knew something about being a target.

She thought of him entering the kitchen in the evenings, tired from the day's work but never slumped. His face was narrow as the rest of him, his skin not as bright as hers. His face strangely wrinkled, his hair beginning to gray. Sometimes in the evenings he sat talking with visiting friends. Her father's friends, a curious collection.

"Train him before he gets to the slappy stage or you've lost him." Her father once said that to a store owner who you would think could not be a friend. They talked about a bear cub, and the store owner planned to exhibit the live bear to attract tourists.

Johnny Whitcomb had been one of her father's friends.

"Dan," Johnny once said, "I go to that little spring backside your hill. Get drunk on that water. Drunk. That spring he is old."

"A good washing place," her father said. "Once I dipped to the bottom of that pool beneath the spring. Came up with a little fox. Looked alive. Dropped him back in the pool. Fox had no luck."

Her father's Cherokee name was Stream.

Streams ran from the mountains, torrential in spring, languid in summer as they crossed slates and eddied and whirled. They carried small pebbles. Sometimes the configuration of rock caused little maelstroms. The pebbles whirled, grinding like ancient stone tools, and slates were pocked with deeps. Through centuries the whirling rocks had cut them out.

"You have done well," her father told her on the day before she left for college. "You will be all right. It is not a big college."

She had been unable to hide fear. "If I study music I may not be able to get a job."

"Ask yourself, do you need a job?"

"In college," he continued, "I think the teachers will say that everything is important. I think, maybe, they are right. You should ask about each teacher, does he feel good about himself."

She had not understood. Later, meeting some who felt bad about themselves, she understood.

Her memory was like an echo. "Train him before the slappy stage. . . ." No wonder her father was a man with problems. He went to war, raised crops and thought of markets, and he respectfully dropped the body of a baby fox back into a pool. A white man would have thrown the thing into the brush. Indians fought conflicting claims like that all the time, but most of them did not fight very well. She hoped her father had fought well.

That evening she arrived at Warwick's house exactly on time. She was dressed in her nicest, most adult summer dress. It was a little old fashioned, a hem line nearly at mid-calf. She chose carefully, this dark blue and collarless dress with the high, nearly demure neck line. It seemed the kind of conservative presentation that would please Warwick.

"You are lovely," he said when he opened the door and invited her inside. This time he dressed in a southern suit of white linen. An old fashioned suit; and entering the living room she felt somehow that history still lived, and she was alive in history.

Old books lay carefully arrayed on a small table. Beside them a yellow legal pad held notes written in a highly styled hand. A reading lamp glowed, making one corner of the room seem like a personal, well-loved and well-used place. She remembered herself as a child, and remembered a small and sunny spot in the forest which she loved. This, she thought, must be Warwick's small and sunny spot.

"Since we spoke," he said, "I've been having notions."

He tapped his temple with one finger. "Somewhere in this old warehouse is a theory that may explain our main mystery." He stepped to the window, drew a curtain aside. "A wonderful storm," he said. "Now that it is gone I miss it."

She found she missed it as well.

"The Gods send such storms," he mused, "as a bit of housekeeping. Now the world is clean and bright and polished again. The wrinkles are smoothed away." He reached for his walking stick, donned a gray summer hat, gave the smallest but definite bow. "Let us proceed."

Dinner was German cooking, the restaurant in a large brick house. She had never supposed she would like such food, thinking it heavy and over-seasoned. This, however, was light, and the wine she knew was excellent. She knew it not because she knew about wine, but because Warwick chose it.

"You have a theory," she said over coffee.

"Not entirely formulated, and it may come to nothing. Tell me what you have learned."

She recounted her visit to Alan, and her phone conversation with Sheriff Blaine. She did not mention that after the storm she had walked and thought of her father.

"Perhaps it is true after all," he said when she was finished. "Perhaps your attorney really did not know the state of your father's mind."

"I am more or less forced to trust him."

"Fortunately," said Warwick, "I am not. I would like to know more about the history of that land. At this time, however, there is little purpose served by asking further questions of him." He peered into his coffee cup as if expecting to find tea leaves that might be read.

"And the sheriff said the perpetrators of our second mystery, the persons of the murderers, were two Indians?"

"The only possible motive." She repeated what Blaine told her.

"The sheriff speaks nonsense," Warwick said. "There is no such thing as a single possible motive. Human beings are too complex. We might here list two dozen motives to fit the case, but it would be a useless exercise." He looked across at her. "For example," he said, "it could be revenge having nothing to do with the land. Some old enemy. It could be wanton, without motive. Perhaps some psychopath simply wanted to kill an Indian. It is possible your father was going to make some economic move which threatened someone else. Jealousy is a terrible motivator, as are fear, prejudice and ignorance." He smiled, but thinly. "Another lecture," he said apologetically, "and I fear one that clouds the issue."

"The sheriff is inept?"

"I doubt it," Warwick said. "These county sheriffs are most generally capable."

"He conceals something?"

"You will perhaps find that out when you meet him."

Warwick signaled the waiter for more coffee. "Tell me more about your father."

The task, she found, was easy. When she was a child her father was playful. She always remembered him laughing. After the war he was quiet. She drew word picture after word picture.

"Your attorney definitely conceals something," Warwick said

when she finished. "The sheriff also. At least so far."

He pushed his empty cup to the center of the table. "Let us stroll quietly in the cool evening." He rose to escort her.

"Because," Warwick said as they left the restaurant to walk the sidewalk beneath great trees, "my impression is that, except for concealing the money he found, your father was never devious. His friends would have known his motives."

"Knowing is not always understanding," she said.

"Was your attorney Alan nervous or fearful?"

"If he was it did not show." She wanted to answer correctly. "Some of the time he seemed a little spiteful, but not at me."

"You must next see Johnny Whitcomb," Warwick said. "Let us plan."

She was, when she saw the sheriff, to pass the information that Warwick must see the files on the murder.

Warwick was certain that this was easily accomplished. He had, after all, a bit of a reputation. She was to contact him occasionally by phone. Meanwhile he would be doing some reading.

"You have a theory," she said.

They stepped from beneath the canopy of an immense tree, and the nearest street light shone a block away. Stars glowed dim above the haze of light from the city, but she followed his gaze at the heavens. "Why," he asked her, "would a man devote an entire lifetime to the history and philosophy of religion?"

Although it was a question it did not sound like a question.

She wanted to ask him about the theory, but obviously this was not the time.

"The answer is there." He pointed his walking stick toward the stars. "In tens of thousands of faces, we humans have created our Gods, and having created them, found that they are real."

He was not concealing his theory from her, she thought. It was as he had said. The theory was not completely formulated.

For the rest of the short walk to his doorway she was content to be in his presence. Warwick did not make her feel like a student, or like an Indian, or like a woman. She fumbled for words and could not find them. The best she could come up with was that Warwick made her feel more human.

She at first felt timid, then bold. At his doorway she said, "I have a gift of thanks for you." She touched his old, veined hand. "At least I have if your piano works."

She played for him, knowing this was what music could be. She played a delicate air and he sat in what must be his sunny corner, eyes closed, listening. Then, loving the music, and because of the music and his kindness, loving the man, she played the "Prayer from Moses," and finally, with all its firm certainty, Donizetti's "L'Elisire d'Amore."

"My thanks," she said.

"And mine," he told her. His blue, nearly gray-blue eyes were moist with emotion. "For a moment," he said, "you returned my wife to me."

His words were like a true, best song in her mind as she walked the dark and quiet streets toward the YWCA.

Chapter 12

NOT all storms lived along the flatlands. In the mountains, in August, storms rose on the voice of thunder as they unpacked their winds and rolled across the Blue Ridge Mountains, across Thunder Ridge; and it was this way in a clearing in the forest during the approach of storm:

Long before the storm arrived birds began to cry and circle, driven by the feel of approaching wind and rain. In the grass of the bottoms mice and rabbits huddled. Squirrels chattered, raced, yelped. Snakes moved to higher ground and were a whisper across the needle-strewn forest floor.

As light faltered bees disappeared from flowering weeds. Deer crouched in the low underbrush, a quick, nervous movement accenting their breathing as their sides rose and fell.

The forest seemed deserted. Trees became narrow spires reaching toward the coming darkness. It seemed, this forest, like an abandoned cavern through which a few giant moths, white-flickering and deceived by the feel of moisture, beat like unsteady birds. In a little while the moths tumbled in the opening winds.

The old woman, Molla, made no preparation. Clouds drove over the far range of mountains. She watched, said no word, muttered no theme or song. Molla approached the stream which was little more than a trickle. It was rapid running. A log lay fallen in the stream. Her voice sounded low and dry. Her eyes were brilliant. She spoke to the stream about rain and storm in soft and metered words. She said to the stream that it would grow now, it would get plenty big. The Cherokee speech filled with gutturals but no harshness. Molla turned and walked slowly down the path to the cabin. She shut the door as the first of the lightnings began to walk on Thunder Ridge.

When rain came the stream rose in quick violence. It tumbled like a falling weight down the mountain. Water rushed, dashed and jumped, over-filling the bed and spreading into the clearing. It thundered between rocks and tore at the roots of plants. It floated the log, dropping it down the mountain like a battering ram which destroyed shrubbery and small trees. When the log floated the partial dam cleared and the stream ran more truly in its bed. Water in the clearing fell away. Until the rain washed down the marks, a line of mud traced against the bottom log of the cabin.

I know this because Molla told the story to Harriette, and Harriette told the story to me. At the time, of course, Harriette did not even know that Molla existed. Harriette was still in Winston-Salem, where she prepared to leave.

Morning was taken up with small chores. Harriette packed her clothes and loaded them in her car. Then she stood in the empty room at the Y, knowing she was about to embark on a new way of living. She did not know that she was about to meet me—the Cherokee girl, Janet Scott—or about to meet a man named Corey.

Beyond the window, streets were still sunstruck, August light somehow thicker than the light of spring. It looked like gold molasses, or watered honey. Her car was down there and would have to be driven. She peered around the room to make sure it was clean. Then, remembering, she pulled the ugly picture from behind the dresser and hung it back on the wall. The room became alien instead of cell-like. Hard to believe, she told herself, she had actually lived in this room for only the past several days. It seemed like months.

Sandy waited at the desk when Harriette came downstairs to keep their date for lunch. Sandy now wore a white summer dress, and she still looked as though she would be more comfortable and attractive in gym clothing.

"Cafeteria by the bus station," Sandy said. "Food's not so bad, and they got no jukebox." She turned to a girl who was taking her place at the desk. The girl was maybe seventeen. She seemed timid, a pale, wispy girl with long black hair. "It's easy," Sandy told her. "If someone cuts her wrists, call the police. If the ceiling caves in, duck. If the old bitch calls tell her I'm livin' in sin on the top floor." She took a comb from her purse and ran it through her short hair. "Let's beat it," she said to Harriette.

The cafeteria was not far away, and it turned out to be a pretty good one.

"Checking out," Sandy said between bites. Her brown eyes just about matched her short brown hair. She enjoyed lunch as much as she seemed to enjoy everything else. "Where you headed?"

"Home," Harriette told her. "Over by Asheville."

"Bunch of snoots," Sandy told her. "Bunch of la-de-da aristocratic snot bags over that way."

Harriette was amused. Sandy had a way of summing things a little unfairly, but pretty accurately. Asheville was not the nicest place in the world. At the same time, how did Sandy know? Her accent was sort of Bostonish. You had to live around Asheville for quite a little while before you understood the aristocracy of Asheville.

At the far end of the cafeteria an old negro man mopped around a section of empty tables. He was a bent, nearly crippled old man who moved the mop like an extension of his hand. Sandy watched. The chatter of the lunch crowd in the cafeteria sounded a low hum, and the cash register rang almost metrically.

"My year in the wilderness," Sandy said, and still looked at the old man. "This gets over, and we're going to do something about that."

"About what?"

"About old negroes working their asses off," said Sandy. "That man's too old."

Off and on during her life, Harriette had heard of northern liberals. In college she even met a few who claimed they were. Still, it seemed to her she was finally meeting one who was real. Maybe the man was too old. On the other hand, maybe he was all alone. Maybe it was nice for him to feel useful, to make money, to be around people. Of course, the people he was around were white.

Sandy, it developed, was a recalcitrant Presbyterian whose mother kicked her out of Boston for a year; whose mother felt that a year of "good work" among the poor would improve Sandy's character. In Harriette's opinion, it did not need much improvement.

"Because," Sandy said, "I was in love with this guy and we didn't want to get married. That's hell on Presbyterians. So now I run kids' games at a Y."

"You are of age," Harriette told her, while remembering that when her own love affair broke up she went into seclusion. Maybe Sandy simply sought seclusion.

"And I'm an heiress who don't want to get disinherited," Sandy said. "We'll play it mother's way for a year." She was going after her lunch in an extremely un-Boston manner. "'f that sounds greedy, then that's because I am greedy." She grinned like a young boy about to shock people by pulling a toad from his pocket.

"Because," Sandy said, "I'm going to need money and there's no time to earn it. Things are starting to happen out there." She gave a little burp, laid down her fork. "It's so exciting."

"What is?"

"Everything. The old stuff is dying out. Everything is building up new. If I want to call the Prime Minister of Peru, assumin' Peru has a Prime Minister, I can get through to the palace or the orpheum or whatever. Fortunately for that poor sumbitch, I can't speak Spanish. So I probably ain't going to do it." She stood. "Got to have a slab of pie. You want some pie?"

Harriette shook her head no. She was not exactly shocked, but she was at least a little bit shocked. She could no more understand Sandy's notions than she could understand the mysteries she had to solve. She watched Sandy walk to the counter, walk to the cash register.

It was true. Things were changing. Penicillin. Talk about space ships. Talk about super highways. Talk about atomic war; but also talk about powering ships and cars with atoms.

Battles over integration. American businessmen going all over the world, and she knew about that and did not like it. Before the war, back when she was a girl, none of this was around. She supposed it *was* exciting to be able to call the Prime Minister of Peru, but she could not tell exactly how. Maybe these days were for the young, and she was too old.

"Because," Sandy said when she returned, "what did the old ways ever do for me? What did they ever do for you?"

"In a way," Harriette told her, "that's exactly what I'm trying to uncover." She was uncomfortable, but still fascinated by Sandy. "I don't think you just get rid of everything."

"Look at it this way. My great-great-grandfather probably shot your great-great-grandfather, unless yours shot first. That's no way to be." Sandy's eyes were excited, but they did not seem fanatic.

"You have a lot to do," Harriette said. "What is it you have to do?"

Sandy quite clearly clamped down on her eagerness. She quite clearly wanted to be understood. "Our country has the wealth," she said, "so nobody needs to be poor ever again. We have the communications, and now we have a court ruling, so that nobody gets shit on or called nigger." She did not blush, and was not apologetic. "I believe in this country, and I believe that everybody can be fed and equal. Won't have it any other way."

"Then you really do have a lot to do." Harriette found herself a little embarrassed in the face of Sandy's idealism.

Sandy was young. Harriette told herself that to injure somebody's dream would be a great wrong. Still, she wanted to warn Sandy, to tell her it was not only difficult, it was probably impossible.

"Which is why," Sandy explained, "I say let the old ways go. They didn't work." Then, realizing she talked only about herself she looked at Harriette. "Got your problems worked out?"

"I've got them sorted. I'll work them out at home." She suddenly did not want to confide in Sandy. For one thing, Sandy already had enough trouble although she did not know it. For another thing, Sandy would try to be kind and that would just be embarrassing. She looked toward the clock on the wall.

"You have to get back," she said, "and I have to drive home. I wish we had met sooner."

"Me too," Sandy said, and her buoyancy returned. "But I'm going to be around for another eight months. You'll probably get to town."

Harriette almost grimly promised herself that she was *not* going to get back to town. "I'll call when I do," she said.

Chapter 13

S UNSET lay pale-glowing along the ridges as she arrived home. The farmhouse stood white-painted, like the ghost of a house in the coming night. Along the drive cornfields stood tattered, and fencerows were not as clean as her father had liked. She understood her sharecropper. He wanted crop, not clean fencerows, and so the rows were cleaned once a year. He was one of the new breed of croppers, a man who ran expensive equipment on land all over the county. A man who was ambitious.

Soon, she would have to see Sheriff Blaine, but this homecoming was all she would now allow to fill her mind. Behind the house, on the lower slopes of the mountain, lay her grandmother's grave. Her mother and father were in a cemetery.

She did not want to administer a farm, and she certainly did not want to administer two of them. She thought maybe she should sell them, although not, of course, her parent's house or the land which held her grandmother's grave. Sell or rent the cropland here, or let it go back to forest, which would be economically stupid.

She sat in the car and peered at the old house which was not pretentious. She loved it because it was home, but now she feared it.

Echoes upon echoes sounded in that house. Across the barnyard, and coming from the barn, a shape flickered as it disappeared silently into darkness. She gasped, caught with fear, and then recovered. Barn owl; the silent flyer moving like a whisper through the air. She told herself that she was modern and civilized, but the owl was ancient and it moved like ancient silence in her mind. She told herself she was not afraid, but some old-time part of her was very much afraid.

Time to get moving. She could not sit in the car all night. It took two trips to unload the car, and she made them without turning lights on in the house. The familiar rooms were easy to move through without light, and she did not want to see them yet. Then she went to the kitchen to heat water for tea.

She turned on lights and waited for echoes.

When she was a girl, back before the war, an old wood-burning cookstove stood where now sat a modern electric. Her mother had been so pleased with that new electric. When electricity came to the countryside, all of the country women rushed to get rid of those cookstoves. Somewhere, maybe in the barn, that cookstove still sat; and she remembered her mother while she heated water.

The memory was nearly dreamlike, the mother dream that permeated Harriette's life like the echoing notes of forgotten piano lessons, the too-hard-to-read books given her, while her mother spelled methodically through her Bible, mouth lip-moving, mouth silent; finally wrinkling, and now dead: finally; the water and soap-burned hands strangely red, the hands impressively silent beside the now unimaginably small and incredibly motionless woman, still, still: quiet finally, encased in a polished coffin of walnut and brass.

Sewing hands, squinted eyes, and the backdrop sound of the hard thumping, squeak-thumping slosh of a wringer washer. Boiling water at canning time. The gleaming, green-blue Ball jars; peaches dipped, the skins sliding off like the fruit was being slipped from jackets, and corn and beans and tomatoes; and the beef cooked and bottled during slaughter time. The slaughter of hogs. The blood-dripping hog carcass, glaze-eyed, skin scraped, and the head later put to boil.

Harriette sat at the kitchen table and told herself her weeping should be past. Her mother had been dead a whole month. You had to stop weeping sometime. She stood, went to the bathroom, wiped her eyes and blew her nose.

Time to get this over with. No doubt she could not seal the past, but it was time to come to terms with it. She moved through the silent house, turning on lights.

The old oak bookcase in the living room still held farming magazines, and the equally old radio stood like a fat little domed mountain. It was like every other farmhouse living room except for the expensive piano. Plenty of farms had a piano, and some still had old pump organs.

On this good Baldwin, though, lay cases that held her oboe, her clarinet and her flute. The side bedroom was almost tiny, filled with its single iron-framed bed. A musty, gray smell lived in that bedroom. Always had, no matter how hard you cleaned. The dining room with the old round table was where her father had sat working over plans for the farm, where her mother slowly placed figures in account books. Where her parents had sat talking to friends. All of the shapes, all of the forms and customs and rituals of their lives seemed murmuring through this room. The china cabinet with its collection of miniatures, of tiny porcelain cups and saucers and little porcelain animals.

The worn linoleum. The rug inside the doorway, the rug for wiping your feet, because this was a farmhouse which lived among soils and woodchips from the fields and forest. The fireplace with its thick gray layer of ash.

She stepped to the doorway. The night shone clear with just the hint of a chill in the air. It was too early for frost, yet she tasted the suggestion of frost. "Winter may come early," she murmured, and looked at the dark surrounding hills above which the moon even now was rising.

She closed the door against the moon, then crossed the room to a closet. She took down a thick candle which she lighted.

"Tslagi," she said. "My great-great-grandfather was a forest Indian. He died in Georgia, shot to death in Georgia."

She thought of Sandy, of Sandy's words. "Your great-great-grandfather didn't miss," she told Sandy. She walked to the stairway with the lighted candle. When she reached the top of the stairway she paused. "A long time ago," she told herself.

She walked the upstairs hall to the furthest room. It was larger than a large closet, about like a YWCA room. Her grandmother had slept here and died here. Harriette stood in the open doorway.

There was a single bed and a small dresser. The room was nearly bare. There had never been curtains. On the dresser sat a clumsily made bowl. She, Harriette, made that bowl when she was a child. Neatly folded on the bed lay a red blanket. Dust covered the room.

"Yours was a hard life," she said to her grandmother who was not there. She stepped into the room and placed the candle beside the bowl. "You had a man and he died of sickness. You had children and they died of sickness. And you could not die."

She paused. "One child lived. My father. Did you bury the last of your dead and then ponder and fear over the child who lived? Seeing me now would you smile? Or weep or wonder?

" . . . sorry. I do not remember you well. Hardly remember you at all. Only things that were done. A spot of sunshine in the forest once. Blackberries. A blackberry picking."

Outside a light wind moved the top branches of trees illuminated by moonlight. She turned at the sound of a small rushing, the back of her neck tight, seized by fear. The sound came from another room. It must be field mice.

The Cherokee, the old ones, did not attend the dead. They did not even go near the graveyard. They tried not to think of the dead. It brought sickness. Harriette shuddered and turned back to the room.

"I have climbed the hill to your grave and wondered at the trees that surround that place, thinking you are not in that place. At night I think of you as a voice on the wind. Or as a whisper from the fire. I do not believe the superstitions, but I am afraid."

She stepped across the room to stare through the window.

"I have met the rattlesnake and not feared because I respected his nature. Yet, in the winter I have walked in these hills and felt fear because rock falls. Thaw and freeze, then great slabs come down and destroy trees that have lived a hundred years. The rock was not like the snake. I did not understand its nature."

The noise of scurrying came again. It was not as startling to her now that she had identified it. A cat killed mice. Still, the mice had never been a problem. Perhaps she could get a dog for company.

She had not felt a lot of fear in a long time. The moon lit the landscape and thrust a shaft of light into the room. A shape moved in the blowing trees. Owl?

She fell on the bed and pulled the red blanket around her. She wrapped herself so that no part of her was exposed.

Red for the east. Red for luck, for the sun, for war. In the silent room she murmured beneath the blanket, murmuring to her grandmother or to herself.

"You loved me," she said to her grandmother. "I was happy when you loved me."

The candle trailed a thin blue stream of smoke above its flame. Harriette huddled beneath the red blanket. Dust disturbed by her movements danced and shone in the ray of moonlight. The house seemed filled with the sounds of small scurryings.

Chapter 14

J OHNNY Whitcomb's bus sat blocked up and wheelless beneath an
old tulip poplar whose canopy was like an umbrella. A stream bed
ran fifty yards away. The bus, made long before the war, had once
been painted dark gray. Now it stood like a small mosaic of imagination. All over the bus and probably, Harriette thought, even on the
roof, Johnny had painted faces of animals and the faces of trees. He
painted forest scenes, and desert scenes with the faces of camels. She
did not know exactly how someone could paint the face of a tree, but
surely Johnny had done it. None of the trees exactly had eyes, none
exactly had noses or mouths; yet the trees were definitely persons.
Bold colors arranged themselves so the trees seemed sighing or happy
or serene or angry. A little black enamel, three or four shades of green
enamel, were all it had taken for the trees. She smiled and thought
Johnny must be a modern version of those first people who painted
on the walls of caves.

"Sure," Johnny said, "Sure, sure. I was on that job. Your daddy die
the day I quit. That next winter I take a crew in there. We clean up
and burn the mess."

He was not a very big man, although he had the arms and shoulders of a big man. His hair shone negro black, negro kinky, but his
skin was lighter than hers. What always impressed her about Johnny
was his tidiness. Even now, wearing an old work shirt and work pants
he seemed dressed to go to town. Perhaps it was the economy of his
hand movements or the small ways he moved that suggested tidiness.

She recalled that he was once a sailor. Maybe sailors and people
who lived in buses or other small spaces developed special patterns.

"You've known me for a long time," she said.

"Since a little girl."

"People are not telling me the truth," Harriette told him. "You will, won't you?" They sat at an old picnic table beneath the poplar. Worn clay around the table showed where Johnny usually walked, a heavily compacted area showed where he usually sat. It seemed he sat where he could watch the stream.

His woodpile was stacked at the rear of the bus. Except for the woodpile and the table, the grounds around the bus held no litter, no rusting carcasses of tools.

"I'll tell you to stay away from there," Johnny said quietly, "that mountain he is a bad one."

"How is it bad?"

"Trees fall the wrong way. The animals are too bold, don't act like animals. Rocks fall in summer." He was not uncomfortable and he clearly was not lying. "On that mountain you got more storm than you got in all the rest of the world, maybe." He looked at her with compassion. "Your daddy have no business there, you got no business there."

"I have to go there next," she admitted. "I have to see a man named Blaine this afternoon."

Upstream a hundred yards a stir of breeze caused a brief, light rain of falling leaves. It was awfully early for any leaf to be changing. She looked upward into the pale sun-green of the poplar. Soon it would be gold.

"Blaine knows his way around. You'll be okay with Blaine." Johnny grinned. "He arrest me once. I get a little drunk, paint a little picture on his squad car. Hound dog picture. Dog look a little like Blaine."

She laughed, imagining the fracas.

"I tell you what happened," Johnny said. "Did not like that job from the first. Did not like the way Dan acted. He had a bulldozer tearing things up." Johnny also looked up into the poplar. It was an old tree but not ancient.

"We fight about a tree like this, but bigger tree. Old, old tree." Johnny laid both of his hands flat on the picnic table, looking at his hands as if asking them questions. "I timber in the north woods, once," he said quietly. "Even there we did not act so bad.

"Old trees like that, they are sometimes not so good. They die in their heart, and when they come down there is only a shell. You cannot make boards from such trees.

"'Dan,' I say, 'let me put an auger in. Let us look at its heart. If this tree will not timber, then I think maybe he should die of old age.'

"Next morning I come to the job and that tree is down. Dan would not speak to me. I never even unpack my tools. Just start my truck and drive away."

Johnny continued to look at his hands, and now he looked apologetic. She remembered how Johnny and her father had been such good friends. It was certain Johnny did not want to say what he was next going to say.

"To cut such a tree is crazy. Crazy. Your wedges will not hold, because that tree did not timber. That tree must have spun in every crazy way when he fall. He maybe waltz on the stump." He looked at her, still apologetically. "I think Dan was crazy," he said. "I think your daddy was insane."

That was it. Or, maybe that was it. That was what Alan hid from her. Maybe Alan told so much about her father's troubles during the war because of that. Alan would give reasons to hide or cloud her father's insanity. She sat beneath the poplar. High up in the poplar leaves rustled.

Insane. Driven too hard and too long; and besieged by awful power. What had Warwick said? That when men usurp the powers of their Gods they are doomed? So her father bought chainsaws and leased a bulldozer, maniacally giving a doomed order and form to a world which would allow him such fatal power.

She looked at Johnny, at his face. He was miserable, having said what he thought, but Johnny did not lie. He concealed nothing. It occurred to her that he really was her old friend. He was brave enough to be honest.

"Thank you," she told him. "I suppose I was afraid of that, and never let myself think it."

Johnny looked away. Looked at his bus. "I was in Merchant Marines during the war. Now I draw crazy pictures. Get a little drunk sometimes."

"Who killed him, Johnny?"

"Two men from over to Cherokee, maybe three men. Maybe not town men. Lot of people still live back in the hills."

There was no uncertainty in his words. He shook his head, as if denying what he was about to say. "Cherokees are funny people. Never know what they gonna do. In north woods you always know what an Indian's gonna do."

She did not know how to repay him for his honesty. Then she thought that you could not pay for honesty. Except with thanks.

"You are a good friend," she told him. "I'm afraid I had forgotten just how good."

"What will you do?"

"I go to see Blaine now."

"No," Johnny said. "What will you do in that house? No husband, no man around. No mother. How is your wood pile?"

"Low."

"You see?"

"I don't know what I will do," she said. "I honestly haven't figured it out yet."

"Figure it out fast," Johnny said. "Dan's friend—me—will take care of your wood pile."

She left him sitting at the old picnic table beneath the old tree, that curious, honest man. She walked down the path to the road conscious that her years of seclusion had probably been a mistake. In the past few days she had met people, Alan and Warwick and Sandy. Now it was like meeting Johnny for the first time. All of those people, even Sandy who was young and a little ignorant, had been good to her. When she reached the road she got her car turned around, then headed in the direction of Cherokee. She had arranged to meet Blaine in the parking lot of a small motel.

He climbed from the cab of a new pickup when she arrived. In the afternoon sun, and across the graveled parking lot, a radio in the pickup broadcast low; but not police talk. Blaine looked like sheriffs in western movies hoped they looked. He was tall, broad shouldered, his hair thick gray with some streaks turning to white. He was blue-eyed, good looking, and it was clear he neither thought nor cared much about either.

On the phone she had heard authority in his voice. The authority was still there. "We'll ride over to the site," he told her, "although it isn't far." He motioned toward his truck, climbed in and pushed the door on the rider's side open. She got into the truck and was glad someone else drove. The truck even smelled new, and the radio must be quite powerful because even here in the hills it picked up a radio station in Charlotte.

There was also a police radio in the truck. She looked at it.

"Force of habit," Blaine said. He pulled into the road and turned left. "When I retired I found out that a man can't stay retired for very long."

They drove about a quarter of a mile, then made another left turn and drove along the base of a mountain. "This is it," Blaine told her. He pulled the truck over. "It is not a long walk."

The logging road disappeared beneath brush. Seedling trees grew in the road. She walked easily, more comfortable out here than she could ever be on city streets. Some of the trees were large, but none were immense.

"It was selectively logged during World War I," Blaine told her. "For some reason the job got scrubbed. There are monster trees further in." They came to a clearing that was filling up with young growth. "Here we are." He rapidly indicated positions in the clearing.

"A bulldozer parked there. Your father's truck stood there. The body lay over there." He indicated a small rise.

"There is no way to make this better than it is. The body was on its back. A regular steel hunting knife was used, and some other kind of knife with a thick blade. It left a ragged wound. No other clues."

"Footprints?"

"Plenty of them," Blaine told her. "The soil was all turned and broken by the bulldozer. Dan's crew made prints all over the place. We checked that. No prints except those made by Dan's crew." He paused and looked upward into the forest as if searching for the mountain top. "I am fairly certain they worked their way down through the forest. Either that, or they were men who are well known around here. No one along that road remembered any strange automobiles, except those belonging to a few tourists." He saw her question before it was asked. "New automobiles are tourists. No one around here drives new automobiles."

She also looked uphill into the forest. It seemed to her like one more North Carolina forest, although more heavily wooded and impressive than most. "Johnny Whitcomb said this is a bad mountain."

"Trust him," Blaine said. "Johnny is crazy as a rabbit sometimes, but when it comes to things like that I trust him."

Now was the time to say it. She had planned to say it later. "I feel there is something you do not want to tell me. Johnny says my father was insane. Is that what everyone is trying to keep from me?"

He actually seemed to relax. "Your mother never knew," he said. "Your mother never visited here. She did not know the extent of damage." He pointed. "Johnny and some other men cleaned up the slash. If they had not I think you would be shocked even seven years later." He motioned her to a fallen log, walked that way and sat down. A young oak rose at the end of the log and placed them in shadow. She sat beside him.

"Dan was not as bad as the worst," he said. "The worst of them end up in the penitentiary or the V.A. hospital." He looked across the clearing as if remembering damage. "I took one to V.A. once. He was lying at home screaming that Jesus was stirring a flaming finger in his belly. The man got wounded in the war, but was still strong enough when he recovered to be assigned to graves detail. He spent six months burying pieces and parts of bodies. Dan was not that bad."

She sat silent. Awed. Alan's stories of her father's experiences pained her, but somehow she had not quite thought of them as real. Or, if real, not so strong they could affect a man who lived with the sanity of a home and wife and daughter; a man who lived with the sanity of forests and fields. Now, feeling the true awfulness of those stories, she blinked back tears.

"I'm sorry," she said to Blaine. "What happened to the man you took to hospital?"

"He's still there and still screaming. He's got company. The ones who went to Korea are beginning to break down now."

Blaine ignored her sorrow. "It will not help you," he said, "but for what it is worth, I turned this county upside down. The men who did it are still here somewhere."

Was he warning her? He seemed passive enough. Was he only apologizing because he had not found the murderers?

"The Cherokee are mountain people," he said, "and mountain people keep their own counsel. You don't know what they are going to do."

"They would revenge themselves on me."

"Your mother feared that," Blaine said. "I did not. I think you were always safe, because you never asked questions. Now you are asking questions."

Beyond the clearing other mountains rose in the distance. They were lower, forested mountains, and on one a line ran up and across the top where a power company cleared land to run its wires. The mountain slopes looked dark because of distance. This late in the afternoon, mist seemed ready to gather. When it came it would put spectral capes across the ridges. In the morning, slow-turning mist would fall down the mountains in silent cascades. She felt the force of the mountains, the great numbers of them.

Blaine watched her. "You could lose an army in these hills," he said. "That is the only thing that saved the eastern band of Cherokee. During the removal, your ancestors hid in these mountains. The best army in the world could not have searched them out." He stood, and for the first time seemed apologetic. "That's all I have to tell you. It is precious little."

She followed him back to his truck. When in the truck she told him there was one other thing. A friend of hers, a teacher of history, wanted to see the police files.

Blaine seemed amused. "Shouldn't be any problem. I'll call Pete. Pete is sheriff. Used to be my deputy." He chuckled. "A history teacher."

Warwick was rather more than a history teacher. She started to explain. Blaine waved his hand. "I'm not laughing at you or him. Maybe a history teacher is exactly what we need."

Chapter 15

THE next morning she woke wondering if she needed a man. It was not a sexual question although it was a little bit sexual. That always happened two or three days into her period. No, the question was practical. Johnny Whitcomb wondered what she would do in this house without a man, and it was a fair question. While her mother was alive it was never a problem. Her mother had been good at planning. Her mother would have hired someone, and the wood pile would be winter-worthy by now. Even if she could handle a saw and ax she would not. Musicians took chances all the time, but she should not take that kind of chance when it came to her hands.

She lay in bed watching the dawn grow along the ridges. The mist up there rolled slowly like gray velvet, and the sun touched redly, bluely, redly. Along the roads birds would fly in confused patterns. This was a crazy time of day for birds. If a bird was going to get hit by a car it was almost always at this time of day. They rose from fence rows, their flight patterns erratic.

In the growing light she lay remembering a teacher she once knew, a conversation she once had with a woman who looked back on a lifetime of playing music. That teacher, Lillian Shuder, was old enough that she could be frank. She had, Harriette remembered, smiling, shocked the confused senses of a young student engaged in her first love affair.

"My dear," the teacher said, "through the years I'd sometimes wake up beside a man. I'd look at him. Maybe a good man. And I'd say to myself, 'Is this what you want for the rest of your life?' And,

I'd say to myself, 'Not worth the price.'"

There was the problem. A man carried a price tag. Maybe, if she were truly modern and if she lived in a city, she could have a lover. In rural North Carolina, even if it was 1957 and the world was on fire with change, you did not take a lover. Not in rural North Carolina.

She rolled from bed and pulled on an old robe, thinking if she wanted she could walk naked through the house; knowing also that she could not walk naked through the house because of the echoes. It would be the greatest discourtesy to her mother, although her father would not have minded. Her father sometimes bathed in the forest, and you did not bathe with your clothes on.

She made morning coffee and ran through a list of men she knew, nearly a fantasy list because everything was a little sexual this morning. It was a longer list than she thought possible. Faces rose, men from her mother's church, men from schools, local men; and she discarded them one by one. Every single one if she could interest them, and she was sure she could, would want a wife who cooked and had babies.

Except, of course, Warwick and Johnny Whitcomb. Why did men have to get so old before they amounted to anything? She mused, nearly dreaming. It must have been perfect to have been married to Warwick. She wished she had known his wife.

Of course, Johnny Whitcomb was no older than her father would have been. Of course, that was pretty old. She smiled and thought of what a psychologist could do with that thought; but, truth to tell, Johnny was attractive. He was not pretty, but his craziness and honesty and ways of living were pretty, if you liked prettiness touched with fingers of wildness.

Some mornings when her mother still lived, and now that her mother was dead, then all mornings she took her coffee to a small table beside the piano. She would work, sip coffee, and in an hour it would be time for breakfast. Dawn was a good time for work.

The light grew steadily, light illuminating the face of the old side-arm bookcase, shining yellowly on spines and covers of the *National Geographic*, on pictured red tractors of the farm magazines, and the unthreatening covers of *Reader's Digest*. Light glossed starched doilies on the arms of chairs, brought up faded colors from the old

American oriental rug. Light rose slowly, perhaps prayerfully, to the feet of a teaching Jesus, the picture a perpetual sermon which had hung on the wall for Harriette's entire life. Light illuminated, re-painted the red of old roses in old wallpaper; and it flowed across all of these possessions and expressions of a dead mother in its bold, broad band.

After breakfast she made the decision that, until then, she had managed to avoid. Johnny Whitcomb said to stay away from that land. Alan told her to stay away. Blaine said to stay away. Only War-wick claimed that the land, itself, was part of the mystery. She would know more when she saw more of the land. She only wished it were close enough so that she would not have to drive. She checked the oil in the car, the way her father always had. She wore jeans and a flannel shirt, and she checked her pockets to make sure her knife was there. A person would be stupid going into the forest without a knife.

Then, about to leave, she got delayed. The new preacher drove up the lane in a black car that looked like it was in mourning, although the engine purred as smoothly as he did. She hurried outside, deter-mined to get rid of him. If he got in the house he would spend a half hour, and the place would smell unctuous for days. She told herself she was unfair. Then she told herself she did not care. Then she told herself she *did* care out of respect to her mother, congregation, and choir.

Tall, thin, blond; his black suit made him look like an undertaker. No, like a Norwegian undertaker. His accent was cultivated. She wondered why so many people from Boston kept showing up in North Carolina. She wondered if his disapproval came because of the way she dressed. Maybe he preferred a house dress. She thought of the kitchen. Had she turned off the stove? Yes. She thought of her thoughts of a man. Smiled.

"It is good to have you back," he said. The conventional words seemed harmless enough, yet they somehow conveyed the idea that she was being scrutinized. He looked toward the house as if suspi-cious that she hid something, then across the farm yard. He looked across the pasture, downhill where an oak stood a little forward of the surrounding forest. It was the oak that meant so much to her, the tree that was nearly totemic. It was the tree where, long ago, she helped save the spirit of another tree. She found that she did not even like him to look toward the tree.

"I was only gone a few days." Was he keeping an eye on her? Why did he look so suspiciously at the house?

"The choir misses you," he said. "The congregation is rather lost without you."

She was in a hurry. She was annoyed. She did not want to be late. She smiled. "Then you must find them. We can't be having them lost." She regretted the words. Then she told herself she regretted not saying them humorously.

"I'm sorry," she said. "That sounded rude."

"I am new here," he told her. His forehead was high and pale. Now it wrinkled. She remembered Warwick, his gentleness. "When one is in a new place a certain amount of misunderstanding, even persecution, may be expected."

Persecution. She wondered if he were mad. Then she remembered sermons, long Sundays where the struggle between forces of light and dark ceased to be heroic in the face of boredom. Maybe the word "persecution" was too narrowly defined. Maybe she was being unfair. She remembered Sandy at the YWCA. Sandy was not stiff, but she was from Boston.

"I have a friend," she said, remembering Warwick, "who claims there is a big difference between southern and northern Presbyterians. Someday maybe you will tell me the difference."

He became friendly again. "It is a long story. The northern church has a strong what you call Puritan background. The southern church is emotional, and derives from the Scots and Irish. The southern church is more or less Baptist no matter what they call themselves."

"I have an errand," she said truthfully.

"We would like you back after your mourning. We mourn your mother as well."

Maybe he told the truth. She wished she did not believe otherwise. She believed he mourned because his church was not mentioned in her mother's will. What had her mother known?

He looked again toward her house, and once more seemed suspicious. It would be good policy to invite him in. Then she told herself, no, absolutely not, no. She had other things to do. "I really must go."

"I'll keep it short." He bowed his head and began to pray. She stood, waiting it out, and thinking that if Warwick did this, which of course Warwick would not do, then it might make a little sense. The preacher said his amen. He shook hands, climbed in his car and left. Before he turned into the roadway she was in her car, heading down the lane behind him.

The land, when she arrived, lay cast in sunlight; although deeper in the forest, darkness and shadow lay like gulfs of superstition. An old, old truck sat parked where Blaine's truck parked the day before. She pulled her car in beside it, got out and did not insult whoever owned that truck by locking her car. She turned to the forest. On this lower part of the mountain the darkness seemed to reach toward her from beneath the tall trees. It would not be difficult to imagine the Cherokee's little men of the forest trickstering on that mountainside. They were a part of the mythology, every bit as real in her mind as the miracles wrought by Christian saints. Of course, she told herself, she did not know how real that was. Invisible men, they were.

Higher up, high among rocks and thinning trees, it was possible to imagine that the Nunnehi still ranged, still hunted, still sat about their fires. In the mythology Nunnehi were not little men, but warriors. In times long past they had become visible and helped the Cherokee in war. The Nunnehi were not gods, but they owned the stature of gods.

And even that was not exactly true. The Nunnehi were not simply godlike warriors. They were Indians like the Cherokee. Maybe they were Indians who embodied every belief the old Cherokee people held as true; whether invisible or not.

The forest was beginning to fade as summer faded. Twigs and small branches thrown by a recent storm littered the decayed logging road. She stepped carefully, not wishing to twist an ankle among rotting remains of logs laid to stabilize the road. The road did not run far into the forest. At its end a gully lay filled with brush. She reckoned that a flash flood brought the debris down the mountain. She looked across the gully.

A man stood there. In sunlight, and on the dark edge of forest, she could not make out his features. She stood shocked, hesitating. The man stepped back into shadow. Harriette stood, wondering if she should head back to her car. Then, more forest-wise than she knew, she stood listening.

Silence. Hidden somewhere to her left, and up the mountain, a spring trickled. A chipmunk whirled, dashed, rose up a tree like a striped spirit. The chipmunk perched on a branch about thirty feet up. He did not scold. She took a deep breath, backed up a pace. He was not scolding.

Johnny Whitcomb said that animals on this mountain did not act like animals. No chipmunk anywhere, no chipmunk ever born would miss this opportunity to scold. She stood almost rigid, more frightened by the chipmunk than by the man.

Silence. Then distant, slightly labored sound of breathing. The man appeared twenty-five yards lower on the hill than when she first saw him. He walked slowly. There was a trail up there.

She waited. The man disappeared behind a cover of brush as the trail went slightly downhill. When he emerged from cover he was no more than a hundred feet from her. He was an old man dressed in faded coveralls tucked into high boots; but he was Indian nonetheless. The boots were proof against rattlesnakes. She thought only touristy adventurers wore them. She waited.

His eyes were dark, deeply dark. Wrinkles circled the eyes like nebula. His dark hands were veined. He did not have trouble walking, but he walked slowly because he had trouble breathing.

"You startled me," she said as he approached. "Good morning."

He did not say a word. As he passed he looked directly at her and his eyes filled with hatred. She had never seen such naked hatred on any human face. Surely, if he had a weapon and enough breath to use it, she would be dead.

She watched as he disappeared. Her heart was timid, shocked. She felt small. It was one thing to be scorned by a couple of teenage white boys, quite another to be hated by one of her own. He disappeared around a bend in the logging road. She listened until she heard the starter on the old truck grind and grind, as the engine chugged into life.

The trail he followed ran narrow, but earth was hard-packed and not overgrown; a well-used trail. She hesitated, wondering if the old man was going home for a gun. Her shoulders rose, hunched. She felt the place on her spine where a bullet might enter. Then she forced a laugh. Maybe the mountain made her fearful. Maybe the old man hated everybody. If murderers still walked this mountain they did not walk in the form of a lung-sick old man.

The easy trail gradually slanted upward. It was cut twice by small streams, at this time of year only narrow trickles. She walked easily. The soundlessness of the forest matched her own passing along the trail. In occasional sunny places she watched for small movement on the littered forest floor. Not even insects buzzed. No wings, no matter how tiny, danced in the sunlit air. The great silence of the forest was broken only by the trickling murmur of streams. No birds, it seemed, were flying.

After another half mile of rising trail, she felt she ascended toward some dark heart of the forest. Here trees were no longer old, but ancient. These trees, some of them, were surely youngsters in the days when forest buffalo penetrated this far east. These trees might have been here when the first voices of Spanish adventurers echoed. Four hundred years were not so long in the life of great trees, even trees of these wet North Carolina forests. She figured she must be near the fifteen-hundred-foot level.

Ahead, a small circle of sunlight rapidly grew larger as she advanced beneath the canopy of trees. The forest began to lighten. Fifty yards, and she could see where the trail entered a clearing. She could not see anything in the clearing yet, but a shadow cast sideways, angular; and no tree or rock would cast such a shadow. It slanted like a roof line. Impossible as it seemed, someone lived back here.

She thought of the old man and his look of hatred. Could this be his? Was it only her intrusion that he hated?

No. A man in his shape would not, could not, live this far from the road.

It would be the worst sort of discourtesy to silently appear in that clearing. She stopped. Listened. Maybe the mountain itself announced her approach. At the same time, maybe not. She forced herself to cough, then she muttered that she was tired and had better take a rest pretty soon. She stepped forward, trying to make footfall sounds. It was difficult when you were wearing a pair of ratty old sneakers.

She did not see the old woman right away because brilliant sunlight left her blinking. As her eyes adjusted from darkness of the forest, the first thing she saw was the cabin.

It was a good two-room cabin. Here and there, on the roof, shone the yellow-white of new shingles. Someone maintained it. Her eyes adjusted.

The clearing covered a little over an acre. At some time a family must have come here and cut the trees. It had to have been long ago because even the stumps were rotted away. On the far side of the clearing, and above a rise behind which ran a large stream bed, a patch of corn stood ready to rattle drying leaves to any wind. Pumpkins or squash grew in the corn and made a dark layer of green.

She stepped forward. Nothing carried a more sacred presence than the corn, in Cherokee "selu." Corn stood at the very base of Cherokee society, and Cherokees raised a high civilization because of the corn. They had not simply been a hunting society.

At one end of the corn patch someone moved. A slow flash of red. A tiny old woman stood there. She wore an old red flannel shirt, a long cotton skirt with a glaring floral pattern. She wore moccasins, and did not turn as Harriette approached.

"Forgive my intrusion," Harriette said when a few yards from the woman. "I was walking the trail, wondering where it led."

The old woman turned. Her face was so wrinkled she seemed to have dressed her face in a web. Her eyes were dark, clear, and interested. The old eyes looked at Harriette, perhaps the way Harriette might have looked at a neighbor's new baby.

"Why are you here?" The voice was dry, like the rustle of wind in the corn. The voice did not sound unkind, only interested. "Your father is not in this place. Your father is dead."

Chapter 16

T HE western land, the shadowing land, the land of death. When Cherokees died it was said of them that they were in the shadowing land. The American Indian had, for the most part, not handled death much better than he handled sex. Taboos and ribald jokes surrounded sex, terror walked beside death. Some Indians were known to flee the dead, while at the same time weeping in inconsolable grief. The Cherokee were not quite so vivid; in fact, their burial ceremonies were sometimes elaborate, but Cherokees did not ordinarily speak plainly and simply about death.

Harriette stood beside the fading corn. She stared into the patch, at small pumpkins with developing streaks of orange, specklings and bands of orange along their green skins. She incongruously thought of Easter eggs, of resurrections, of doxologies. She blinked, shook her head.

"You know me?" She wondered if this was a magic woman. All of the magic women were dead. All of the great medicine men were dead. All of the old medicines were dead. At least she thought that was true. Then she vaguely remembered stories of people living in the old ways, but those were common stories. If someone told of this particular old woman she would probably have thought it but one more of those stories.

"People from town. Some say you are your father who has returned. One man has dreams of big machines." The voice betrayed no emotion, although the voice still sounded interested.

That was the reason the old man on the trail hated her. Harriette, in the midst of startlement, did some rapid thinking and summation.

How could such a story get around, and how could it get around so quickly?

Obviously, someone saw her with Blaine. Some gossip spread rumor simply because she set foot on the land. Probably the man who owned the motel. He would have seen Blaine parked in that new truck, waiting for her.

"I don't have any machines," she said. "It is not me who causes bad dreams."

"That is good," the old woman said. "I think maybe nobody will believe that."

"They must..." She fumbled her words. Here she was, indicted and convicted by some man's bad dreams. "Of course they do not have to believe me," she said, "but whether they believe or not I'm telling the truth." She stared at the ground, at wheat-colored grasses. She raised her eyes but did not look directly at the woman. Most Cherokees did not do that. A direct look would mean she was shameless, bold. Instead she looked upward. From the clearing she could see above trees, could see the dark ridge rising, stretching across her vision and filling the sky. For a crazy, silly, insane second she thought of a man's back, of how if she were holding a man to her—in her—over her—his form would seem like the spine of that mountain.

Then the thought did not seem crazy. Watching the ridge, feeling this old woman's presence, she felt the gathering of power up there on that ridge. Power lived in the forest, power in this small patch of corn. If she thought of having a man because she looked at a ridge then maybe that was a good thing to think.

Power. Naked, non-threatening, but absolute. Absolute as egg and sperm, absolute as storm. Power, that if unleashed, would bend the sky, would make night and daylight whirl, would make the invisible world visible.

Power. The power of the sky world. Power as sacred and unremitting as the sun. The power of the middle world, the power of the underworld. Indifferent, inexorable, serene.

Power. She stood awed. Her feelings came not from fear, but from the great indifference of the power.

"I will be alone now," the old woman said. "You go away." The rustling voice seemed edged with fatigue. The woman waited for

Harriette to leave. She seemed fragile. Standing beside the corn, and no taller than the corn, she appeared to Harriette like some old goddess, an ancient expression of the land. Savagery was this way, for savagery was straightforward. It did not paint in pastels. It occurred to Harriette that Johnny Whitcomb did not paint in pastels, either.

"But you will come again tomorrow," the old woman said. "When the sun is straight up. Maybe we will eat." She turned from Harriette, showing her back and stood waiting for Harriette's shadow to move away.

"Yes," Harriette said. "I mean well, yes tomorrow." She left, walking rapidly, feeling humiliated. She blamed herself. She had been rude, barging in here and violating the old woman's privacy. If some stranger came walking up to her house, and demanded her time over some issue that bored her, she would be angry.

Still, the old woman had not seemed angry. At the edge of the clearing Harriette turned back. The old woman was nowhere to be seen. Doubtless she had disappeared into the patch of corn. Harriette looked toward the ridge. It stood dark, nearly black against a sky stacked with high cumulus. She told herself she was a trained musician with a trained ear, and yet she did not know whether she heard what she seemed to hear. A pulsation lived in the air, like the distant beat of drums. At the same time she could not actually, technically, say she heard anything. Silly. Her imagination, so trained to sound, now creating the illusion of sound. Still, the power of the mountain remained unshakeable. That was no illusion.

And after all, during a storm there was music in the sky. In the forest music lived in the streams. It sounded wild and sometimes uncoordinated, obeying different musical forms; but music certainly. If the beat of drums seemed invisible above a mountain, what was so surprising?

Harriette entered onto the trail. Giant trees shadowed the trail so she could not see well at first. Somewhere in the underbrush beside the clearing, a heavy body moved. Bear, no doubt, because deer did not stomp around like that. She walked rapidly. Black bears were rarely a problem. A black bear could live in the neighborhood for years and you would never see him. They only became a problem when they got civilized, got too near garbage cans or tourists who fed them. Sometimes a bear would stalk a person, either from curiosity or simply for fun.

Bear sign lay along the trail. She noted it automatically. Here and there rotted logs were shredded as effectively as if exploded by dynamite. The bear was after grubs. She wondered for a moment if the old woman knew about the bear. Then she told herself yes the old woman knew about the bear, and that bear had better not try to cross that old woman; because it would rapidly be one awfully unhappy bear. She did not know why or how she knew that but was serene in her knowledge.

Further into the forest, as she looked down the trail, came a flash of white. She told herself this was not a trail, this was a thoroughfare. Half the people in North Carolina must be on this mountain today. She waited. She heard someone whistling. He was a terrible whistler, nearly tuneless and with no more sense of pitch, no more ear, than an ear of corn. Still, he sounded happy.

He was about her age, and very good to look at. He was tall, whiter than she but sort of darkly, and he carried a lumpy pillow case over his shoulder. She stepped from the trail and waited. He came up to her. Stopped. His eyes looked like polished, happy chocolate. His mouth smiled wide and not thin-lipped. His black hair hung a little shaggy, too long between haircuts.

"You must be the Johnson lady," he said. "Are you going to log this?" He nodded at the forest. Then he sat the pillow case on the ground. A loaf of bread tumbled out. He reached down, stuffed it back in the pillowcase. Grinned. "I bring soft stuff," he said. "She hasn't got many teeth anymore. Roasted her a squirrel one time but she could hardly handle it."

"I wouldn't dream of logging it."

"People can *dream* all they want. Just don't do it." He reached in his shirt pocket for a pack of cigarettes, offered one, lit one. She had not smoked in a long time but it seemed a friendly thing to do. He broke the burned match, rubbed the head between thumb and index finger. "Woods get pretty dry this time of year."

"How do things like this get started?" Harriette asked. "I step one foot on this mountain and it looks like half the world starts having hysterics." She gave an experimental puff on the cigarette, coughed.

"It's a rube town," the man said, and grinned. "It is a real *nice* rube town." He dragged on the cigarette. The tobacco put a pleasurable scent in the air. Among Indians tobacco had always been important, even sacred, even medicinal. Of course this was Winston-Salem treated tobacco, so maybe it did not count. "Don't worry about the grumblers," he said. "They sit around and talk. They feed on it."

"Tell them," she said. "Make them understand that nothing is going to happen."

"And break their hearts? Nothing this big has happened around here since Andrew Jackson set up his hired guns." He paused.

"This is serious."

"I know it," he said. "You know it. The mountain knows it. The old woman up there knows it. The mountain wouldn't let you do it anyway." He looked into darkness under great trees. He shook his head. "Tried to log it after World War I. Tried to log it after the Second War. Mountain won't allow it." His voice was matter of fact. He might use the same tones in discussing the weather.

She suddenly feared him. Not terribly afraid, but uneasy. It seemed he felt, rather than saw, her alarm.

"Nothing to be scared about," he said. "You been up to see my old friend?"

"I did not know she lived there."

"When you go," he said, "don't talk so much. She wears out easy." He picked up the pillow case. Grinned. "Name is Thomas Corey," he said. "You get over to Cherokee then check in with my dad. Lewis Corey. He knows all about this mountain."

She felt young. Silly. This man was no older than she, yet he was completely comfortable with this place. Be honest. After all, he was being honest. "I don't understand what I feel here. I've never felt this before."

"You don't *try* to understand it," he said. "Just live beside it. It doesn't mind. I'm going now."

He walked away before she could be more fearful, and before she could ask more questions.

She called to him. "There is bear sign up there."

He called back. "That's a real good bear. Known her for the last six years." As he disappeared up the trail he was once more whistling.

She came off the mountain without meeting anyone else, and she came quickly. Back in the forest she felt the gathering of enormous power. The power seemed indifferent to her and her concerns. Yet it was power that even few Indians would want to live beside. It was power no white man could even experience, maybe. She thought of Warwick, and thought she must call him. She figured that Warwick, of all white men in the world, would be the one most likely to understand that power. It was not the power of the Hebrew God on that mountain, but there was the power of some kind of Gods up there and they were ancient.

She arrived at her car. Stood, looking back into the forest. She opened the door; stood shocked. On the front seat lay a redbird, the eyes dull, the body slightly decayed.

She stood, feeling the ugliness, the meanness of this. Was it a warning? Was it only something that a spiteful, sick old man did? The feathers were covered with dust. Someone had gone out along the road and found this, had returned to place it here.

She looked back to the forest, back past the spot where her father's body had lain. She remembered her father. She remembered her grandmother. In Cherokee mythology the redbird was the daughter of the sun. She took a handkerchief, picked up the bird and placed it on the floor of the car. She would bury it when she got home.

Chapter 17

T HE earth holds its sacred places, places where unknown dimensions intersect; or maybe where bones of original creation lie
bared or near the rocks' surface. That creation need have been
no more than a big bang. No matter. It is ancient, it is real. Whatever
powers run in the universe are sometimes made evident on earth.
I, Janet Scott, who have studied so many religions, say this.

And power, itself, comes not from ways and beliefs. It rises not
from gods, but from the power that created the gods. In different
places, it takes different expressions because of the people of those
places.

In Georgia, for example, the Moravians, whom Harriette did not
understand, carried enormous power. They arrived in Georgia in
1734, did not get to North Carolina until 1765. They were always a
small group, but their power exercised influence in American history
out of all proportion to their numbers. That, however, is another
story. For Cherokee purposes the Moravians were the only European
group who did not try to change the Cherokee. They learned the
Cherokee language. Their message was simple. "Do not kill. Be quietly pious." I mention this only because Warwick had announced
himself as the last Moravian worth hanging, and because Harriette
hurried home to call him.

"I suspected as much," Warwick said over the phone, after she told
of her experience on the mountain. He paused. "Also I feared it.
Have you ever made a pilgrimage?"

She knew vaguely what the word meant. People in Europe did that
sort of thing. It was like being a religious tourist. She was going to say

no. That would hide her ignorance. Yet, even on the phone, Warwick's way of asking a question assumed a careful, considered answer.

"I think maybe I have now," she said. "Except I didn't intend to, and maybe that doesn't count." She was vaguely puzzled with Warwick. A man that brilliant would not spend a lifetime studying something unimportant. Yet, everything she knew about religion in North Carolina showed that religion was only important when it made people miserable.

"I have," he said. "Made pilgrimages. Three times. They came to nothing."

"What my attorney was hiding," she said, "and what the sheriff was hiding, is that my father was insane." She paused. "Johnny Whitcomb says the same. I believe Johnny."

"We have a costly change of plans," Warwick told her. "Can a man as old as I get on that mountain?" Even over the phone he sounded almost eager, and almost reluctant at the same time. He paused. "The greatest error any scholar can make is to deny evidence."

She was startled. Warwick coming here. She remembered the lung-sick old man who hated her. He managed the mountain. "You can get on it," she said. "I don't know how high you can get."

"It will be, of course, a last pilgrimage," Warwick said. "Old men have a restricted amount of time." His voice actually sounded amused. He changed the subject. "Is there any evidence of your father's insanity?"

"Only what he did."

"It is not overwhelming evidence," Warwick said. "I accept it, but there is no conviction in it."

"What shall I do?"

"Visit the old woman, of course. Beyond that, nothing." He paused, spoke, had obviously been doing some calculations. "I have a bit of reading to do. I have also made inquiries of the county, checking the tax rolls on that land. When all of the facts are in I shall come there."

She was pleased. Also not pleased. "I will come for you." After all, the man was her friend. No matter how badly she hated the trip, she must offer.

"I will take a bus," Warwick said. "It would not be a pilgrimage otherwise. Phone me in a week."

"You have a theory."

"Not worth expressing just yet," he told her. "In fact it was probably a smoke screen after all."

When she hung up the silence of the house did not seem as lonely. The rooms felt nearly friendly, as if her parents worked outside and would return at dusk. The warm feeling did not last, but it was worth having and treasuring. From the roadway, then coming up the lane, came the sound of an engine in low gear. She looked through the window. Johnny Whitcomb's truck carried a heavy load of firewood.

It was an old red truck with high farm racks, but it did not puff smoke and the engine did not pop or sputter. She thought it looked like Johnny would look, if Johnny were a truck. Slightly faded enamel, strong, working. Against the background of the forest the truck looked altogether natural. It was as natural as an axe, a bowl, a clarinet, or any other human tool. Perhaps humans and their tools could actually help give sense and shape to a forest.

She opened the door and called to him that she was making coffee. He backed toward the woodshed.

At least she could help stack wood. A person might bump a finger, but you could not permanently damage your hands. When the coffee perked she took two cups and the pot with her.

He looked up. Grinned. Proud of a simple but beautiful thing, a load of firewood. "I cut it zip, zip," he said. "New saw." He pointed to a red chainsaw riding high on the pile. "Back in old days, saw weigh fifty, sixty pounds. This one he's a feather."

"I want to pay you for this."

"Dan's friend. You invite Dan's friend for supper sometime." He was not smiling, and it was obvious there was no chance of paying without insulting him. "You did not visit that land?"

"I did."

"Stubborn. Dan was stubborn." He grinned again. "Blaine said you were gonna."

"Johnny," she said, "I must understand something." What she had to understand was why, when she had been reclusive and out of sight, why suddenly the entire county knew every move she made. People like Johnny and Blaine discussed her affairs. Mean people went down to the road and found dead birds. Everybody talked, but no one seemed talking to her. She poured coffee as she spoke.

Johnny took the coffee, then sat on the bed of his truck. He looked unhappy. "Dan was murdered. Murdered. That is a fact." He sat on the truck, the forest in the background; the forest where he mostly lived his life. Drinking from springs, watching streams, cutting wood, a man of the forest.

"Everybody is not so nice as you," he said. "This is the south. You know this is the south. These are the mountains. You know that."

He was trying to explain something that was obvious to him, but not obvious to her. "Your mother was not silly," he told her.

She began to understand. Her mother had tried to protect her. "They would hurt me?"

"Who knows what killers will do? Who knows why they do?"

It made no sense and she said so. Her motives were not dangerous. She was not hurting anyone.

"You wonder who kill Dan?"

"Of course."

"Somebody will not want you to know." He reached for the pot, refilled his cup. "Cherokee," he said, "you never know what he will do. In this south revenge happens a lot."

Revenge. She was shocked. Maybe it made sense for someone to try to keep her from knowing her father's murderers. But revenge? For something her father did?

She looked into the familiar forest, the second-growth timber. At the bottom of the pasture the stream ran slow at this time of year. In a couple of weeks, halfway into September, the rain would arrive. At her back the hill rose. Her grandmother's grave was on that hill. She had lived in this land all her life. Now, she suddenly felt she did not understand a single thing about it.

Either that, or she did not understand a thing about the people of the land. She had not even dreamed of the pressure that had been on her father.

"Johnny," she said, "what happened during the war? What happened to you?"

"Scared crazy," he said. "Crazy all the time." He seemed puzzled, and she thought he should be. After all, they had been talking about revenge, not war.

"Because of Dan," she said softly. "Did other men go through that?"

"Rode a T2 tanker," Johnny said. "Big ship fella. Death trap." He slid from the bed of the truck, turned and picked up two balks of wood. She sensed that he would keep talking, but he did not want her to watch as he talked.

"T2 worst damn ship ever made. Don't maneuver. Get the wrong kinda storm and he breaks in two aft the house. Don't have a storm then torpedoes come after you. Cargo of airplane gas. Can't smoke. Afraid to pray."

"Why?"

"Afraid God pay attention. Don't want nothing or nobody paying attention." He worked steadily, his large hands moving about the yellow-silver grain of pine and fir. Almost, she thought, like the hands of a lover. "Seven convoys," he said, "last one started with thirty ships. End with three left." He turned, and his face, which he had not wanted her to see at first, now seemed trusting her for understanding she knew she could never have. "Ships go down. Men in the water. We steam away and leave them." He picked up an armload of wood, like a closing statement. "Got to make them die, 'cause if we stop torpedoes get us too."

She told herself she just plain wanted to sit on the running board of that truck and cry. Then she wanted the piano, to sit at the piano and strike notes of pain and anger to fill the room, the forest, North Carolina, the world. She wanted more than she could have, and besides, she told herself, her wants had no place right now if Johnny had needs.

"Dan," Johnny said, "he have it worse. Had a woman and a little girl."

This was something she did not know. Her father? A woman. Another woman?

Johnny saw her surprise. Maybe, she thought, her shock.

"Not that," Johnny said. "Damn." He hopped up on the bed of the truck. Enough of the load was off so he had to get on the truck to reach the next rick of wood. "That train station where Dan hid.

Woman and child there. Dan didn't know. They were hiding in a little room. German infantry come through. Shots. Dan found them later. Could have hid them. Didn't search building good enough." Johnny looked as near tears as she. "Scared and crazy," he said. "Just scared and crazy all the time."

It seemed too much for her to comprehend. It seemed the world suddenly spilled every ugly thing from history into her mind and hands.

Death. Even her mother's death seemed sort of an abstraction, seemed a lonesome but necessary part of life. Now death, violent death, seemed to lie all around her. It was not natural, not the normal flow of life and death in the forest. This was ugly, premeditated, violent.

"I tell Dan maybe he searched good. Then everybody hide in that basement. Then maybe that woman, little girl, come in afterward. Dan don't buy it." Johnny looked apologetic. "I'm sorry I tell you this."

"I asked you," she said. "Did my father feel guilty all the time?"

"Maybe so." Johnny seemed to be puzzling something. "He say once why does white man's God give all the miracles to Indians and got no miracles for women and children? Question maybe drives him crazy. Drives me crazy sometime. Get a little drunk." He looked apologetic. "Thirty ships," he said, "and three pull through. Why us? Why me?"

Chapter 18

Too much war. Too many tales of war. Pain came and went, came and went, although sunrise poured red and silver above surrounding hills. A night of dreams, a night-filled room—house—forest—of dreams. Her father, her mother. Johnny. They all appeared wearing blood. Bloody faces, bloody hands, clothing soaked in blood. In her dreams she tried to wipe the blood away, soaking it up with cloth, with sheets, with towels. There was too much blood. She finally stripped naked to use her own clothing, and blood ate the clothing.

She fled into wakefulness, running water into the sink, turning on the radio, rattling cups, coffee pot, dishes. She avoided the piano, the clarinet. What was the use of music? Music meant nothing.

She had to get out, get away; had to see some form and sense and familiarity out there. Then she remembered she also had to bury the redbird. It took only a minute, but she was hysterical for minutes before and a couple of minutes after. A shovel full of dirt in the pasture, respectful placing of the bird still wrapped in her handkerchief; refill the small hole and pat the dirt with the shovel. She looked across the pasture. On the downside the oak was not yet changing to red. She murmured to the tree. Got control of herself. Red, red, red. Red for luck, for the east, for the sun. Red was the color of war.

At noon, or at least when the sun went straight up, she had to visit the old woman.

She returned to the house, poured another cup of coffee. The piano still sat like an alien thing. The phone rang. It sounded alien, and a voice's concerns were as surreal as her dreams.

It was the sharecropper, and he was mooching again. Could he use the pasture and barn to winter three head of cattle?

She pictured him, small but lithe and ambitious and corporate and singularly focused on gain. Not a nice man or a good one, but a cropper who made money. Not all of them did. She wondered if he had been in the war. She nearly asked. Instead, she wondered to him if there was room in the barn because so much of his equipment was stored there.

He was a weasel. That was her next thought. He fawned, suggested a meeting; suggesting, somehow, that after the years since her father's death he was like a member of her family. He once more mentioned buying the land. Like he was doing a favor. A man on the place, bringing it back the way it was when Dan was alive. Insulting. When Johnny asked what she would do without a man she did not feel insulted. This man was dissonance. A scamp. She half expected him to propose marriage so he could get his hands on the land.

"Use the pasture," she told him, "use the barn." It was a price and not a cheap one, because he would be there every day to feed the livestock. At the same time any price seemed better than listening to him fawn. "The land is not for sale," she said. "Not yet." She hung up expecting him to call again, but the phone remained silent. She finished her cooling cup of coffee then hurried from the house.

She got the car started, turned around, and onto the road. The need to flee was so great that it was a task to drive slowly. When she arrived at the mountain no cars or trucks were parked. It was only mid-morning. This time she locked her car.

Forest silence. Sun glazed dull leaves in beginning change. No sound of tires or engines came from the road. Far away and high a hawk rode the air like the very wings of silence. The distant voice of a stream existed on the bare edge of silence, and she could not actually say she heard the stream. She avoided the spot where her father's body had lain, and rapidly walked the short logging road.

Standing on the trail. Certain of what she must do, but not certain how to go about it. This close to the mountain it was impossible to see the ridge because of the forest. From far away the mountain was different from surrounding mountains. The ridge stood black, cut with deep red bands of rust from iron ore, bands that only showed on those rare mornings when mist had not gathered and sun was over-flooding. The ridge ran straight and dark, like a roadway of the im-mortals. But that was from a distance. This close, the mountain looked like any other mountain.

"Tree's Friend," she told the mountain. It was an act of trust. You did not tell your true name, unless there was a lot of trust. A person's true name was as much a part of them as their heart or arms or legs.

"If there is harm in me," she told the mountain, "then it is only the harm of ignorance. I have no bad thoughts."

Silence. The gathering of power. Beneath the dark canopy of trees power lay more indifferent than the brilliant sunlight glossing the leaves. She did not understand it, could only comprehend that it partly rose from tens of thousands of people who had lived on and walked this land. Those people were dead, forgotten, maybe never known. A hundred generations, two hundred. And they were not the source of the power, but they were part of the power.

"I know you hear," she said, "although you do not speak. I think maybe you hear my heart and know it is good." She stepped forward along the trail.

Sounds. The rustle of the distant stream, the flight of birds, the call of birds. Small movement in the underbrush. A little snake crossed the trail, wiggling a path through light dust. A twig fell beside the trail, and a bee circled a patch of blackberry, then flew away.

The sun was not yet straight up when she arrived. Fifty yards be-fore the clearing she stopped and waited. The bad dreams tried to come back. "Wrong," she told herself. "You are trying to set your thoughts somewhere else." She thought of the old woman. How did you set your thoughts so the old woman would like you?

What was it like to live up here? Apparently the old woman had plenty of company.

Something moved in the forest. Grunted. The bear still rummaged in about the same place. Usually bears ranged more widely, scaveng-ing for food. What was a bear doing at this elevation, anyway? It should be following the streams, looking for pool-trapped fish.

In the mythology, bears once were men. She could almost believe it. No other creature in the world except people were as capricious as bears. You could always be pretty sure what a bear would do, but you could never be absolutely sure. Mostly, because a bear did not seem to know from one minute to the next what he was going to do himself. Another grunt, more distant, as the bear moved away.

When she entered the clearing the old woman sat dozing in a chair beside the cabin. Harriette hesitated. Walked softly to the center of the clearing. Harriette's shadow lay like a small circle at her feet, the sun straight up. Above, the ridge seemed suspended like great architecture. She could not tell whether it had grown from the earth or been suspended from the sky by invisible lines of force. Below the ridge and in the tree line a thin spiral of smoke or maybe a tendril of mist rose above the trees. It was not dark smoke, smoke mixed with the burning of the forest carpet. It was not a forest fire.

"What do you know? I know a lot." The voice was dry, falling leaves dry. The old woman did not move from her chair, but she watched with the bright—buckeye bright—horse chestnut bright—of deeply polished shells.

"Nothing," Harriette said. Then she stopped to think. "I know many things," she told the old woman, "and some of them are big. I know about drums. What is that smoke above the ridge?"

"I hear no drums."

"I hear none either," Harriette told her, "but I know a lot about drums."

"We will eat. I do not believe this about the drums." The old woman stood slowly, went through the doorway of the cabin, and brought back white bread, greens, corn bread and beans. The meal was on two dimestore plates. Harriette waited for the old woman. The old woman ate, a little. Harriette tried to eat slowly and felt she was making a bad job of it.

"Maybe you don't know so much," the old woman told Harriette.

This was a part of the Indian world. This was negotiation.

"I think maybe," Harriette said, "that I know more about drums than anybody."

"I think you say a lot but have no drum."

"I have my hands." Harriette bent forward, placed her fingers on her knees. She took a last bite of the cornbread, and began to play drums.

It was easy, patting her knees with fingers, patting them soft and hard. She went through rhythms, through range; $2/4$ and $4/4$, $3/6$, $8/12$, $7/8$. She was suddenly happy, playing the metres of her imagination. Playing, playing and music is the drums. She beat $11/12$ with easy fingers when she thought of the stream, the smoke—if it was smoke—but the stream was real—and she searched for the pattern.

Rippling, crazy, against any known music. There was a horn player doing this kind of thing. Somebody named Davis, Miles Davis. She listened to the silences, not the sounds surrounding the silences. Soft drumming of her fingers, her palms, the heels of her hands on her knees seemed to her a truth of all she knew. It was a little surprising. She did not know that she could play this way.

"That is as good as good," the old woman said. "I think maybe you know about drums."

It was difficult to stop. The stream was in her mind. "I think you know so much," she said. "Maybe you will tell me what to do."

"I will not tell you anything what to do," the old woman said. "Maybe Corey will tell you what to do."

"Lewis Corey?"

"He is still young. His son Tom is a good man. His wife knew about fish, but she is dead. Susy died. She could call fish to her."

"My father," Harriette said, "did something wrong. His friends say he was insane—" She corrected herself. "His friends say he was crazy."

The old woman looked at her, the old woman's bright eyes accurate but liquid-seeming as polished nuts.

"Dan Johnson," she said, "did one bad thing. He hurt a tree. Your daddy was not crazy. There was nothing crazy about him. He did a good thing and a bad thing. He had to do the bad thing so he could do the good thing."

"I don't understand." She really did not, and was shocked. Only Warwick doubted her father's madness.

"Corey will tell you about this." The old woman looked to the ridge, and Harriette followed her gaze. The column of mist was gone in evaporating sunlight. "I think he will tell you a little about this. When you know more maybe he will tell you a lot."

"You will not?"

"My father used to take us across the river. Whole family. My family used to pick blackberries. Then I got married to Jimmy, and two years I didn't have a baby.

"I say to my mother, 'How do you have a baby?'"

"She tells me, 'You go into the forest and you pick up this leaf here, this root here, and you talk nice.'"

"Then I had a baby. Then lots. Too many babies.

"Then Jimmy got killed in the war. Down in Cuba. I liked Jimmy all right. I liked him pretty good. We could have had a good life to-gether."

Cuba. The Spanish-American War. Harriette sat dazed, feeling the great weight of years behind the old woman's voice. The old woman was not wandering. This was Indian. She had said as much as she was going to say about Dan Johnson.

"People say now, people say the white man has a medicine that stays away from babies." The old woman's eyes were interested, calm. "The white man is getting pretty big for his britches." She paused, looked toward the forest and not upwards to the ridge. "You go see Corey," she said. "Maybe Corey will tell you something." She turned without picking up the plates and walked into the cabin.

Harriette stood in sunlight among the tall grasses. She was sud-denly hopeful. The old woman would not tell her anything, but she had the name, Lewis Corey. Now she had heard it twice. He must be powerful. She walked across the clearing and entered onto the trail, musing and a little amazed. She was five hundred yards down the trail before she was aware of something behind her.

Bears could be silent when it suited them. This bear was an old one, the muzzle grayed, and when she stopped it stopped. The bear walked the trail behind her in the same way a human would walk the trail. She stood almost rigidly silent. It was a big she-bear, the face scarred, one ear partly missing from some old fight. The bear sat on her haunches, yawned.

No sense running. She could lie down, play dead, and the bear would get bored and go away. Or she could move slowly, and that might do the same thing. She took three slow steps, looked backward. The bear yawned. She began walking at a slow pace, looking over her shoulder. The bear followed, not closing the distance, just ambling. Its footfalls were light on the trail. A bear out for a midday stroll.

It took an hour to get off the mountain, walking slowly, looking backward. The bear never closed the distance. If anything, the bear already seemed bored. A hundred yards before the logging road it disappeared.

Her father had done a bad thing. She understood that. But Dan Johnson doing a bad thing so he could do a good thing? It made no sense. There was nothing good in what her father did.

Her car was a comforting, civilized sight as it sat at the end of the logging road. She walked toward it, fishing her keys from her pocket. Stopped. Wanted to scream.

Wrapped around the radio antenna, tied with an old shoestring, hung a little snake. Dead. Its small striped body made the antenna look like a miniature barber pole. Except, of course, barber poles were not these delicate colors of brown and yellow and gray.

The snake was a great friend. Cherokee did not kill snakes. Of course, if someone had killed her father, then it was not likely he would be timid about a snake. Her fingers trembled as she fumbled with the shoestring. It finally came untied. She held the snake, the body sun warm. "I did not do this," she said to the snake. "If I have done anything that caused this, then I am sorry." She walked into the forest, found a small tree blown down in some storm. She rolled the tree a little, placed the snake beneath it, and let the tree roll back into its place upon the forest floor.

Chapter 19

THE road into Cherokee wound off the face of a hill to run along the river past new motels, until a fork turned left into the main shopping area. Harriette drove into town, turned her car around, and drove back out. She did not know whether she carried more anger than scorn. Some sneak, some nasty and violent little man threatened her. He would not come right out and say anything. He just went around leaving dead things. All she knew is that with this much anger, it was not yet time to walk in the town.

A few miles outside of town, and at the base of the mountain, stood the motel where she first met Blaine. She pulled into the parking lot. The place was ordinary. It could just as easily sit in some seedy section of Cincinnati.

She did not want to go home just yet. Bad dreams about war and blood were past, but she did not want to be alone. She decided to check in, call Blaine, and get her anger under control.

She was asked no questions by the motel owner who looked full-blood and probably wasn't. Not too many people were full-blood anymore. The man's darkness was not like her darkness, but deeper, fuller, more obvious. His hair was coarser than hers, his face quite racial.

"I have a friend," Harriette said, "who says that some terrible person is telling lies about me." She looked at the motel owner. She knew she should not be saying this, but her anger made her want to strike him. "No timber will be cut on that land."

He passed her the key to the room. "Check out time is noon," he said. He turned and walked through a curtained doorway, disappearing back to his own rooms.

She went to her room, still trying to get her anger under control. It was a plain room, flooded with sunlight in middle afternoon. Above, the broad dark back of the ridge hovered.

It was always a fair question in Cherokee which asked how much of what was seen was true. The mountains and the streams were true. Maybe the motels and gift shops were also true, but a different kind of truth. Both mountains and stores were consistent with Cherokee history.

That history was one of exploitation in both directions. When they were finally removed, having survived two major plagues of small-pox, a Revolutionary war, and the French and Indian War, the Chero-kee were a wealthy people. From first contact with the Spanish they were a people in transition. Other Indian nations were conservative, but the Cherokee were traditionally interested in new ways of think-ing; also in accumulation of personal property, especially horses and slaves. They had not had their religions stolen by missionaries so much as they simply gave a lot away because they attended to other business. In the nineteenth century they had a written language, but they did not write history. They used the language to run a news-paper and engage in politics.

In fact, she told herself, each time she came to Cherokee it was not a homecoming. Deeper down there were thoughts like that. The mountains were the mountains. The country was all traditional. She lived in it as well as the motel owner.

She walked to the bathroom, the bathroom mirror. Her nose—and she had suffered because of that nose when younger—was just the tiniest bit knobby. Just fractionally. If two layers of skin were shaved away it would not be knobby at all. Her cheeks might be oriental. In fact, she might very well be oriental except for the skin. The skin saved it.

When younger she hated the nose and the skin which made her so different. Also her then-gangly, light-breasted figure, but it was the skin which bothered her most. That was no longer true. She knew how pretty she was. She smiled, telling herself that if she had been white she might have done something dumb like marry right out of high school. She would have been a wife and mother married to God-only-knew what white man who might have been gentle but would probably have been a bastard. Maybe her sharecropper.

She returned to the bedroom and the telephone. She called through the motel switchboard. Blaine's phone rang several times before he answered.

"I have a horse with a barbed wire cut," he said. "Takes me a minute to come from the barn. Are you making any progress?"

"If I am, I don't know it." She paused, decided to tell him. "I must be making some. Someone seems to be threatening me." She told him about the bird and the snake.

"Somebody's got his back up," Blaine said, "but I doubt if he is one of the killers."

"Why?"

"Because I think anyone set to kill is not going to put you on guard. Whoever these killers are, they acted without warning when they killed your father."

"Still, it makes me nervous."

"It at least makes me wonder," Blaine said. "Because I could be wrong. Will you be at home this evening?"

"No." She told him about the motel, about being in Cherokee, about her plans to stay at the motel for a night.

"I'll take a swing past your place, since the house will be empty," he said. "Probably nothing to it, but I'll be out there anyway. Sometimes I assist the sheriff on Saturday nights." He paused, as if trying to remember something. "The sheriff sent that file to your history teacher."

"He's coming here."

"Who?"

"Warwick."

Blaine sounded interested. "Let me meet him. Got some talking to do. Nothing about this case. Couple questions about local history."

"I'll call if I find out anything. . . ." Then she remembered. "There is an old woman living on that mountain. Did you know?"

"I know it," Blaine said, "but I've never met her. Went up there one time, but the trails were so criss-crossed I never found her. Call me when you get something." He hung up.

It did not make any sense. No trails criss-crossed up there, at least none she had seen. She checked her watch. Nearly 3:30. If she did not go into town she might not find Corey.

She walked to her car. Off on the hill came the belling cry of a hound. She stopped, puzzled. That hound should not be there this time of year. Hounds would not be let off their lines until the weather turned cold and rattlesnakes went to cover. At the same time the voice was reassuring.

The hounds were always there. More than horses, more than many people, hounds were a presence. You could live nowhere in the hills that was beyond the baying of hounds. Black and tan, blue tick, even the little rabbit-running, spraddle-running beagles sang and called and echoed through the mountains with their separate, easily identified voices. Sometimes it seemed they were the voice of the hills.

The hills had always been sanctuary when the losses got too great. Sometimes she wondered if there were dogs up there at all, or only the crying of lost spirits.

She drove into town knowing that, with tourist season over, there would be plenty of places to park. When she arrived in town the streets were deserted. The stream forked and ran behind buildings, and she entered the built-up section. The museum to the left, the school to the right, and then restaurants and craftshops. An old car drove by, its driver silent, unmoving, enigmatic. An old man, but not the old man who hated her. She wondered what this old man knew.

Maybe nothing. Each time in Cherokee she was aware of a lot of ignorance, and not just her own. She thought she probably knew more than plenty of the people who lived here. They were not historic enough, unless, she had heard, you got far enough back in the hills. There were always those rumors of old ways being practiced.

How to find Corey? She figured she would start asking. She stepped into a small craft shop. It was not phonied up with totem poles chipped from logs following a book of Northwest Indian art. She looked around. Amazing luck. Corey's business papers hung framed on the wall. This was his store. Of course, maybe the luck was not so amazing. It was an awfully small town.

There was no one in the store. Of course, with the tourists gone, there was no one around who was likely to steal. She walked between center islands. She did not carve, but if she did carve she would do it better than this and she could weave at least as well as what she saw. The store was fairly denuded. It must have been a good tourist year. At the front of the store a clock hung over a small glass display case. Nearly four o'clock.

In the case, like dark jewels glowing dully against a piece of white material, lay three bird stones. Three. She bent to examine them through the glass, excited, then thrilled. This was Cherokee art at its highest. This was like music. Well-made bird stones were like life itself, and not an imitation. They were of dark rock, not large, and could be mistaken for Impressionist art since they captured the movement of life but did not actually try to capture all the details of a bird.

They were almost small enough to be concealed in an adult hand. These had to be old. It was impossible that three old ones had been found, yet these had to be old. No one could hit that simplicity of line in the stone. There were good woodworkers, but this stone work seemed beyond the ability of the twentieth-century mind. It was something she felt about the truth of form. Somehow you had to get under, not beyond, the current confusion in the world. It was not possible to live with contradictions or complications, and still produce such work.

She wanted to feel the water smoothness of the stone. They would cost too much, even if they were for sale. If they were old, and she was sure they were old, they would probably not be for sale.

A man entered the store and she turned. He was white, in his early sixties, lightly built and wearing old army clothes. His hair was thin and so was his face. He moved as easily as a boy. Once his hair had been brown. Now it was almost all white. He walked to stand beside her and peered into the case.

"I was at the restaurant," he said. His voice was soft and high but would be harsh if it were loud. "This one is mine." He pointed to the stone on the left. "These two are by my son. He's thirty. You can see the difference."

She could not. "I thought they were old."

"In a manner of speaking. The rock is as old as any other rock." He walked behind the case and picked each stone up carefully to arrange them on the glass in front of her. He had small hands, weathered and brown. "I made four last winter. This was the successful one."

She touched it like a diamond buyer pushing an immense and precious stone with one finger. Then she held it. The weight was a contradiction to the form. Wingless. Eyeless. It had the smooth-flowing motion from a beak-like protuberance through a living, arching, slightly plump fatness of living body, and ended in another protuberance that was nearly round and spoke only of flight. Here, in a rock, was the most simple and unornamented statement of life she had ever seen. The implications about the man who created it were immense. It held the truth of a straight line, although it contained not a single straight line.

"I want it." Her voice was forced.

"It is almost prohibitively expensive. Look at the others."

She examined them and did not believe anyone so young could do so well. The son's work held a feeling of rapidity, excess movement, wasted motion. Yet, with a micrometer she was willing to bet that though of different sizes the spatial proportions would be the same. Was she imagining?

"I see the difference. These are quick."

"Yes," he said. "The price is less now."

"There is nothing so good in the museum."

"There is one. Badly worn, but you can know how good if you hold it." There was no ego in his voice.

"Who are you?" He was white. How could he? Some trick? She picked up the stone. No trick.

"Lewis Corey," he said. "I live here."

"I am Harriette Johnson."

"I know," Corey told her. "You don't come here often, and now you have come to talk about your father." His smile was gentle and his small face showed sympathy. "This is not a very big place," he said. "Everyone has an opinion. To some you are beautiful and proud and they are glad. Some others despise you, and will never forgive you for what your father did. Some think you are young and silly and they pity you."

Pity. To be hated was bad enough.

"I do not pity you," Corey said. He looked at the stone. "You see more than most."

The conversation would have frightened her even if she was dead, yet the man was not frightening. He only said simple things. The room was filled with electric light and the fading sunlight in the windows. The electric clock hummed over carvings and clutter that had probably all been produced in a factory.

"You live alone now," he said. "Inagehi. It is an old word for people who live alone in the wilderness. The question is always which wilderness?"

He took the bird stone which was now warm and, she self-consciously felt, wet from her hand. He wrapped it in tissue paper, found a small sack and handed it to her. "I want you to live closely with this for awhile. Then come back and we will talk about price."

"Yes." She involuntarily reached for her purse.

"Because you must pay a lot. We will see what you will pay."

"What?" The fear kept coming back.

"Come with me." He turned out the lights in the store. "We will go back to the restaurant." This time he locked the store. "Have to go soon. My son Tom is coming to pick me up. Early dinner at his place. Then I have a little trip to make."

"I met your son. On the mountain."

"I know," Corey said. "He mentioned it."

They entered a restaurant which might have been built on any road, anywhere. He directed her to a booth, then stepped to the counter to bring back a scarred fiber tray with cups of tea. From the back of the restaurant came the sound of someone moving about.

He sat across from her and spooned sugar into the tea. "Weakness. I think real tea drinkers never touch this stuff." His voice was matter of fact. "You are trying to find out who murdered your father."

"I thought so," she said. "Now I don't honestly know." Beyond the window, over on the school ground, two young boys tried to get a kite aloft. Their problem was that there was no wind. "Other people want to know."

"Blaine?"

"That's one. Another one's name is Warwick. He does it because it interests him, and because he is a friend."

"It is better to ask why your father did what he did."

"Warwick believes that," she told Corey. "He is fascinated with the question."

"It is the only question worth answering. I can save you time," Corey said. "I would not waste much time on the killers. If there was much likelihood of them being caught, Blaine would already have done it. Concentrate on the other question."

Was he protecting someone? Did he actually know the names of the killers? Probably, she thought, he did. "The old woman said my father did a bad thing in order to do a good thing. Do you know what my father intended?" She did not know whether she trusted him or not, but if he knew the state of her father's mind, he would know why her father behaved so badly.

"I did not know your father. I met him a couple of times, but he was a solitary man. The old woman may be right." Corey sipped his tea. Checked his watch. "Tom will be here soon. Meanwhile, your answer will not come right away. Maybe you should think a lot, and spend some time on the mountain. I think the answer is there."

"Visit the old woman?"

"You should sit with her in silence. She is not going to tell you anything, except with silence. Some still think she is a magic woman. There aren't too many who believe that anymore."

"Do you?"

"No," he said. "Not in that old way. But I believe she has a lot of power."

"I believe it too," Harriette said, "but I don't understand it."

"You don't have to understand it," Corey told her. "You feel it. People die, but power lives. It's the simplicity that confuses you." He drank and wiped his mouth with the back of his hand. "I have some power." He touched the paper sack which held the bird stone.

It was disconcerting to have a white man knowing impossibly more than she did. A man who could bring that kind of form from stone.

"Do you visit her often?" Harriette asked.

"Not so much these days." He paused. "I think, although some disagree, but others agree, that she is part Catawba but of the Cherokee. There were a lot of mixups and child savings going on when she was small. At least she had a Catawba grandmother, because of some speech patterns."

"When was that? How old?"

A slight bitterness crept into his voice. "The popular belief is that all Indians become ancient in spite of a forty-five-year life expectancy. She is an exception. She is at least in her nineties, probably a lot more. I will guess she was born during the Civil War." He looked through the window, into the parking lot. "My son is here. I will talk to you at another time. I think the people here who do not forgive you are wrong." He stood, turned back. "The mountain can be unsafe. Stay only on established trails."

He left and she wondered if she was supposed to pay for the tea. There was no one around. She sat, struck, thinking of a twenty-cent obligation because her mind rebelled against what he said. Catawba. She knew little about the Catawbas. She thought they were all dead or something.

She fumbled in her purse and laid change on the table. Outside a truck disappeared around a bend. She felt abandoned, angry, given careful attention and then mislaid.

Harriette returned to the motel grumbling. She did not know whether to go or stay. He said he would see her another time, but did that mean tomorrow or next year? He said only selected things. He left advices, if they were advices, open. After all, how could anyone tell you anything with silence? She felt that Corey knew everything she needed and could tell it to her in a minute, in an hour or so anyway, but would not. She arrived at the motel, parked her car, and went to her room. She felt the weight of the bird stone.

What did he mean, pay? And what about power? The hallmark of the Indian had always been reverence, not power; although powerful men were great men. And the greatest men and women were people of peace. Maybe there was something there.

When she arrived at her room she unwrapped the bird stone. She expected it to be different now, thought the work had borrowed from the presence of the man who made it. When she unwrapped the small figure, serenity and life still breathed in the stone.

To simply exist, although eloquently. She examined the stone. The surface held a dull glow, like it had been polished by water for centuries, then hand rubbed for a year with soft cloth. Maybe it was not technique. Maybe it was a matter of finding the right material. It was close-grained black rock. A lot of it washed in the stream beds.

A wingless, eyeless bird capable of evoking knowledge of flight and motion.

She turned to look through the window at the ridge. It stood tall, nearly gaunt, with ripped spots of burn from lightning. Splotched with fire and ricocheting electricity, billions of volts over hundreds of millions of years swallowed into the heart of the mountain. For an instant the mountain also lived in the way the stone in her hand lived.

And now there was this man Corey who had been living so near to her, and so invisibly, for probably all of her life. He was more Indian than she. He was in touch with his luminous self. Surely. What he knew he must have learned here, and she turned again to look at the mountain.

She felt firmly and with despair that for all of these years she had been playing. She acted a part without understanding the meaning of the lines. If there really was reality that lived beyond skin and knobby nose and myth—and there must be that reality because this birdstone could not be denied—then it was here, and some of it was on that mountain. In spite of dangerous people who might harm her, it was necessary to be brave. Tomorrow, she decided, she would not visit the old woman. She would walk a different approach to that mountain.

Chapter 20

DREAMS of blood did not return, but night filled with dreams. Her mind puzzled to itself, feeling that one more logical step could be made that would allow her to solve every problem that had ever been engaged by history and philosophy. Since she knew little history or philosophy, except those of music, she knew as she was dreaming that she must be mistaken. Still, dreams insisted and she dreamed of a struggle with logic. Her father had destroyed a tree and she had saved a tree.

When she woke the sun still rode the far side of the hill, and she thought she should be exhausted. Instead, she felt refreshed and looked forward to the day. She touched the birdstone, felt its serenity. She wrapped it in a handkerchief, put it in her pocket, and went to breakfast.

The restaurant owned by the motel stood deserted except for a young girl. Harriette took a seat at one of four small tables beyond a box-like counter and watched the girl. She was a child. No more than thirteen or fourteen. A tall child who must be the daughter of the owner. She moved slow and sleepy. It was still an hour before the sun would get over the ridge, but the sky grew light, fog blue with thin streamers of clouds that in the beginning day looked like a spirit's passage.

Harriette smiled at the thought. She was about to walk on a mountain she absolutely respected, and feared more than a little. A mountain of power. She had no doubt it was the source of Corey's power, of the old woman's power.

The girl listened to a radio station from Asheville. At a break for news the girl quit her busy work and came to the table. She made a point of moving slow. Harriette watched, the sullen child face drawn, mouth pouting and thin shoulders slumped. The girl's hair was cut short, which was unfortunate. Her ears stuck out. The pout made her round face look like a tan balloon.

"Good mornin'." The girl's voice sounded low, listless, and managed to convey the information that she was ordered to say good morning to customers. Harriette decided to try a conquest. She smiled and it was sincere.

"I've been watching you," she told the girl, "wishing I was that pretty when I was your age." She flipped the menu over. "It's early to be working." She looked exactly at the girl's eyes and smiled again.

"Awful early," the girl said, but the slump came from her shoulders. "Have to come down, get everything ready like always, and we don't have ten people this time of year."

"Let's have coffee," Harriette said. "I guess your father figures that ten people or a hundred he should stay open."

"He's my uncle." The girl said it quick and her face showed she lied.

"I worked for my uncle once," Harriette lied back. "He always expected too much." She had never had an uncle, one who lived.

"I'll get the coffee." The girl turned, came back with two cups, but did not take a seat. She did not know whether she was invited.

"Please sit down," Harriette said. "I'm not often where I get to see many people."

"For a minute." The girl was more shy than anything else, her belligerence a cover.

"My eyes are too dark," Harriette told her. "I wish they were like yours."

"That's what Davey says." The balloon look was completely gone. "He's my boyfriend, kinda."

"I'll bet he says more than that. I think of how you'll look when you fill out." She touched the front of her own shirt and smiled what she hoped was a conspiratorial smile.

"Where you from? Just a minute until I turn down that damn radio." The girl stood quickly and when she returned brought the Silex with her. "Saves trips."

"I'm from right around here," Harriette told her. "That is, I live here now. Before that, though ... you could say I'm from more or less all over." If she were the girl's age she would be crossing her fingers under the table for telling that whopper. She pushed one hand up the side of her neck to move her long hair toward the other shoulder. Her hair was tied for moving in the forest, so the gesture did not have all the worldly suggestions it might if her hair hung loose.

"Tell about San Francisco." The child's voice was like she asked for a favorite story.

Harriette did a quick riffle through her information on San Francisco. She came up with cable cars, a bunch of weird new poets whose names she could not remember, earthquakes, Chinese and Jack London. How had she gotten herself into this mess?

"I had a friend ... a very dear friend. We used to meet at a Chinese restaurant for tea and have our fortunes read in the leaves...." It was probably gypsies that read tea leaves. Get out of this mess. "I haven't been back in a long time." She was amazed at the touch of nostalgia she heard in her own voice. Maybe she should have become an actress.

It worked too well. The girl's eyes came alive with interest. It was kind of hard to take. Imagine such interest, when the girl lived surrounded by the calmest and most peaceful way of life that ever existed; at least that was true in Harriette's opinion.

"Davey says that's the best city in the world. He's got a book."

"Like a travel book?"

"No." The girl's voice indicated that travel books were for children and idiots. "This here is a book about big names and bands and stuff...." She looked over her shoulder. "Dancers, and some of them girls are near naked."

"It's a hard way to live."

"Did you ever?" The girl was excited. Harriette tried hard to remember how it had been at fourteen.

"I had friends," she said. "They didn't like it much." The conversation was totally out of hand. She was not only uncomfortable, she was doing more harm than good.

"It's a nice place," she said. "I've seen a lot of nice places." She thought that a small college in Pennsylvania did not exactly count for a lot of nice places. Still, she had to make a point. "Seen a lot of them, but I came back here."

"Did you have to?"

"It's nicer here."

The look on the girl's face expressed the opinion that Harriette was insane. "Here?"

"Do you know Lewis Corey?"

"He's nice. Davey spends a lot of time over there." The girl's eyes widened. "He's lots older than you."

"That isn't it." She felt trapped and foolish. She supposed by now she had started a local scandal. Corey had a son. Maybe she had started a double scandal. She turned at the sound of someone entering the room. A tourist couple argued in low voices.

"Damn." The girl's voice was half angry, half sad.

"I should go anyway. Give me two donuts to take with."

The girl leaned forward, her eagerness painful to watch. "Will you be here tonight?"

"I don't know." It had been wrong for her to get into this no matter her good intentions.

"This afternoon. You come by this afternoon. My name's Jan."

"Jan."

"I'm not here you ask at the desk...." Jan was shy again. "They call me Janet.... I got to go."

"I'll ask for you, Jan." She could not allow the girl to go away hurt or embarrassed, or, yes, she could, but it seemed a bad thing to do.

Jan smiled, reached quickly to touch the back of Harriette's hand, then crossed the room to the bickering tourists. Harriette took two tired-looking donuts in a small paper sack. She told herself it served her right. There was little satisfaction in that. Two donuts were not much preparation to take to the forest.

As she walked toward the rear of the motel and toward the first reaches of the mountain she heard a scuffle and clink of chain. Beyond an old tool shed two hounds stood ground-tied. They were good, big-footed dogs, and she wished it were possible to take one with her. She looked at the dogs, then back over her shoulder. The sun would be over the ridge in fifteen or twenty minutes. Corey said to stay on established trails. She decided she would climb until she found one.

"You're pretty," she said to the dogs, and it was true. They were especially pretty if one knew anything about hounds. One was almost fawn-colored, the other a big black and tan. They wagged and thumped their tails and shivered along their shoulders when she bent to touch them. Hounds were dogs that could be made pets of and still be good hunters. These dogs had slick, shining coats and were lean muscled. Someone ran them through the summer.

The bitch was the fawn color, going deeper brown around the muzzle, and with excited youthfulness in her eyes. It was a good bet she was quick, but there was no guessing if she had the endurance for an all-night run of twenty miles over rough country. With the male you guessed the endurance right away. He looked no older, but the puppy-flash was already gone from his eyes. In its place was the hound stoicism that would not leave until he ranged. He was a dog that would not call often, a silent-running animal that would not destroy his energy with constant belling. A dog that ran low, ran fast, but ran within limits to extend his range far beyond any following pack.

She picked up his foreleg and examined the pads. The dogs were beautifully cared for.

"I wish you had puppies. I would like to raise one of your pups." She flopped the fawn dog's ears, told her she had to leave, and turned toward a small stream.

The stream ran a narrow line, shallow through surrounding trees. Forest trails were up there somewhere. Sooner or later one would intersect this stream. As she started upward, she hesitated one last time and remembered her grandmother. Somehow, she, Harriette, was mixing two different levels of knowledge, but it was difficult to figure the mixture.

The first level was about being. People, animals, things, existed distinctly. At the same time they could become one; and the best words she had ever read to describe it were in a book about an Indian who hunted a bear. He rested his rifle on a rock because the bear was a grizzly and that meant he got only one shot. The line that was so important was, "He became the rock." She thought no white man would ever understand that. Now, having met Corey, she was not so sure.

The other level might be myth, but on this mountain some of it was surely true.

Some things adhered to no fact or form, things that read like ancient shadows. From the blood haunts of Europe, through two thousand years of crucifixions, through the great story-tellers of all nations ancient shadows spoke in whispers through the night.

And with the Cherokee it was the same. Witches took any form, man-killers, animal spirits, invisible tribes, but, except for witches and a few others, Cherokee spirits could be comic, could even be friendly. Only sometimes were they malevolent, and only with certain formulas might they be combatted.

Everything had its nature. Yet, the true horror was that some things in myth had no true nature, were changeable, were inconstant. The supernatural was acknowledged by every human society and religion in every country through all of history. History agreed that horror arrived only when what was normal fell before forces no logic could explain.

The forest on either side of the stream stood filled with brush. She walked into the forest to a depth of a hundred feet, found her way blocked, and returned to the stream. Humus gave back a small bouncing pressure that would be less if there were more water in the soil. The storm had not hit this part of the mountain. The forest stood tangled, but not roughed up and freshly broken. Trees at this level were deciduous, leaves changing, the first and middle textures of gold and red.

Further up, the mountain would be covered with conifer, the brush lower, and the forest floor cushioned with small twigs and the deep mat of needles. Dead lower branches, tree-discarded like old needles in a climb for the sun, would hang from living trunks like forgotten gestures. Further south and west she knew that moist climates caused trees to shed dead limbs fast. Further north it might be impossible to walk in some forests because the trees might never lose dead branches. In North Carolina, in the conifers, it was often possible to walk long distances unimpeded. It was also possible to get lost. She stayed close to the stream.

It was a trickle at this time of year. Ground water. A good time to become acquainted with a stream because the particularities of pooling, the slide surfaces of flat rock, the roiling surfaces of larger round rocks were easy to see. This stream seemed too fast and shallow to have many deep pools. She moved slow and looked for the kind of material Corey might have picked for his work. Most of the rock was sedimentary, but round, hard stones were there. They were water-smooth and possible. After a hundred yards she admitted that one rock looked pretty much the same as another. She arrived at a shelving of slate and stopped to rest.

Through reaching tops of trees, and at maybe three thousand feet, she could see churning rolls of mist, the silver-gray, unhesitating movement in slow-motion cascades down the hill. An inexorable tumbling of blue into gray into silver into white; that always, deep in the center, one knew descended into a black shadow that lived under the mist. In the heart of mist, living nearly like a presence, there would be a singular chill that would retreat last and die slow as sun burned off the protecting layers.

For a moment it seemed the mist accelerated, jumping down to surround her. She told herself it was impossible. It hardly ever fell to a low level. It would certainly not fall low today. The sun now stood over the ridge and in the mist.

In the mist it would be like walking in clouds or heavy fog. Trees would disappear and only the trunks and only a few of them would be visible. She had walked through it before on familiar mountains.

Silenced shattered before the high yelping, fearful sound of a dog. Scream yelping. It was the fawn dog. She was joined by the heavy voice of the male, dropping back to silence when he must be snarling; un-yelping but afraid. The female's voice screamed high. Stopped. Gained stance, and now, although a hundred yards off, vibrations of snarling rose beneath the trees like whispers, knotted under living branches like ancient echoes, hard and brutal with defense.

Harriette searched the forest. Dog fear was real fear and could be trusted. Whatever was after the dogs was behind her, downhill, between her and people. She froze.

Then the tones changed. First one voice, then the second, started a long, low howling but ascending cry, followed by long drawn strokes. Then it changed again and they were calling. Harriette could imagine them—heads raised, braced into a direction, straining at the chains and forward-leaning into the sound. Her confidence returned. There was a yell from a distant voice and the dogs quieted. Then the yelling stopped and the only sound to break the quiet was the trickle of the stream.

She stood debating whether to continue or return, knowing if it were not for the dogs' confidence she might already be stumbling quickly down the hill, toward the fear but toward other people. Worse, she might be going further, maybe even trying to fade into the forest.

She searched downhill, looking along the stream and into the undergrowth. She identified movement in low-growing, stream-clustering plants fifty yards away. She called it a fox as she caught a glimpse of his brush moving in the thicket. She watched as he tumbled through and emerged to cross a clear space. She called it a dog.

She stood shivering. It was either a red fox or a gray dog and neither would cause fear in a hound. Her eyes were better than to miscall a fox for a dog. She looked back up the mountain.

It was wrong to stay and wrong to go on. The sun already made the mist lighter. Shadows of trees darkened the stream so that slates looked oily. She walked upward expecting at any moment to be terrified. When nothing happened after fifty yards some of her confidence returned and that was good, because it was another three hundred yards before she found the trail. She rested. The weakness from fright departed. Maybe the reason for the dogs' fear was because they stood upwind, or were pocketed in some way that caused them to be startled. At fifty yards it was probably easy to miscall any small animal.

The stream narrowed. The cross trail led from a grass bald, and the trail was one season overgrown. It hooked off to the right and up. To the left it led down and southwest.

Harriette stood in the glade weighing her unease against her real need to understand the power of this mountain. She might find that power, and there was a ninety percent logical chance she would find nothing. It was always like that when her feelings knew things, and her logic knew things, and the things were opposite.

She disliked the weakness of facts, and stepped almost defiantly onto the trail, arm-pushing branches from in front of her face. The trail followed a mountain deformity. It wound under a face of rock caused by a cleavage, an upward pressure on the hill, or a downward falling that caused the mountain parts to shift a few feet. Sedimentary layers were thin. In other parts of the hills one found layers as wide as thirty inches. Sun on the rock face dispelled some of the feeling she suffered at the stream.

Once beyond the glade the trail became easier, although blackberry had hold near the shelving. It was scrubby, not the strong twenty foot running branches of blackberry found in the bottoms. Two or three times she had to work her path carefully through it. In the bottoms and lower hillside patches, blackberry often meant rattlesnake. She remained alert, but expected no trouble. The chill left the air. In another month or so it would be time for the rattlesnake migration into the hills.

Traditionally the rattlesnake was honorable and respected. Traditionally the rattlesnake once was a man, as were the bear and the pine tree and the star.

The trail continued across the side of the mountain and followed the cleavage. After another quarter mile it branched, one side dropping right and down, the other continuing along the rock face. She followed the high trail, blinking in sudden sunlight because a dirt wash stood dry and choked with fallen trees. It was a small wash, not much more than a gully, and once she crossed it the shadows returned. She followed the trail and searched the forest, then heard movement on the rock above her head. She watched, startled, as she would not have been startled in a familiar forest, then moved slowly. Nothing. She turned to where she had been and looked up, looking with sudden horror into the yawning face of a red fox fifteen feet away on the rock above her. He seemed enjoying the yawn, stretching it, laugh-yawning and red-furred, sitting on his haunches, lazy in the sun. She wanted to scream.

She turned, walking quickly, almost trail-running. The easily-pushed year's growth was now an impediment holding her back. She looked over her shoulder and saw the fox padding after her. He paralleled her path, bright-gleaming, easy-trotting, and red, red, red, which was the east and luck and war, which was power and mystery. He trotted curious perhaps, but Harriette tasted fear—copper on her tongue—and ran. Her hair, which she should have tucked beneath her shirt, was jerked by branches. She stopped. No human being could outrun a fox.

The fox stopped. He was still a fox. She walked rapidly and he followed. A break in the forest lay ahead and she walked for that, glancing constantly over her shoulder and still terrified. At least she was not running.

The trail emptied into a natural clearing so large it surprised her that she had not seen it on her approach to town. It covered fifteen or twenty acres, and while there were traces of old burn there was no trace of trees. It was long, and not more than a couple of acres wide. The trail wound into the clearing badly overgrown with tall grass, wheat-colored and tangled. She moved as fast as possible, turning, seeing the fox sitting on the fault ridge and no longer following. She walked on, determined to put the clearing between them.

As she walked she looked toward the other side and saw she tended downward. The forest grew thicker, heavily shadowed, but a part of that was because she stood exposed in strong sunlight. Thirty yards from the forest edge she stopped again, feeling boxed in, small and dying.

Alien sound came from the forest. It was a low, whickering lyric that held elements of speech. It came from the east and moved closer. She stood in sunlight with coldness at the back of her neck. She waited with the kind of numb fatality that would happen if she were standing beside a dying person, the difference being that the person was herself.

She wanted to lie down, to close her eyes and huddle trembling like a spirit-broken dog before a kick. The sound came closer. Guttural now, rough and smooth like an interrupted chant pushed here and there by the wind.

Nunnehi, Yunwi Tsunsdi, she had read in the books. She had also read books about fire walkers and angels, levitation and the Holy Ghost. But, this was North Carolina and it was here that forest spirits walked. When she saw vague movement in the forest she tried to run;

made two false starts on legs that seemed stiff and riveted. She willed herself to move and could not. She searched the edge of the clearing. The movement was gone. Then, from what seemed a great distance behind her was a repetition of the whickering, rustling sound of almost speech. Harriette stood afraid even to try to run, afraid to turn, knowing if a bird's shadow flickered on her shoulder it would start her; would bring a fear so compulsive that she would scream and run. A rustle sounded in the underbrush across the clearing. She stared.

Lewis Corey stepped from the shadow of the forest and stood blinking in the sun.

He seemed tall. As he approached he must have stepped off a slight rise of ground and the illusion faded. Behind him another man broke through the growth before the clearing. He was tall and obviously full-blood.

Harriette tried to step forward. Then she waited. Corey came closer and smiled.

"Alone?" He stood in front of her. Actually shorter than she was. He did not sound angry but his voice was lower than she remembered.

"I needed to come, and there was no one to bring along. I've been so frightened." She actually seemed to be panting.

"Why should you be frightened?" He smiled again. The man behind him stood sleepy-eyed and passive.

"I heard a sound."

"There are plenty of sounds." Corey's voice was gentle, but the syllabication sounded guttural. He spoke to the man beside him, speaking rapidly in Cherokee that she could not follow. In the run of his words was the fluttering suggestion of the sound she had heard. The other man muttered back, his voice deep, his words slow. She started. The Nunnehi had been known to take familiar forms.

"Lewis...Mr. Corey."

"Yes." He turned back to her and now his voice was without inflection. His old-child face had the calm smile of the day before. She felt a fool.

"We talked yesterday."

"Yes," he said, "about power and my son and the old woman. I gave you the stone. I told you to stay on established trails."

She felt weak. "A mistake."

"You are in the forest alone."

"Another mistake."

"Maybe. Give me your knife." It was a compliment, his assuming she would not be there without one. She fished in her jeans for the jack-knife, specific for snake bite. She handed it to him and he walked from the clearing. She looked at the man who still stood sleepily in sunlight. He dressed in jeans and an old work shirt. "I'm glad you came," she said. He seemed nearly asleep. From the forest came a sharp, small click, and Corey emerged to hand her the broken blade and handle of her knife. "You must study this thing," he said.

It had been a perfectly good knife, in fact, the best you could buy and it cost six dollars. She accepted the halves dumbly.

"I don't understand."

"Study. The main trail is just above." He took her arm with his small hand, his touch gentle. They walked fifty yards through the overgrown clearing and entered a broad trail. After the overgrown trail she had followed, this one looked like a boulevard.

"Follow this. No side trips."

"I'm afraid."

"There is nothing to fear. Nothing. Now we must go." He dropped his arm which he had placed around her shoulder. "Go straight."

He turned and the other man followed, silent-walking, moving like a shadow. She watched and then turned to look down the trail. Turned back. They were gone, around the face of the mountain or back beyond the clearing, or become invisible. She held the broken knife like a charm and followed the trail. It was broad and fast. She heard no sounds. The trail emptied onto the main road. She followed the road a half mile, came to the motel and picked up her key. It was almost noon. She lay on the bed, exhausted and ashamed. A radio sat by the bed and she turned it on for distracting noise. Then exhaustion caught her and she slept; restless, dry-mouthed and tossing while the station broadcast a program of Christian prayers at midday, and a smooth-voiced announcer spoke intermittently and with warmth of a particular brand of soap.

Chapter 21

Harriette woke to a low knock on the door. It was Jan, me, Janet Scott, who did not then much understand the weight of past things. I still had my past to gather.

The radio sounded loud. Harriette turned it off.

"What time is it?" she asked the door. I told her it was two o'clock. I also told her Blaine called, and wanted her to call back. Then I left and went to the restaurant.

Harriette felt her face, her puffy eyes, and went to the bathroom to cool her face with a wet towel. She did not want to go into another situation at any disadvantage. Blaine had called. She tried her voice to see if it worked correctly. Her voice sounded husky, unmusical. It took her fifteen or twenty minutes before she felt in enough control to call Blaine.

The phone rang and rang. He was not at home.

She sat on the edge of the bed, remembering. It seemed impossible that only a little over two hours ago she came off that mountain, down a wide and well-worn trail, with fear too great to articulate, because articulated, it was too awful to consider. She reached to the dresser, picked up the two broken pieces of the knife.

The most likely possibility said that she had actually met Corey. That was easy to discover. Should it happen that by some one-in-a-million chance she had not seen Corey then she could only choose between acceptance, or the protest that she had hallucinated. She had read of mushroom and peyote rituals of Mexico and the southwest. She knew that induced hallucination was part of religious ceremony in some places—but self-induced by the mind?

When she felt in control she left to find Jan. Spending an afternoon with a rebellious child was among the least of the things she wanted, but she had promised. The weather was getting colder. When she rounded the corner of the restaurant Jan waited outside. Either Jan felt daring and worldly, or feared her presence might remind someone of work that needed doing.

They walked toward the road, the girl suddenly shy, and Harriette wondered where they were going, or if they were going anywhere. As they passed her car she turned to Jan. "Walk or ride?"

"Let's ride." The girl's voice sounded neutral. Maybe she had second thoughts. Maybe she had built her expectations and believed that Harriette would magically turn the day into a great and exciting time.

"Good." Harriette forced briskness into her voice. She had lied to this girl. It was her responsibility to mend the lie. Intentions were nothing. Results counted.

As she seated herself behind the wheel it occurred to her that it was the first time she had ever been conscious of her car. It was a few years old, she could not remember how many. It always ran. The steering had a little play, but it was otherwise a good car. It was simply not the kind of car a renowned world traveler would own. When she started the engine it seemed louder than usual, probably because Jan sat on the unused side of the seat wearing what was probably her best dress.

"I suppose I should get another one," she said about the car. "Never get around to it. My friends think I'm crazy."

She rolled from the parking lot and Jan's silence seemed an agreement with Harriette's friends. Harriette turned right, toward Bird-town. As they passed the spot where she had joined the road earlier she looked for the broad trail and saw nothing.

"There's a trail about here, isn't there?" She pointed.

Jan grunted.

"What?"

"There's a path leads over that way."

"I could have sworn a broad trail ran across the mountain just off to the right."

"Could be." Jan's prim voice said she was uninterested in trails, trees, mountains, countryside, spirits, religion, peace, warfare, the millennium, or anything else that was not San Francisco.

So be it. "When I was your age everyone headed for New York. Actors, painters, writers and business people."

"It's a good place," Jan admitted. A touch of enthusiasm entered her voice, a touch of expertise. Harriette figured this would be the blind leading the blind.

"But they went to Chicago for the music."

"It's a good place," Jan admitted.

"And New Orleans."

"Catch me in the nigger-lynching south."

Harriette was shocked. Shocked. She turned to Jan, nearly ran off the road, corrected and began to pay attention to her driving.

It was a shock to find it here. Here, of all places. Here, from all people. No society in the entire history of the world had enjoyed more individualism, rights, and freedom of thought than the Cherokee. At least that was true in the past. It was one of the reasons they had been so easily defeated in the past. No one could agree, and both men and women had a voice.

"It's probably different than you think."

"I doubt it." Jan's anger was not at Harriette. "Suppose you think these white sons-of-bitches don't let you know. Reckon they don't look?"

Harriette smiled. The old sick feeling she intellectually knew was ridiculous drew her into a knot. She had to make herself smile, because liar or not she was not going to teach anyone to hate.

"What do they do?"

Jan stared. Incredulous. "What do they *do?*"

"What do they do? I've never lived in this town."

Jan's voice sounded low and small, but not childish. "Is it different other places? Is it different in San Francisco?" Her voice seemed to come from a place so withdrawn she would even be unable to cry. Harriette felt helpless.

"It's different everyplace. You don't get away from it any more than you get away from being a girl. Some places it's an advantage, and that's really true."

"Where?"

Harriette had to admit she had never been anywhere that her mixed blood did not cause her to be different. Either good or bad distinctions were still distinctions. Only a few people did not grant her extra room or less room because of it. Her old teacher, Lillian Shuder, Warwick, Johnny... Trying to keep the car in the road, trying to find an answer for Jan, it was a little shocking to find that perhaps only those three were completely unimpressed. Something of her feeling must have shown on her face. Then she was smiling happy.

"What?"

"Thinking of a couple of friends." She felt warmth for them she had really never felt before. Jan was quiet and obviously impressed by the truth of Harriette's feelings.

"Is it the joking?" Harriette asked.

"Sometimes."

"Not hating."

"Sometimes."

She turned to Jan. "Be honest. It's the joking. Some fat drunk called you Pocahontas."

"Or Sacagawea, on account she did it with them white men."

"That was a different world," Harriette said, "and she also saved those white men's lives. You have to be kind. There's all kinds of fools, except in the west people mostly don't hate Indians. They just think everyone is big chief something or other."

"Ain't true, ain't true, ain't true."

"It's pretty true. Contempt sometimes, but mostly people just don't take you serious."

That was the really deep down feeling that got you. Lots of times she would have rather been actively hated, because there would be a solid reality she could direct her own hatred against. It was hard to hate idiocy, the usual rain-in-the-face, Hiawatha...John Wayne—watching cretins who would be happy to have an Indian chief in the family tree if he were far enough back not to show. In a way, to not be taken seriously was worse than being a candidate for a lynch party.

"Sometimes we do it to ourselves," she told Jan. "Look at all the phony feathers of the men who are 'Chiefing it' during tourist season. Look at the blocked-out carvings, the tourist junk, the 'white man's burden' attitude."

"I wish all the sons-of-bitches was dead." Jan did not explain whether she meant Indian sons-of-bitches or white ones.

"What about Mr. Corey?"

"He's different."

"What about your...uncle?"

"Ooooooh." Jan pounded her fists on the seat and dust flew out. It was embarrassing.

"The people were poor before the tourists."

"And still are."

"Your uncle?"

"Ha."

"Have him send you to college," Harriette told her. "It's all right in college, and that's the truth." It was not the truth but it was close enough. "You and Davey could go to the same school."

"U.C. Berkeley," Jan said quickly.

Harriette told herself grimly that what Jan needed was a good smack, but she did not believe that, either. What Jan needed was to grow up, and apparently nothing could be done to speed the process. "I'm thirsty," she said. "Look for a restaurant."

"There's none open this way on Sunday."

"We'll turn around and go back. Maybe we can find Davey."

"He's in Asheville," Jan told her. "Mr. Corey took a bunch of the boys. Next time he takes the girls."

It startled her. "When did they leave?" How could he have gotten off the mountain and be gone so soon?

"They left last night," Jan said. "Hey, whatinthehell's the matter?"

The car was getting away from her. She fought it, tires running the shoulder, the front end slipping toward a ditch, and she snapped the wheel hard. The front end pulled out, the back end sliding across to the ditch, and the car seemed to rumble sideways for an hour before it finally began to straighten. When it was once more straight in the roadway she got on the brake, stopped. Trembling. Jan opened the door. Began to get out.

"Please don't," Harriette said. "It's all right. Just something you said was shocking."

Jan paused, closed the door. "Whatinthehell?"

How much to tell her? Have to tell her something. "Do you remember I asked you about a trail? Is there a trail over there?" She could not get the tremble from her voice.

Jan seemed relieved that there was some kind of reason, even if she did not understand. "Just a short path. It runs in back of all the buildings."

"And goes onto the mountain?"

"No."

"Are you sure?"

"I lived here all my life."

Harriette did not doubt her memory. "When will Mr. Corey be back?"

"Tonight. There's school tomorrow. They just went for a ball game, and they have a pretty good time when they go."

Harriette began to drive. The road commanded too much attention. She felt confused, wondering, and the fear she should have, and did have, seemed a weight apart from this normal thing of driving and talking. She had never almost had a wreck before, and she was compromised in the presence of a child.

"I don't expect you to understand," she told Jan, "because I'm not sure how much I should tell you about what has happened. Do you remember the dogs this morning?"

"No."

"Something frightened the dogs."

"Yes."

"I met what frightened the dogs on that mountain, and nobody but Lewis Corey is going to believe it, I guess."

"There's nothing on that mountain." Jan's answer was too quick. She looked at Harriette, frightened. "There isn't a damn thing on that mountain."

"There is now," Harriette told her grimly.

"Sometimes we go to Winston-Salem," Jan said wistfully. "There's a real nice lady at the Y over there. Named Sandy. Sandy knows about real stuff."

"There's more power on that mountain than you're going to find in San Francisco and New York combined." She did not mean to frighten Jan, but she frightened her. She had to get back to the motel, get calm, think of all this. First she had to take care of the girl.

"I don't mean to scare you," she said. "And honestly, I'm not crazy.

Some new things got mixed up with old things, you know about that?"

Jan nodded.

"All the time," Harriette said. "Of course you know about that."

"David and I," Jan said. "We are going to get out of this crazy mess. We are going to the University of California in Berkeley." Her voice was as formal as her words. She seemed suddenly grown up, her posture unchildish, her whole self stretched toward dignity and reserve.

"I understand that," Harriette told her. "When the time comes I'll understand it. Until the time comes I hope we can be friends." She tried to match Jan's dignity without letting it sound cold, and admired the tone in her voice. The tone carried it. Jan forced a smile. Dignified. Reserved. She nodded yes, and a situation that was impossible turned barely possible. Harriette vowed inwardly that she would do well for this girl. Then she speeded up a little, and drove back to the motel, where Jan rapidly disappeared as Harriette went to her room. And, when she called, found that Blaine was still not at home.

Corey arrived after dark and she saw him at the restaurant. He did not seem old or fatigued, which to her was a small magic. Dealing with a carload of boys would have been a big job.

She feared Corey would think of her as some sort of neurotic, seeking woman, knowing that is how she must look.

He had better sense. He listened, asked a question in two or three places, his boyish face serious but unperturbed. At the end of her story he seemed nearly amused. "What surprises you? Are you really surprised?"

"When something happens that is impossible."

"These things happen rarely," he said. "The Nunnehi were reported once in this century from a reliable source. Two or three other times when alcohol might have been involved. Several times in the last century." If anything, the wrinkled, young-looking face regarded her with respect.

"I don't know what to do. I don't know what to think. We are talking about the impossible."

"We are talking about the Nunnehi." He was so calm, sitting over what must be the perpetual cup of tea. The modern restaurant seemed as natural a place for him as the forest. "The Nunnehi are documented on good evidence. Maybe they are invisible, maybe they are a separate tribe of people, but they are of that mountain. Even in those cases of alcohol one should not dismiss all evidence. Psychology has a long way to go before it understands alcohol."

"Could auto-suggestion make me do that?" She had brought the broken knife with her, had laid it on the table.

"You know as much as I do. Maybe more." He placed her knowledge right back where it belonged. With her. She admired him, but it made her afraid. He would not argue, support, dissuade.

"Study it," he said. "That was the instruction."

"What do you think it means?"

"You will tell me after you study it."

"You'll be here?"

"I think so. I almost always am here." He stood. "It was a long drive. I have to go now."

She wanted to detain him. Get his reassurance. There was not much to say.

"Next time the girls?"

"We go every two or three weeks. Maybe some day you'll join us."

"I like Jan."

"You should. There is a lot of life there."

"San Francisco."

"They almost always come back," he said. "Those who are not lost." For a moment his composure slipped. "A lot of them are lost. Cities eat them. Bad times, no work, booze." Then his serenity returned. He paid for the tea this time, touched her shoulder and left. His light form moved well, intact, and he was not envious of her experience. He did not doubt it, either. She did not quite understand how he managed, but for the second time in two days he had given her an enormous gift.

Light wind began moving darkly in the trees, and she felt more than saw trees through the lighted window. She must go out there in a minute, millions of trees, and the ancient, powerful mountain. The wind pressed through cracks in the window frame and she felt in it the first true touch of winter.

She would go back to the motel now. Tomorrow she would go home.

It all fit together somehow, and she felt herself closer to making it fit. The music, the old woman, her grandmother, her blood. She sat thinking of those things and found she actually looked forward to the future. Wind probed and searched around the window frame. It was still early in the autumn, but the wind probed with frost on its breath as if predicting future snows.

Chapter 22

S HE arrived home early next morning, driving up the lane and surprised because the big barn door stood open. She rarely went to the barn. When she did she always used the small door. The morning hovered gray and cloud-filled, low scudding mist blown through the valley. Her house would be cold.

Then she saw smoke from the chimney. She braked, stopped in the middle of the lane. Then she realized she had to go ahead into the barnyard because there was no place to turn around. As she entered the barnyard she saw Johnny Whitcomb's truck parked beside the house, hidden from the road. It was a relief. If Johnny was here nothing could be wrong.

He came from the house as she opened the car door. He looked relieved, happy. His short, muscular frame moved as if he were still half asleep, but his dark eyes were bright.

"It is all right," he told her. "Nobody. All night. I cook some of your coffee." He opened the door of her house, nearly bowing her inside.

"What is the matter?" She hurried inside. She had not gone dressed for cold weather, and the car's heater did not work very well.

"You talk to Blaine?"

"I called him twice," she told Johnny, "but he wasn't home. Is something wrong?"

He brought her a cup of coffee. "Then you don't know nothin' about it. Here you are, and you find Johnny in your house." His eyes were still bright, but looking at him, she could see his fatigue. Had he been up all night?

"Blaine comes and gets me," he said. "Blaine says somebody got to be here, 'cause maybe something ornery happen." He set the coffee down, but remained standing. "On account something ornery already did happen." He was unhappy, having to tell her.

"Blaine swing by here Saturday afternoon. Something awful. Big deer. Been shot then lynched from a tree. Doe. Just hanging with a rope around her neck. Ugly thing."

Her cup rattled against the coffee table. All of her recent experience fled, her feeling that she was about to discover some understanding about herself and her situation; well, that feeling was gone. Nunnehi or no Nunnehi, an enemy lurked out there. A deer was not a decayed bird, not a little snake. A white-tail deer was a big animal, heavy. No sick old man could hang a deer from a tree.

"Blaine take it with him," Johnny said. "In the back of his pickup. Takes it to game warden."

She felt little, like a little girl. For a moment she wanted to be a little girl, tucked warmly in bed with the sound of her parent's voices coming from the living room. Wanted the warmth of safety, wanted to know the adults were in control.

"Blaine say this time he catch the killers. This time he has tire prints, and he digs a bullet from that deer." Johnny grinned. "Wanted to leave me with a gun. I say, 'naw, man, don't want to shoot nobody. Got an old axe handle in the truck.'"

"You've been up all night?"

"Saturday, Sunday, pretty much. I sleep afternoons there on couch."

She stood, walked to him. "You are such a good, good friend, and Johnny, I'm afraid. Could you hold me for a minute?"

Like a father with a child, except she was taller than he, and yet like a father with a child. His arms, his large hands were gentle. He kind of patted her shoulder as he held her. "Gonna be okay. Blaine gonna get those fellas." Then he released her, and that made her lonesome.

"You have to sleep," she told him. "Have you eaten?"

"I open some cans."

"Then you will sleep, and when you get up I will fix something nice." She held his hand and led him to her mother's room. She thought momentarily she would have to push him inside. "Dan's friend," she said. "His friend would always be welcome here."

"You watch close," he told her. "Anybody, anybody, come up that lane or cross that barnyard you call me quick."

"Yes." She closed the door behind him, and moved silently toward the kitchen. The kitchen window looked onto the lane.

She sat drinking her cooling coffee, and watched lane and pasture and the distant oak tree. This house, which had always been safe, always been home, sat under attack. It occurred to her she did not know where the key to the front door of this house was. Then it occurred to her that she did not even know if there *was* a key to the front door. This was rural North Carolina. She was willing to bet there were not two houses in the county that were locked. Things like that must drive men like Blaine crazy.

Then she told herself, no. No. It was not the house that was under attack. It was she. All because she stepped foot on that land.

Somewhere, at the bottom of the antique sidearm bookcase, beneath *National Geographics,* were some of her father's old books. She crossed the room, nearly on tiptoe so she would not wake Johnny.

Strange goings-on had been happening toward the end of the nineteenth century. A lot of ethnologists tried to save the cultural history of the American Indian. Some of those ethnologists used some pretty underhanded tactics to get what they wanted, but she was glad they had gotten the information. No Cherokee saw fit to write it down. She hefted the heavy old books. Among the Cherokee the ethnologists were Mooney and Powell and Olbrechts. She liked Mooney best because he wrote so simply and sincerely, and it was in the Mooney that she found the account which read:

> There was a man in Nottely town who had been with the Nunnehi when he was a boy, and he told Wafford all about it. He was a truthful, hard-headed man, and Wafford had heard the story so often from other people that he asked this man to tell it. It was in this way:
>
> When he was about ten or twelve years old he was playing one day near the river, shooting at a mark with his bow and arrows, until he became tired, and started to build a fish trap in the water. While he was piling up the stones in two long walls a man came and stood on the bank and asked him what he was doing. The boy told him, and the man said, "Well, that's pretty hard work

and you ought to rest for awhile. Come and take a walk up the river." The boy said, "No," that he was going home to dinner soon. "Come right up to my house," said the stranger, "and I'll give you a good dinner there and bring you home in the morning." So the boy went with him up the river until they came to a house, where they went in, and the man's wife and the other people there were very glad to see him, and gave him a fine dinner, and were very kind to him. While they were eating, a man that the boy knew very well came in and spoke to him, so that he felt quite at home.

After dinner he played with the other children and slept there that night, and in the morning, after breakfast, the man got ready to take him home. They went down a path that had a cornfield on one side and a peach orchard fenced in on the other, until they came to another trail, and the man said, "Go along this trail across that ridge and you will come to the river road that will bring you straight to your home, and now I'll go back to the house." So the man went back to the house and the boy went on along the trail, but when he had gone a little way he looked back, and there was no cornfield or orchard or fence or house; nothing but trees on the mountain side.

He thought it queer, but somehow he was not frightened, and went on until he came to the river trail in sight of his home. There were a great many people standing about talking, and when they saw him they ran toward him shouting, "Here he is! He is not drowned or killed in the mountains!" They told him they had been hunting him ever since yesterday noon, and asked him where he had been. "A man took me over to his house just across the ridge and I had a fine dinner and a good time with the children," said the boy, "I thought Udsiskala here"—that was the name of the man he had seen at dinner—"would tell you where I was." But Udsiskala said, "I haven't seen you. I was out all day in my canoe hunting you. It was one of the Nunnehi that made himself look like me." Then his mother said, "You say you had dinner there?" "Yes, and I had plenty, too," said the boy; but his mother answered, "There is no house there—only trees and rocks—but we hear a drum sometimes in the big bald above. The people you saw were the Nunnehi."

There it was. She had read the account before, knew what she was going to read. Yet, there it was, and she knew now who had killed her father.

It was impossible. Totally unreasonable. Maybe a little insane. But there it was.

Her problem, as she sat holding the old book, was not that she believed the Nunnehi had protected the land. Her problem was that she *knew* it. It had nothing to do with belief or disbelief.

And yes, it was crazy. What was she going to tell Blaine? That the reason he had not found the murderers was because the murderers were invisible Indians?

No. She was not going to tell that to Blaine. She wasn't going to tell it to Warwick, or Johnny, or maybe even Corey. At least she thought she would not. Then she remembered Corey advising her to concentrate on the main mystery which asked why her father had done such a thing. Did Corey already know that the mountain killed Dan Johnson?

From her mother's bedroom came a muffled snort, a snore, then silence. She smiled thinking of Johnny. The house felt better, now, not so empty. It was nice having another person in the house, a trusted person. Maybe she was pretty solitary, but at least for now it was just plain nice.

Her mind began striking balances. If the mountain wanted revenge, if the mountain wanted her dead, then she would be dead by now. Either that or dying, lost somewhere on a criss-cross of trails, or entangled in a rhododendron bald with no possibility of escape.

So the mountain did not want her dead. Maybe, she thought, the mountain was her friend. That broken knife could mean a lot of things. Maybe it meant there was no enmity between her and the mountain. Maybe it was a sign showing that she was powerless. Maybe it meant the mountain was her protector.

Whatever it meant, she understood that the situation was now more complex. Someone out there wanted her away from that mountain. That someone had not murdered her father. Whoever sent warnings had a motive which did not include hiding the identity of the true murderers. Somebody wanted something, but it had nothing to do with an old murder.

A flicker of understanding crossed her mind, then left before she could grasp it. Why had the Nunnehi felt forced to kill her father? With such power, surely they could have frightened him away.

Invisible Indians. She sat, leafing through the old books which had lain so long beneath piles of farm magazines. This was the twentieth century. Mountains bigger than that mountain out there were being strip-mined, torn apart, denuded for a million years. This was a century of technology, of force. And here she sat, not worried about belief in invisible Indians, but trying to understand her absolute knowledge that Nunnehi existed.

She looked across the barnyard at the open barn door. Of course Johnny would have opened the door. From the roadway the open door would signal that someone was on the place and working. Another understanding flickered past, but she caught this one.

The mountain may have killed her father, but it meant her no harm. Someone out there apparently meant her a lot of harm. She understood that she was safer on that mountain than she was in her own house.

It was still a gray, chill day. She slipped into a jacket and walked to the pasture. In a day or two the cropper would have cattle in there. That might be a good thing. The farm would almost seem like a farm again. The pasture had been hayed twice, and now clover and grass rose only a little above the stubble. At the downside of the pasture, but before the oak tree, a small mound of hay sat black and abandoned. She walked to the tree. Touched the rough, cold bark.

What did it know? Maybe nothing. This tree had its own affairs. Much of it was subterranean, roots spreading, the tap root reaching like a dark anchor in the center of darkness. When she was a little girl she had nearly expected the tree to speak with the congregated voices of the valley, the stream; speak with the voices of breeze and rain and thunder. Maybe as a little girl she expected the tree to thank her.

On that mountain she was safe. She turned, looked at her house. It was necessary to be brave, to fight back; necessary to be in complete control of her life. Standing beside the tree which would soon move to dormancy, she thought not of the mountain or the pasture, but of her old teacher; that woman who weighed the prices of love and chose to pay the price of music. It seemed that some price must be paid.

Chapter 23

I recall that night after the bad afternoon with Harriette. It was the night before Harriette returned home and found out about the deer.

After Harriette dropped me off and went to her room I felt betrayed, neglected, treated like a kid. It was one more Sunday afternoon and evening, one more day of looking toward school on Monday. At least in school a few things happened. In my world of that time, nothing much happened except fantasy. I dreamed of leaving home, of going to miraculous cities, of people who drove fine cars and who danced or played music or acted on the stage. Sometimes I dreamed that Sandy Smith, over at the Y in Winston-Salem, would become my best friend. We would travel around the world together.

That Sunday evening, after Harriette dropped me off, was one more evening of chores and silence. I understand now that my father was a worried man. I understand now that in his way my father was a good man, but his way ran narrow. Like most of the Cherokee he had been poor. Then, when my grandfather died, my father inherited a little money. He built some cabins. Then later he built the motel. It was a small motel, and it would never make my family prosperous, leave alone rich; but it was his, an assurance against poverty. On that evening—and doubtless for many evenings before—my father worried about losing the place.

His problem was this. He built on ground that he believed he owned. Surveyors in the North Carolina hills during those times surveyed as much by local knowledge as they did by surveying tools. Now, with Dan Johnson long dead and Harriette Johnson in control of the land, my father feared Harriette would learn just how far her land extended. The motel was built at least partly on the Johnson land.

I think maybe my father always felt he could deal with Dan Johnson. Dan had a reputation for fairness. Dan was Cherokee, a known quantity.

But Harriette? She was educated. She was even a teacher. She was, as far as my father could see, a white woman. In other words she was intimidating. She had the upper hand, although she did not know and would not have cared.

So my father did a foolish thing. It was he who started the rumors which said Harriette would timber the land. When he first saw Blaine and Harriette in the parking lot, he called a hate-filled old man named Peter Lee. I do not know why my father was Lee's crony, never will. Nobody else had anything to do with Lee. Lee held a grudge against the memory of Dan Johnson. Nobody knew a thing about that grudge at the time, or about its origins. It was Lee who originally sold the land to Dan. It was Lee whom Harriette had met on the mountain, Lee who looked at her with such hatred.

My father no doubt hoped he could force Harriette to sell the land, and that he could buy the part he needed. His action was short-sighted, but he was a desperate man. Instead of frightening Harriette off, he forced her to deal with the land.

On the next day, for example, she would understand that the mountain had killed her father. Practically every grownup in Cherokee had known that for years. Some people even believed it; but whether they believed it or not they all knew it. A few old ones said "Nunnehi." Most said that some men living in the old way came across the mountain. It was worn-out news. And, of course, it was news that belonged among the Cherokee. No one would have told Blaine, even if Blaine would have believed it. Dan's death was a Cherokee matter.

Be that as it may, on that Sunday evening, my father had a visitor. No one in town knew about the decayed bird or the little snake, but on that Sunday evening everyone had heard about the deer. On that evening Harriette slept in her room at the motel. She was probably the only person in the whole county who had not heard.

The visitor was Lewis Corey's son, Tom Corey. Most everybody liked Tom because Susy had been his mother. He was married to Susy's third cousin, Mary Ford. Some of the old people did not like that, because in a matrilineal society Tom had married where he should not. He could have married his first cousin on his father's side, or even his aunt on his father's side; but marriages to the mother's side had once been unthinkable. At the same time, everybody liked Mary. Since the Cherokee trace lineage through the mother's side, Tom was Cherokee no matter how light his skin.

"I think, Frank," Tom said to my father, "that things are maybe getting out of hand. Lot of talk." They sat at a table in the restaurant. I dawdled, putting kitchen tools away for the night and filling sugar shakers. They paid no attention to me. Maybe I was an invisible Indian.

"There's always plenty of talk," my father said. "*My* people are good at talk."

Tom Corey ignored the insult. Tom did not like what he was doing but knew he was the only one who would do it. At least he was the only one who would do it nice. After all, he was talking to a man fifteen years older.

"I ask Lee what's going on," Tom said, "and he gives me the old Lee grunt, and then he spits."

"Lee is a bag of pus," my father said. "Too sick. All he can do is spit. He says he was cheated on that land."

Tom stared into his cup of cooling coffee. He did not look for an argument, did not want one. "Lee got that land from his grandfather," Tom said, "and his grandfather stole it in the first place."

"Lee says he got cheated. Cheated when he bought it, cheated when he sold it."

"He didn't buy it. His grandfather willed it to him."

"Lee's grandfather got cheated," my father said. "Lee claims white lawyer business."

"Dan paid fifteen thousand cash for land you can only walk on. Can't timber. Land killed him." Tom sounded really puzzled. "How can that be cheating?"

"Lee is bad sick," my father said. "He can't do anything."

"He can talk," Tom said. "Could be he talks and some hothead hears the talk. Somebody did something pretty mean." Tom looked pale beside my dark, solid father.

"We never get snow in September," my father said. "Feels like snow though, don't it?"

"Suppose whoever is doing this is one of our young ones? Suppose he figures he's a big man? What's he gonna do?" Corey's eyes, which were always so happy, were not happy now. "That Blaine is hell on wheels," he said. "Since he retired. Got lots of time now."

"Blaine," my father said. "Couldn't find a skunk in a hollow tree."

"He's going to find something," Tom said. "Maybe," he said, "I'll find something." It was not said like a threat, but like a question.

My father looked at Tom, and my father was as serene as an old log. "What you're gonna find," he said, "is a white man. That damn deer is white man's business."

Tom looked relieved. His eyes looked almost happy. "I thought about that. Seemed right. Lynching is white man's business. I was just scared some of our young ones were running around with rifles and ideas."

"I got nothing to do with the woman," my father said. "Don't care either way."

"I might tell that around."

"Maybe you better. Maybe then you won't have to come here and talk." My father stood, taciturn, serene; left the restaurant and headed for the office. There would be no tourists coming through, but he headed for the office.

Tom Corey sat at the table, a cold cup of coffee in front of him, and he looked like he felt good and he looked like he felt awful. He was a man who had given offense. The fact that he felt he had to do it did not matter. At the same time, he was happy because my father said what Tom already felt, that this was not an Indian matter.

I did not even know who or what they were talking about. The next day in school everybody knew about the deer. I more or less understood the conversation I had heard, but it made no impression. It was a white matter, and at the time I did not care if Blaine threw every white man in his county into jail.

I did not care if Blaine put Lee *under* the jail, but, of course, Blaine was not looking at Lee, because Blaine was not Indian.

He did not know that when Lee sold the land, and Johnson began tearing up the land, people blamed Lee every bit as much as they blamed Johnson. After all, if Lee had not sold it, then Johnson could not have attacked it.

Nobody would tell that to Blaine. It didn't make white sense.

Also, Lee had not been cheated. He had caused his own shame, and he was blaming it all on Johnson. He behaved so badly that people began talking about witches. Of course, some people always talk about witches. That was the shape of things after Harriette returned home and found Johnny guarding her house.

Chapter 24

COLD mist lay across the pasture all that Monday afternoon as Johnny slept. Harriette moved quietly through the house, and she had things to think about. A letter from Alan, for one. He wrote details of the estate, mostly matters requiring no decisions from her. One matter did require a decision:

> I've been approached by attorney Jay Richards. He has a client who inquires about the flatlands farm. There is an opening offer of twenty thousand dollars. The place has been producing an average share of twenty-three hundred dollars a year. The expenses with taxes have been running about one third of that. While no one can know the future, I estimate in eight or ten years the tobacco base will be worth around ten thousand dollars. In other words, this does not look like a sufficient offer. However, it is only an opening offer, and I must ask if you feel the matter is subject to negotiation.

Her problem, walking through the house and looking occasionally into the cold mist covering the pasture, was that she did not understand why she even had to make a decision. None of her work was in that property. She could not even recall having ever seen the property. Other men and women thought of it as home. She was not certain, but believed the share croppers on that farm had been there for years. It did not seem fair for them to work so hard, be there so long, and have someone come along and buy the place. They would have to move.

It also seemed unfair to get money from something she had hardly known, leave alone loved. In the white world these things happened all the time. They also happened sometimes in the Indian world.

Because when you boiled it all down, boiled all of the history and push and shove of centuries, the basic difference between the American Indian and the European whites who settled America was the difference over property. No American Indian—not even the property-oriented people of southeast Alaska and the Pacific Northwest—could really understand white ways of looking at property. Before the whites, and among the Cherokee, people owned their personal things: tools and weapons. The idea of anyone's owning the land was inconceivable. There were no words in the language.

The Cherokee, of course, learned pretty fast, and learned the hard way. These days some of the most avaricious people in the world could be found among the Cherokee. The old ways were still there, but new ways were there as well.

About her own place, this farm, there were other feelings. The cropper for this farm was not poor. She wondered why the cropper had not yet brought his animals to pasture. And this farm could not possibly be as rich as the flatlands farm. This farm had, at best, eighty or a hundred acres which could be cultivated. It held another forty or fifty acres of woodland mountainside. Even if cleared, you could not get a tractor up there. It would roll off the mountain.

It seemed to her, thinking about it, that she must write to Alan and ask who wanted to buy the place. If the people on the land wanted to buy it, then she was honor bound to sell. If some speculator wanted to buy, she was honor bound to refuse. Maybe that made no economic sense, and maybe Alan would think she was crazy; but if a person's parents raised that person to believe in decent behavior, it would be a betrayal to behave badly.

Alan wrote further:

> And, if I may depart for a moment from my role as your attorney, and speak to you as Dan's daughter and as a friend, that forest land is a luxury. It is presently non-productive. While the taxes are not high, no income is produced. It cannot be regarded as forest crop land, because the crop is already grown and not cut. It has been a source of tragedy for your family. I continue to believe you should divest at any reasonable price.

She remembered him. Tall, relaxed, a nice-looking older man who showed genuine concern for her. A man who concealed her father's

madness. But her father was not mad—at least according to Warwick, and according to the old woman Molla. She wished she could
absolutely trust Alan, but honestly told herself she could not.

In the cold mist, looking onto the silent pasture, this place which
had always been her home seemed small, attacked, shriveled. She
looked toward the barn, the large and open door, and remembered
the farm when it had been alive.

The chickens, the pigs in their pen, the few cattle there in the pasture. She had a pet pig when she was little, a big one named May. And
there was a chicken named Molly; the two named after characters in
a children's book. And each evening after school she came home, got
an apple, and went to sit on the fence rail of the pig pen. And she and
Molly and May shared the apple.

And now it was all gone, quiet, the old barn with no fresh-cut hay.
No animals. Only the barnyard, where every year it was necessary to
mow the weeds at least once.

Maybe it was cold mist, maybe it was the fact that someone hated
her. The afternoon pressed like a frozen weight and she fed the heating stove more hugely than was strictly necessary. When the house
got too warm she opened the back door, allowing heat to escape and
churn the cold mist.

A depressing day. She could not work at the piano, because it
would wake Johnny. Thinking that, she smiled. At least she could
make a nice dinner for Johnny. They could sit and talk. Later she
would play music, and he would like that.

Which is exactly the way it turned out. She cooked in the manner
farm women had cooked for centuries. It was automatic, intuitive,
educated; and she did it all without thinking. Those country
women—on the only time she had ever thought about it—cooked by
sound. The only reason she thought about it was because she found
herself working by sound and wondered if she did because she was a
musician. She had watched her mother, her mother's friends, and
never seen a single one of them taste or measure a thing. They knew
the sounds that told them all was well.

Johnny was quiet, tidy as always, polite. He even acted formal at
first, and appreciative as if she had done some wonderful thing for
him. He, who had been up two nights protecting her, acted as if she

were the one doing the favors.

He was sitting relaxed, listening as she played, as they had been for about an hour, joined together with the music, when headlights appeared coming up the now-dark lane. Johnny stood, moved toward the doorway. She stopped playing. The sun had set and darkness encroached.

"Okay-okay," Johnny said. "It's Blaine. Come to tell about it."

Once inside the house, Blaine looked nearly as tired as Johnny had looked earlier that morning. His hair seemed more silvered, and was rumpled. He took a chair, waved off a cup of coffee and was finally persuaded to drink hot chocolate. He slouched but did not slump. His face showed fatigue, but it also showed success.

"I know the name of one of them," he told Harriette and Johnny. "Say nothing about this to anybody. I've got my man, but I've got no proof." He looked at Johnny. "Anything happen?"

"Nary a nothing," Johnny said. "Quiet like the mouse."

"Drove past every old truck in this county," Blaine said, and he talked directly to Johnny. "Needed a seventeen-inch wheel, bald tire on the left front, knobby tire inside left rear. Last truck I checked was the last one you'd expect. Old Pete. Pete Lee."

"Naw," Johnny said. "Think about it, man." Johnny sounded discouraged, like a man who had just seen some great hope shattered. "Lee so sick he got to hire people tie his shoes."

"He can afford it." Blaine still slouched, but comfortably. "All these years," he said, "Lee's been sitting on money. Won't even buy himself a decent truck. All these years I've been looking for some young bloods, been looking for hot dogs. Not some old man choked up with money and hate."

"Lee hate everybody. Lee hate Indians pretty good, but white men oh boy. Hate white cows, white pigs, white horses, white chicken...." Johnny stopped, thought, and a look of amazement and admiration for Blaine was in his eyes. "Lee sell that land to Dan."

"Please explain." Harriette listened, somehow resenting that Blaine talked to Johnny and not to both of them.

"All these years," Blaine told her, "I've been going on the notion that there was only one possible motive for your father's murder. It was the only visible motive. Two men tried to protect the land."

She privately agreed. Two men had protected the land, but they were men Blaine would never see. "Now you see another motive," she said.

"I called myself a sheriff," Blaine said, and seemed mostly speaking to himself. "And there, right under my nose..." He looked at Harriette. "Your father bought that land from a man who is vicious. What I missed was that I thought Lee was never vicious except with his tongue. Now I think we have some kind of personal revenge, and that amounts to a different motive."

She had stood when he arrived, had prepared the hot chocolate, and now she found herself sitting on the piano bench as if she had never moved. The bench felt familiar and somehow safe.

"Old people," Johnny said, "say he didn't use to."

"I am not understanding this at all," Harriette said to both of them.

"I've heard that story," Blaine said to Johnny. Then he turned to Harriette. "Lee got gassed with mustard gas in the First World War. Old people say that before the war he was not so bad." Blaine straightened in his chair. "Makes no difference. He was one of the men who murdered Dan Johnson. Lee is one of the men who threaten you. He is a man I will bring to trial, convict, and send away for what little life is left him." Blaine's mouth was not cruel, his eyes were not hateful, but there was no kindness about any part of him. "Someone younger is his accomplice, and that one is looking at life without parole. In a grim way this is almost a comedy. If they had lain low and ignored you, I would probably never have found them."

Johnny stretched, pretended a yawn. Harriette watched him. Johnny was not devious, but he was not sleepy, either. Why was he acting for Blaine?

"Maybe we take him the other way around," Johnny said to Blaine. "Dan, he is dead. Nothing we gonna do for Dan. How 'bout you go to Lee, tell him these things that you know. Then Lee get scared, never bother my friend no more."

She loved him, loved Johnny. Not like a wife or a lover, but as a strong woman might admire and love a strong and decent man.

Johnny was right. Blaine, whether he was talking about white law or not, still talked about a form of revenge. She did not want to hate. She did not want revenge.

And Johnny called her his friend. Always before Johnny had been here because he was Dan's friend. She sat, filled with the man's kindness, his loyalty. It was almost worth it to have Blaine here, if it meant having heard this from Johnny.

"Because that is not the way it works," Blaine told both of them. He paused, as if carefully considering Johnny's words, but his expression did not seem to pay any attention to those words. At the same time he respected Johnny. "If it were only Lee," he said, "maybe there would be some sense to it. Someone younger is out there, and he is a murderer. If he killed Dan, then he is capable of killing again." He paused again, and Harriette wondered at Blaine's respect for Johnny, because Blaine had also once described Johnny as being crazy as a rabbit. "Maybe," Blaine said to Johnny, "I could tell Lee that. Lee would tell the accomplice. The accomplice would stay away from Harriette. That does not mean he would stay away from someone else. It does mean I'd still have a murderer out there in this county."

Johnny did not yawn again, but he managed to look as if he were holding back on a yawn. "Maybe so," he said, "but think him over, that accomplice. He know you gonna tell the sheriff, and the sheriff gonna tell the next sheriff, and the sheriff after that..." Johnny paused, almost elaborately. "So all you gotta do is find that man and say to him that everybody is watching."

"Who," Blaine said, "in the hell's side are you on?"

"My friend's side," Johnny said, and he no longer pretended to be bored or sleepy. "You go along like hound dog. Those men got more time to do orneriness. Maybe you solve a murder while you get somebody hurt?" He phrased his last statement like a question, but it was really not a question.

"Lee could have done it," Blaine said, and he somehow argued with Johnny while not answering Johnny. "Dan was killed seven years ago. Seven years ago Lee was in bad shape but not feeble."

"C'mon Blaine and stop it." Johnny stood, walked to the window, and he did not look short or silly at all. His voice held as much authority as Blaine's ever had. "Do not get this woman hurt. Do not have to answer to me. Do not have to answer to you."

"She will not be hurt," Blaine said, "because Johnny will not let it happen. I know you, Johnny."

"That is not fair." Harriette heard her own voice even before she decided to speak. "You can't ask somebody to stop his way of living and take care of somebody else." She stood, headed for the kitchen because she wanted to be busy doing something; even making more hot chocolate if nothing else. "I feel like a pawn," she said to Blaine, "and I've never even learned to play chess."

"Because," said Blaine, "I will have the sheriff appoint Johnny a deputy and Johnny will be paid. Johnny can likely use the money."

Johnny turned from the window. He looked at Harriette, nearly apologetic. "That was lousy," he said to Blaine, and he enunciated the words carefully. "You are as full of hate as Lee. First murder you never solve."

Blaine looked like Harriette thought he should look, which was confused and apologetic and stupid. It was not the way Blaine was accustomed to looking, that was clear.

"That was a wrong thing to say," he told Johnny. "Between old friends that was real bad." He stood, but he did not approach Johnny. "It's going to take everybody awhile to get over that."

Johnny said nothing. He turned toward the window, staring into darkness and cold and mist.

"So I'm asking an old friend, a good friend, a favor." Blaine's voice was genuinely freighted with apology and shame. "Give me ten days. All I need is to trace Lee's associates. I can do it in ten days."

Johnny turned. "Man, go ahead and do it. Maybe then all that hate leak out. Maybe then you come around here and you start talking like Blaine, 'stead of the way you talkin' now."

"I am sorry," Harriette said to Johnny. She did not know why she said that, and she certainly had no reason; except, maybe, somebody ought to be saying some kind of apology to Johnny.

"I'm sorry too," Blaine said, "but saying it doesn't amount to much." He stepped to the door. "Stay close to home," he said to Harriette. "These men are not clever, and men who are not clever do unpredictable things."

Blaine left, the red tail lights of his pickup disappearing down the lane like two small eyes fading into mist. Johnny watched the disappearing tail lights. "In his whole life," Johnny said, "Blaine see maybe eight or ten dead men. Don't know anything about dead men. He know anything, he would not act so bad."

Chapter 25

HARRIETTE and Johnny alternated watches. For two days a pattern rose in which Johnny watched through the night, occasionally leaving the house to walk like a short, light-footed ghost drifting through shadows and listening for sound along the mountainside, or watching for movement along the lane and in the pasture. In early morning, around five or six, Harriette would wake and Johnny would sleep. In late afternoons Harriette cooked, and Johnny worked around the place.

At first it seemed to her there was not much work that needed doing. She had forgotten the demands of a farm, even one that was not a working farm. Her mother would not have forgotten. Johnny tsked and tsked as he did minor repairs on the house, the barn and outbuildings. In the evening she played both the piano and the clarinet, remembering the way she had drummed with her fingers for the old woman. She experimented with time frames, tried to get the clarinet to sound like the many waters of a stream—rushing—trickling—roiling. When she departed from that and played boleros, Johnny patted his foot, rolled his eyes a little bit, and was a short and happy spirit. On the morning of the third day, Wednesday, Warwick called.

"Geology is a fascinating science," he said. "I regret never having spent much time with it before."

Someone was threatening her, a man filled with hatred, a man wanting revenge; and Warwick talked about geology. Of course, Warwick did not know about the threats.

"A half-billion years ago," he said, "a part of that mountain range rose. A half-billion years." Even Warwick, even though he was in full possession of the facts and had clearly thought about the facts, still sounded impressed. "They are named the Ocoees. Then, three hundred million years later, a second range arose, incorporating some of the original range. That range was named or misnamed the Appalachians."

She knew that Warwick was not telling her something useless. Warwick did not waste time with chatter.

"Which means," Warwick told her, "that parts of those mountains are among the oldest structures on earth. Parts of those mountains are as close to the original creation as may be discovered on this planet."

She did not understand which way he tended, and she said so.

"I am not a missionary," he said, "and I have no dogma to peddle. However, one school of theology holds that divine force is expressed as original creative energy. Should those theologians be correct, then what you report feeling on that mountain is one expression of that energy which some call God." The word "God" existed as comfortably in his voice as would the words "cat" or "mountain." She had never met anyone before, not even preachers—or maybe especially not preachers—who could talk seriously and casually about God.

"At any rate," Warwick said, "you will understand why I am a wonderfully excited man. I will arrive late Saturday evening."

About that, she could do something.

"You will stop in Asheville," she said. "I will come for you in the car. When does the bus arrive in Asheville?"

"It is not necessary."

"It is necessary," she told him. "Geology is more reliable and a good deal faster than our local bus."

"Then I accept. Meanwhile, there is another matter. I have been over the sheriff's file. You recall we agreed the sheriff hid something?"

"My father was insane," she told Warwick. "Sheriff Blaine really believes that."

"He hides something more," Warwick said. "The reason he hides it from you is because he hides it from himself. The sheriff denies evidence." Warwick's voice became more gentle. "There is no easy way to speak of this, for the dead man was your father. That was not an assassination, it was not revenge, and it was not murder in the sense we usually understand murder." Warwick paused again. For the first time since she had known him, his voice sounded apologetic. "It seems a ritual killing. Your father's body was laid out in the manner for burial. It was not crumpled. There were signs of struggle, but someone closed the eyes, which denotes careful respect."

"I don't understand."

"I do not yet understand, myself," Warwick told her. "Perhaps when I arrive I will understand more. At any rate, our Sheriff Blaine has denied the evidence of his senses. What he saw made no sense in his terms, and I doubt not that he has by now forgotten he even saw the evidence."

She had sworn that she would say nothing about her father's killers to anyone: not Johnny, not Warwick, not Corey. She had sworn it, so why was she saying, "The mountain killed my father." She could not bring herself to explain invisible Indians.

"It seems likely," Warwick said. "It would be consistent with the mythology. If the mythology can be tested, your knowledge will quite possibly stand. The problem is how to test it without disrespect."

She took a deep breath. "That is already accomplished," she told him. "It's a long story."

"Then I shall look forward to its telling," Warwick said. "I have also collected a history of the ownership of that land. Meanwhile, have you visited the old woman?"

She was suddenly angry. Angry with Warwick—and that was not fair because she had told him nothing of the threats—angry with the mountain, with Blaine; finally, angry because some sick and sad little man threatened her. She held her hand over the phone, took a couple of deep breaths. How dare some old man intimidate her? How dare some old man cause her to be angry with her friends? "I visit her this afternoon," she told Warwick. "Some people are unhappy because I visit the old woman, but those people are going to have to live with it."

"When one has taught for many years," Warwick said, "one becomes sensitive to the inflections in speech. Something frightens you."

"Something has," she said, "but maybe I scare too easy. There is nothing to worry about."

"Until Saturday, then. The schedule says the bus arrives in Asheville at noon."

After she hung up she sat staring through the window and onto the pasture, at the tree, and she thought about power. There was power and there was *Power*. Lee was exercising the power of fear over her, and she wondered how much came about because he was a man—even an old, sick one—and she was a woman. Thus presumably frail. Thus needing protectors? How much of his power came from underhanded tricks, cloaked ways of causing fear?

Then there was *Power*. There was Power on that mountain, but the same thing existed among people. Lewis Corey had some, fashioning flight and life in stone. She realized she had some—some of what Warwick had just called original creative energy—and Johnny had some because Johnny was loyal and gentle and kind. No one but Johnny could paint the faces of trees.

Which meant she could fight back. She did not want a gun, any more than Johnny wanted to take one from Blaine. Only nasty little men with nasty little powers needed guns.

Could you actually take music and with it defeat guns? She told herself you blessed well could. She also told herself she did not know why she knew that, but she knew it as firmly as she knew the mountain had killed her father. If she took music to that mountain it would be her way of talking to the mountain. The mountain would defeat the guns, because it would hear her talk.

When Johnny woke at noon she had already checked oil in the car. Her clarinet lay cased on the automobile seat. Her hair was not simply tied back, but braided, and she was dressed for the mountain. Her knife was broken, but all a snake bite needed was a blade. The broken blade was wrapped in a handkerchief. She carried it in her side pocket, along with the bird stone.

She listened to what she knew Johnny was going to say, "Naw, think him over. Naw." And she watched him turn from reluctance to admiration.

"Okay," he said. "I call Tom Corey. Never thought 'til now about Tom. Tom's a farmer."

She sat listening to the phone conversation. Tom did not ask questions. The only question in her mind was why Blaine, and now Tom, acted with such respect toward a man who described himself as getting a little bit crazy, a little bit drunk. She knew Johnny was a good man. She was simply surprised that first a white man, and now an Indian man, understood it as well.

"Let's go," Johnny said. "Tom be here in half an hour."

"You drive."

"You bet." He slid behind the wheel, started the engine, and turned the car around in the barnyard. Grinned. "Been all the time piddle around fixing barn. Tomorrow right away, fix them ball joints. This old car he steers like a T2 tanker."

Chapter 26

W HEN they arrived at the mountain and locked her car, Johnny turned toward the forest and crossed himself. "Saint Jude," he said in the direction of the forest, "now he was not a bad man. Saint Jude, Saint Therese, they pull me through a lot." To Harriette, he said, "Those two pull me through a-plenty."

She waited for him to explain, then saw that in his mind everything was already explained. She stepped past the place where her father's body had lain, and onto the trail. After cold nights the forest showed a tangle of slowly growing color. Trees expressed yellow and gold. In the thickets, red and yellow and purple tangled beneath great trees like a faraway canvas by an Impressionist artist. The silence of the forest seemed normal silence. At this time of year some snakes would be moving to higher ground. Squirrels and chipmunks would be stuffing themselves in preparation for winter. Bears would do the same, building winter fat for their short hibernation.

In the middle of normal silence, power lay across the forest like a light, non-touching and indifferent hand. She felt again the old forgotten people who had walked this land, felt their presence in the way she had so often—while playing music—felt the living presence of long dead composers. Warwick said this was some of the most ancient land on earth. A half-billion years, and people had been here perhaps no more than twenty thousand of those years. If she found herself not speaking to Johnny, it was not from fear or awe of power. It was from awe of the many echoes walking this mountain. She did not wish to break the silence. When the silence did break, she was a little indignant even while being startled.

A heavy body moved in the undergrowth about fifty yards above the trail.

"Bear," Johnny said happily. "Hi, bear," he said. He continued up the trail behind Harriette, and his voice sounded light and free. "This mountain feel okay," he said to Harriette. "Not like before. Not like when we logged."

She wondered if that bear up there was the same old bear which had followed her. If it was, it made no sense. Bears, and especially at this time of year, would range. She wondered if Johnny felt the indifferent power of the mountain.

"But he is still a full-time mountain," Johnny said.

She figured he felt it.

"When we get there," she told Johnny, "we must not talk very much. She gets tired awfully fast."

As they ascended, it seemed autumn mist descended to greet and wrap around them. Beneath ancient trees, mist lay across the trail. The clearing, when they arrived, seemed deserted, haunted with mist. Behind mixed and low-blown clouds the sun gave a pink glow. Even dressed in jacket and warm shoes, Harriette felt chill covering the clearing like a thin blanket. The pink sun illuminated the corn patch. The patch stood in mist and shadow, the drying leaves with a layer of pink mist in the middle afternoon. She looked toward the ridge, but it already stood covered with mist. The forest disappeared toward the summit.

She turned. The door to the cabin was closed. No smoke rose from the chimney.

It would be the worst kind of rudeness to knock on that cabin door. On the other hand, suppose the old woman were ill? Johnny looked into the mist, looked at her, looked back into the mist. He did not understand why they were here, because she had not explained very well. She did not know herself, except she was fighting back.

On the other hand, if the old woman were sick, she should be cared for. Harriette watched the single window of the cabin. There was no movement.

"Johnny," she said. "Sometimes you get a little bit drunk, paint pictures." She did not wait for a reply. "Maybe scared is worse than drunk. I'm going to paint some pictures." She assembled the clarinet.

As she did, she thought that a person would have to be a musician—or be Johnny—to understand.

She began to play, the notes low and firm as they walked into the mist, across the grass, toward the forest. She focused on the music, on the perfect and magnificently deliberate expression of a Bach chorale. The music became full, of itself. You could not modulate from a Bach chorale, because a modulation would spoil the statement; and it would be as disrespectful a thing as a musician could do. When the chorale was done, she lowered the horn and allowed silence to return. The silence had its space as well. Johnny was beside her, although she felt rather than saw him. She could not even hear his breathing.

Think of the stream. Think of the mist. Think of the great, dark ridge which had made her imagine a man over her, held to her, inside her. That which was elemental, think of it.

She breathed into the horn, not planning, only thinking, but mostly feeling. She played the horn and listened to what it was going to do.

What the horn found was more than she knew. It seemed to settle at first into a slow, accented, 8/4 beat—like a chant. Moving then, modulating, toward the layering mist so that the beat gradually vanished. No musician could play without a controlling time frame, a structure; but apparently clarinets could do it. It seemed the horn built layers, like the quiet of mist. The music walked slow, like the eternal ocean, the eternal mountains.

And then gradually, quietly, the music found a beat. She followed blindly, not thinking, only following what would come next. She did not know how long she played, but thought it was a pretty long time. The beat was established, firm. The music knew what it wanted to do.

Then playing, listening, she suddenly felt more happy, more safe than she had felt since she was three years old. She played, telling herself she felt exactly all the things she should not be feeling. She told herself she should be fleeing in terror; yet here she was, happy and safe.

Because that beat did not come from the clarinet. The clarinet followed the beat. She listened for drums, heard none. Yet she felt the beat the way any musician feels the French horns, the deep basses in the foundation of a symphony orchestra. The sound was not there, at least not hearable. Yet the beat was set, and the horn followed. And then, as she realized what was happening, the foundation faded and she was once more alone and playing into the mist.

Think of the stream. Think of the centuries-old tulip poplars, their canopies like giant umbrellas across the land. Think of the black rocks in the streams, of birds, of the sky world. Think of movement, of life pulsing like the strong beat of wings. Think of the sky dome, of earth, of the underworld.

The music quickened, like flight. It had the power of the eagle, the dark and great power of the vulture. Music swept like wings across the sky. It ran mid-range, certain-stepping like deliberate movement of cloud stacks above the mountains. Anthem.

Think of storm, of thunder. Think of thunder.

The music rose, the clarinet reaching and reaching and reaching until every technique she knew took it above its intended range. High trilling like flashes of light, like the ornaments of storms. Vivid, like the brilliant robes that thunder wore. Then sinking to mid-range, to the tumbling voice of the stream as it ran with storm. Hymnal. Doxology. And the clarinet praised the storm.

When the music stopped her embouchure remained so tight she almost had to force the horn from her mouth. The pink spot of sun had moved in the mist. The corn patch cast light, longer shadows. She turned to Johnny, and Johnny's face was wet. He put his finger to his lips, asking for silence.

She turned further. A small trail of smoke rose from the chimney of the cabin. Only the driest hardwoods burned so cleanly. Of course, Tom Corey would have seen to the woodpile.

"Everything is all right," she whispered, and spoke to herself and not to Johnny. She did not even sort out all of the things that might be wrong. All she knew was that she was safe, protected, invulnerable.

The door to the cabin opened and the old woman stood framed in the doorway. She seemed unchanged, but less feeble than at other times. "That is good as good." She stepped into the clearing. She dressed the same, but now also wore an old wool hunting jacket. The reds and oranges of the jacket made her face seem washed, pale. "Why are you here?"

"It would take a lot of explaining," Harriette said. She stood holding the clarinet. She did not move toward the old woman, did not look directly at her. "A man named Peter Lee has made me his enemy."

"That is a good enemy to have," the old woman said. "Lee is sick."

"He has a friend who is not sick," Harriette said.

The old woman looked at Johnny, at Johnny's face, but not into his eyes. "You have a friend," she said about Johnny. "You have power. Lee don't have any friends."

"He has an associate," Harriette said. "Somebody who helps him."

"Maybe he pays money to somebody," the old woman said. "Lee don't have any friends." She looked again at Johnny. "This is the man who makes pictures. We will smoke." She turned back, stepping into the cabin.

Harriette hesitated. She did not know whether they were supposed to enter the cabin or not. When the old woman did not reappear she stepped to the doorway, then stepped inside. Johnny followed.

It was a plain two-room cabin. There seemed nothing remarkable about the place. It might have been built by any settler on any mountain through the entire southeastern United States. The furnishings were two rope chairs, a deal table, old and battered, pots and pans hanging beside the chimney. The other room, the sleeping room, was dark; but afternoon light saw its way through the single window and combined with the glow of a small fire. The old woman sat in a chair beside the fire. Leaves of tobacco hung on one wall. The old woman held a stone pipe, ancient, blackened. Harriette sat in a chair before the fire. Johnny sat beside the fireplace.

She, Harriette, expected some ritual. She sat unmoving. The old woman crumbled tobacco, fed a small portion to the fire, and lit the pipe with a common table match. The sweet, strong scent of tobacco filled the room, while the draft from the chimney drew smoke toward it. The old woman lightly blew smoke toward the four directions, and then to ground and sky. She sat smoking in silence.

At least, Harriette told herself, she had enough knowledge to remain silent. She accepted the pipe and did not look at Johnny. Johnny—and it occurred to her that maybe Johnny knew more about the ways of Indians than she did—sat equally silent, reposed, expressionless. She smoked, contemplated the smoke, watched it drift toward the fireplace. The stone pipe she held was surely a museum piece. It was so heavy she rested the base in the palm of her hand. It was long-stemmed and fashioned in the shape of a bear. In late afternoon light the smoke tinged blue, like the mist of the mountain. She seemed to hear again some of the notes she had played into the mist. She passed the pipe.

How had the old woman known that Johnny made pictures? She watched the smoke, trying to feel the question rather than test its logic.

It occurred to her in a quick, sliding sort of way, that the land down below where people bought and sold things; the land where people drove cars and made love and had babies—well, and maybe—maybe that land was not the center of anything. Maybe the center was right here in this clearing. Maybe this was the crossroads where everything that could be known was known.

In a logical way it even made a little sense. This old woman, this Molla, was Inagehi; but the rest of the world was not Inagehi. Important parts of the world came here. Peter Lee came here. Tom Corey came here. No doubt others came as well. Logically, this could be the center of information for all that happened in that world of highways and money making. It could even be a center for those people back in the hills who lived in the old ways. Those people must exist, or others would not believe in them so strongly.

Johnny passed the pipe. He remained silent. The old woman smoked.

The smoke layered in the fading light. The old woman spoke, but not to them. She spoke to the smoke, but also and directly to the fire.

"When that old man comes," she said, "I think it is all right. I think maybe the old one knows plenty." She passed the pipe to Harriette.

Smoke. Mist. Layers like the insubstantial memories of dreams. Smoke drawn toward the fire, like the passage of a spirit.

What old one? Lewis Corey? No. Molla would have used Corey's name. Warwick? Impossible. Only she, Harriette, knew that Warwick was coming here. She had not even mentioned it to Johnny. Some old one from the hills? She smoked, passed the pipe.

Johnny sat in silence and smoked. He leaned forward, fed a small piece of oak to the fire. Quietly, slowly, crossed himself. Smoked. "Maybe," he said, "this mountain is getting stronger." There was little fire left in the pipe. He passed it.

"Maybe so," Molla said. "What is the old one's name?" she said to Harriette. She emptied the pipe. A small amount of tobacco remained. She fed it to the fire.

"Warwick."

"Then you will say to Warwick that it is good that he comes here." Johnny sat, imperturbable.

"He is called a holy man." Harriette listened to her voice which was making all this sense in a situation that made no sense.

"That is white talk." Molla sat, as imperturbable as Johnny. "Pretty quick the trail will be dark."

Johnny still sat, like a squat statue. "This Peter Lee is not so bad?"

Harriette was startled. It took some control to remain passive, unperturbed.

"He is a man who has bad things happen."

"Then he is not a witch?"

"I think," the old woman said, "that a witch is after him. He will die pretty quick."

Harriette was a little shocked. This was the second time the old woman had referred to death. Maybe, she thought, when a person lived long enough to become so old, that person learned that death was not frightening. Silence lay in the cabin, seemed to lie all around it. Slowly, Johnny stood, looked toward the fire.

"We will think about this," he said. He beckoned to Harriette. "Before it gets so dark," he said to her.

When they were on the trail and descending, Johnny walked before her and seemed alert, as though looking for danger. The afternoon light lay like faded yellow shadow. Movement came from the forest. "Bear," Johnny said. He relaxed.

"What did you mean," Harriette asked, "that Lee is not so bad? Lee has been frightening us."

"Blaine is not so bad," Johnny said, "Blaine is even pretty good, but he act bad. Lee act bad."

There was so much about the afternoon she did not understand, that she wanted no more mysteries. Now Johnny talked like some kind of oracle.

"Because I understand something up there," Johnny said. "Johnny has been fooled. No Indian, no Cherokee unless a witch, would do that with a deer. That old woman say Lee is not a witch. If Lee is not a witch then Blaine is chasin' smoke."

"You may understand," she said. "I do not."

"Don't care how modern. Go to college, even. Don't care if Baptist or anything, no Cherokee do that to a deer."

She understood. There was a balance of forces in the Indian way of life, and no Indian ever quite got beyond the idea of those balances. The traditional Cherokee had both rituals and tricks to avoid offending deer. In a greater sense, to hang a deer like that was an offense against everything, not just a deer.

"So Blaine wants himself a white man," Johnny said.

She did not believe in witches, but apparently Johnny did. She followed him. When they reached her car she feared something dead would be tied to it, but there was nothing. Johnny slid behind the wheel.

"Let's sit for a minute and talk," Harriette said. "I have a friend named Warwick. He is an old man. We go to Asheville on Sunday to bring him here. How did the old woman know?"

"She is magic woman," Johnny said. "I don't know how she knows." He looked toward Harriette. In the dying light his face was serene. His hair, which at his age should be gray, was nearly all black. To Harriette, Johnny looked nearly spiritual, like an old dweller in the forest. "This don't amount to anything," Johnny said. "We been fooled. Lee don't have any power, he would have used it."

"Somebody is still pulling some mean tricks." Her voice sounded grim. She did not want to argue with Johnny, but it seemed to her that Johnny denied facts.

"Sure. Sure," Johnny said, "and maybe Lee is chased by witch. Maybe Lee hire someone cause trouble." He touched the clarinet case which lay on the seat between them. "On this mountain," he said, "you have the most power. Your power make this mountain strong."

Behind the darkening hills the sky faded red toward the west, and was light silver and mist toward the east where the moon rode high. In the mythology the moon was the brother of the sun, and he pursued her. At one time the moon had been his sister's lover.

"I don't understand."

"Me too," Johnny said. "Johnny don't understand, but the old woman does. Maybe this Warwick, he does. We go to your house, see Tom Corey. Maybe Tom does."

Chapter 27

I have known of witches all my life. As a young girl I reluctantly believed in them, and as I grew into a woman I came to *really* believe
in them. It is simply that the Cherokee witch was different from the
witches and warlocks imported to this country from Europe.

What is not different is that witches are the products of small communities. In the old, dark days of Europe people did not travel. They
lived in villages. The manor was on the hill, the church right there
among them; and they had their work. Any aberrant behavior in a
place where—if a man ever made a journey of twenty miles—that
journey would be the largest event of his life and he would speak of it
all his life, had to be explained by association with dark powers. The
Cherokee also lived in small communities. Their witches were natural
to their way of life.

In Europe, and latterly in America, witchcraft belonged to people
who made a compact with the Devil. In America, there were witch
trials as late as the eighteenth century. Witch trials lasted elsewhere,
as in Ireland, until the 1890s. In modern America, witchcraft still
lives, sometimes even in its original form.

A Cherokee witch came to power not by dealing with a devil. A
Cherokee witch found power sometimes through knowledge, sometimes through the facts surrounding birth. No matter how the power
was gained, it was expressed when the witch violated the spirit of balance the Cherokee sought.

The Cherokee understood that there were three worlds. There was
the sky world, the middle world where the Cherokee lived, and the
underworld. That underworld was often a source of chaos. The

Cherokee knew that people lived in the underworld, and they knew the seasons in the underworld were different. They knew this because springs which fed the streams were cold in summer, warmer in winter. A person lived by trying to keep the power of the sky and the power of the underworld in balance. The belief greatly resembles the yin and yang of eastern religions. Harriette's father—Dan Johnson—was named Stream. This name denotes a lot of ambivalence, for streams coming from springs derived from the underworld. Dan Johnson fought against chaos all his life.

At any rate, the Cherokee witch was an offense against the balance of the worlds. That witch would do unspeakable things, like lynching a deer.

What Harriette did not understand at the time, but what Johnny did understand, was this: The old woman, Molla, said that Lee was not a witch but might be pursued by one. It then followed that Lee was a victim and probably doomed. I, Janet Scott, am glad that as a young girl I did not know of all the events then taking place. My fear would have been too strong. After all, how much can a child understand about the ways of adults? To me, Blaine was not human at all. He was a white sheriff.

All I knew, as Johnny and Harriette drove to Harriette's house, was that Blaine came to the motel and took my father. That happened early in the day, and as Johnny and Harriette arrived home, my father was still being held over at the county jail.

Tom Corey had been at Harriette's house all afternoon, but when Johnny and Harriette arrived, two pickup trucks sat in the barnyard. The first belonged to Tom, the second to Lewis Corey. Johnny brought Harriette's car to a stop beside his own stake truck.

"Lewis Corey," he said. "Something is no good." He opened the car's door. A faint smell of smoke lay like a memory in the mist. "Lewis would not come here without Tom call him."

The house, when they entered, smelled vaguely of Tom's tobacco. Warmth from the heating stove seemed to make the house smaller, more intimate and friendly. At the same time Tom looked troubled, and Lewis—while not anxious—was not sedate. Lewis Corey simply showed no happiness, but he also showed no grief.

Johnny closed the door. He stood, waiting.

"Hell to pay," Tom said. "Blaine picked up Lee, and he picked up Frank Scott. One set of tire prints and he tries to make a federal case."

Lewis Corey sipped at a cup of tea. Remained silent. He took a pack of cigarettes from his pocket, offered them around. Johnny took one. Harriette carried her clarinet to place it on the piano, then sat on the piano bench.

"We had a fire," Tom said. "Late afternoon. Didn't see a soul. All of a sudden, that little haystack at the bottom of the pasture was burning. Kerosene. You could smell it."

"And now Blaine is busy driving Lee crazy. Lee, he got enough trouble." Johnny sat cross-legged on the floor not far from the heating stove. He reached for a piece of fir. A knot was knocked from the fir. Johnny used the space for an ashtray.

"Blaine may have killed Lee," Lewis Corey said. "Lee is not a well man. He would not have been with us much longer."

"Lee got so mad," Tom said to Harriette, "he started choking. Lee is in the hospital."

"Frank," Johnny said. "Frank Scott he is all mouth. Frank don't do nothin'."

"There is a further problem," Lewis Corey said. "Tom spoke to Frank about that lynched deer. Now Tom must prepare for a difficult time. It will be generally believed that Tom told Blaine that Frank was involved. People will think that Tom accused Frank."

To Harriette, sitting in a confusion of information, the whole thing seemed insane. Worst of all, she felt in some way guilty. Nothing would have happened had she not stepped foot on that mountain. Now Tom was in trouble, and Lee was maybe dying, and Jan's father was in jail.

Jan. She would be frightened. Harriette half rose, sat back down. She looked toward Lewis Corey. He did not slump, but trouble replaced the ease and happiness she had seen before. Still, his face held authority. His hair, now mostly white, was not rumpled. It was simply that there was no boyishness about him.

"Right now," she said to Lewis Corey, "I care more about a young girl than about Lee, or Blaine, or murder. We must go to Jan."

"Tom's wife is over there," Lewis said. "Mary will do better with Jan than any of us."

"I will call Blaine," she said. "This simply has to stop." She found herself looking across the room, at the picture of the teaching Jesus which hung on that wall for all the years she could remember. "This is not Blaine's business. This is Indian business. Those men did not kill my father. They did not kill Dan Johnson."

Lewis Corey turned from his place beside the stove. Johnny looked toward her. Tom butted his cigarette and waited.

"Who?" Lewis Corey's voice was low. It was kind.

She lightly touched the keys of the piano. She did not strike notes. Johnny looked puzzled. Then Johnny did not look puzzled. He did look shocked.

"Everything about this situation is crazy," Harriette said. "So it is all right if you know that I am crazy." She touched the keys, pulled up a quiet, slowly running explanation with a phrase of music. Forest music. Something she remembered from the mountain. "Nunnehi," she said. "The mountain killed my father."

"I expected you to understand that," Lewis Corey said. "I did not expect you to understand it for a long time. I knew you saw more than most." He turned to Johnny. "The other explanation is that some people came from across the mountain."

"What difference?" Johnny said. "That mountain he caused it. I tell Dan. I tell him stop. Get rid of bulldozer." Johnny spoke only to Lewis Corey. "The old woman say Lee is chased by witch."

"I do not understand witches," Lewis Corey said, "not in that old way, but I understand what she means. Something very wrong has been after Lee for years." Lewis Corey looked first at Johnny, then at Harriette. "Lee is now a bitter and vengeful man. I am not trying to excuse Lee."

"Perhaps we can understand him. After all, he does visit Molla." Harriette knew that she sounded puzzled. Molla would probably not tolerate a completely bad man.

"He does not visit the old woman," Lewis Corey said. "He walks that mountain. Lee was gassed in World War I. After the war he got tuberculosis. He got healed, but all his life Lee has felt that something was after his breath. What no one remembers about Lee is that he did well in the war. Maybe something was after his lungs, but his eyes were all right. He saved two wounded men. One crawled into brush to die. The other was buried by shell blast. A white man would have likely seen neither of them."

Corey paused. "The Cherokee are just as foolish as other humans," he said. "Every single one of them thinks he is a warrior. In World War II, one third of all American Indian men between eighteen and fifty went to war. Some of them had not, until that time, even learned to speak English."

Harriette sat, fingers touching the familiar piano keys. How and why, in the quiet of rural North Carolina, did war keep intruding? Every bad thing she knew somehow led back to war.

"It was after the war," Lewis Corey said, "that Lee became cruel." He looked at Harriette. "Lee is not a smart man," he said. "Lee's grandfather died, and Lee inherited that land. In some manner, maybe from what his grandfather said, Lee believes there is gold on that land. For all these years he has walked that land, because to him gold meant power. There is no gold on that land."

Johnny stirred, opened the stove door, fed a balk of pine. "He believe that? He still sell it to Dan."

"If you find Lee's witch," Lewis Corey said, "then you will find the reason why Lee sold the land." He looked again at Harriette. "Lee is not smart, but if the contract of sale is examined, I expect he retained mineral rights."

"Gold?" She was appalled and did not know why.

"There was a gold rush in North Carolina. One of the world's largest nuggets was found here long ago. Stories of gold die hard." Lewis Corey spoke with certainty. "Were there gold on that mountain it would have been found by now. People have been looking since the days of the Spanish."

Why had Judge Alan not mentioned this? No wonder Peter Lee wanted her away from that land. Why had Peter Lee ever sold the place? It seemed he had money. She felt she had to do something. "I'm going to call one of Lee's witches right now," Harriette said. "In fact, I'm beginning to think Blaine is after all of us." She crossed to the kitchen and the telephone. As she walked she looked onto the pasture and the lane. Headlights pointed up the lane. "Maybe I don't have to call." She waited. Johnny stepped to the door, stood standing in the doorway.

When Blaine entered the warm house, the intimate, if troubled, feeling of the rooms seemed to draw back. Harriette told herself she did not hate Blaine. In a way she admired him. At the same time, she did not like him very much. Blaine was clearly uneasy.

"Fireman's convention," Blaine said as he sat, "or a council?" He looked at Lewis Corey. "Lee is on oxygen at the hospital. Frank Scott is on his way home. He is still figuring out answers to questions, and he has a night's work ahead of him. If Lee lives he'll make a mistake, and I know blamed well Scott will make a mistake. Scott is running scared."

Lewis Corey did not look in Blaine's direction. It was nearly insulting, the way he refused to look toward Blaine. "I do not think you can prove a knife murder seven years after the fact. I think the most you can do is charge someone with poaching a deer."

"Maybe," Blaine said, "maybe not. There is no evidence, and so I'm doing the only thing I can do. I can ask enough questions so that one man may accuse another. I don't like to do it, because it might not work. It's all I've got. Lee owns an .03 Springfield. Scott has a Marlin .30 .30. Something that size was dug from that deer. Men who are frightened do some pretty stupid things." He looked frustrated, as if he did not trust his own judgment. "I have to frighten them because there is no evidence."

"Yes yes," Johnny said. "They burn little haystacks even when the sheriff has them in jail. You lookin' for a white man, Blaine. Think him over."

"I have," Blaine said. "They could not have set the fire, but when one of them makes a mistake I will find out who set the fire. Lee did not wash the deer's blood from the back of his truck. Frank Scott's land abuts the Johnson land. Something is wrong with the title."

"You'll find a white man," Tom Corey said.

"The point," Blaine said to Tom, "is what you saw or found. People, tire tracks, a vehicle."

"I smelled kerosene. The haystack was wet. No good. Got rain the day after the cropper cut." Tom's voice was guarded. He seemed ready to defend himself, ready to believe Blaine would be accusing him next.

It seemed Blaine had something like that in mind. "You went to see Frank Scott," Blaine said. "What did Frank say?"

"Nothing," Tom said. "Frank said it felt like snow." Tom's voice was suddenly noncommittal, passive, imperturbable. If silence could be a weapon, Tom used silence.

"Blaine," Johnny said, "you my friend but you got to stop this now. Don't plague people who help."

"This is the second time," Harriette said, "when you have visited my house and I've been made to feel like I should apologize to someone. You concealed information about my father's death. You have frightened a young girl for little or no reason. You threaten my friends. You act like my friend, but look what you are doing." She stood and started toward the kitchen, angry, angry, not wanting to look at him.

"A question you might well ask," Lewis Corey said, "is the one which wonders why an arsonist would burn a small haystack when he might more easily approach through the forest and burn the barn. Any man who would lynch a deer will burn a barn." Corey sat, still not looking at Blaine. "It appears you have a rather timid criminal."

"I concealed nothing," Blaine said to Harriette.

"The killing of my father was not wanton. It was ceremonial. The body was arranged for burial."

Blaine sat, and he seemed to be seriously thinking, or remembering. "I don't see what you are driving at," he said. "I honestly don't."

"That it was not a murder. Not revenge. Not wanton."

"It was a murder," Blaine said. "A man was alive. Someone stabbed him with knives in pursuit of their illegal intent. That legally constitutes murder."

She found herself becoming as quiet as Tom. She suddenly understood the trick all Indians learned. Taciturn, noncommittal, she turned away and began filling the coffee pot. Her mind, unobligated to move her mouth, felt calm.

"You seem," said Lewis Corey, and he was still not looking at Blaine, "to have been doing quite a bit of homework. What else have you found?" He finally looked at Blaine. "I have an .03 Springfield," he said. "Tom has a .30 .30 Winchester carbine. There must be a hundred such rifles within a ten mile radius."

"Me," Johnny said. "Johnny is guilty. I have a .30 .30 back in 1948. Traded the damn thing for cans of paint."

There were a couple of rifles or shotguns sitting back in one of the closets. At least Harriette thought they were still there. Her father had occasionally hunted. For a moment she thought of joining the fracas. Then the silence came back to her. Taciturn. Noncommittal. She looked at Tom Corey. Tom winked, grinned—irrepressible even in the middle of trouble. Harriette smiled in spite of being taciturn.

"What is wrong with Scott's title," Blaine said, "is that the survey was off when he bought his land. His motel sits halfway on the Johnson land."

"How much is halfway?" Harriette found herself startled from her silence.

"Maybe two acres are involved," Blaine said. "Scott's problem is that he legally owns half a motel."

Harriette turned to Lewis Corey, to Tom Corey, to Johnny. "Does any of this make sense?"

Lewis Corey smiled. Some of his boyishness was coming back. He seemed to be having a good time fooling with Blaine, and she had not exactly expected that from him. She looked at Johnny, at Tom.

"Legally," Lewis Corey said, "you may own half a motel. Do you think you will enjoy being in business?" He was not smiling now. He grinned the way Sandy, back in Winston-Salem, had grinned—like a young boy about to shock people by pulling a toad from his pocket. "Of course it makes no sense," he said. "Maybe it makes a little sense to Frank."

"Slop jars," Johnny said happily. "Thunder mugs. Empty 'em every morning. Make piles and piles of money."

"Lewis," Harriette said, "Mr. Corey. Lewis." She paused, uncertain not of what she wanted, but of how to go about doing what she wanted. "Phone him right now. Tell him he has an easement, or let him buy it for a dollar. Or something. You know about these things. Phone him now."

"Don't do it," Blaine said. "That is roadside land. It has some value."

"I am proud to say," Lewis Corey told her, "that I do not know a whole lot about these matters, but I know enough to tell Frank that everything will work out easily."

"You need an attorney," Blaine said. "You are not taking care of yourself."

"I am taking care of a young girl," Harriette told him. "A girl who right now has to be scared to death." She spoke again to Lewis Corey. "Call him now."

Lewis Corey slowly stood, appeared to think about a yawn; stretched, decided against the yawn. "A long and exciting day," he said. "But one that ends well. I am so seldom able to be a bearer of good news that I will go over to Frank's right now. It will make him glad."

"The man who killed Dan Johnson," Blaine said, "is the man you are now letting off the hook." He controlled his anger, but just barely. "You give a gift to your father's murderer."

She was taking care of Jan. That was really all she was doing. There was no way to explain to Blaine. She did not even like Frank Scott.

"And if pressure is off, maybe Frank don't make no mistake." Johnny looked at Blaine. "My friend, stop acting so bad. Best you going to find is that Lee hired some white man for dirty tricks." He turned to Harriette. "Best you get some sleep. I'll stay up for awhile." He turned to the others, waving his hand as if shooing chickens. To Lewis Corey he said, "You give us a call tomorrow. Say did Frank faint away when you tell him." To Tom he said, "You are a good friend." To Blaine he said, "I sure hope Lee dies of meanness, and not choking."

Chapter 28

PETER Lee died that same night from choking. His was a hard and bitter death that followed a hard and bitter life. It was not that his weak lungs—what was left of them—could not take in oxygen. His lungs were flabby, distended, and could not expel his breath. Peter Lee died while a desperate nurse stood over him, bearing as much weight as she could on his chest while she tried to get his lungs to expel used air. The only doctor on duty at the small hospital was saving a young boy who suffered a broken back when his father's truck left crumbling two-lane pavement. The father was unharmed. In later years the boy went to school and became a pharmacist, one who filled prescriptions from a wheelchair. I recall these things because for the next day or two the world filled with good things and bad things.

A bad thing came the next day when some people said they heard ravens. In Cherokee mythology that meant something terrible for Peter Lee. The Raven Mockers of the mythology deal most cruelly with the dead.

I do not know what Lewis Corey said to my father, Frank Scott, on that night, but knowing my father I can guess. Corey probably told my father that he was behaving stupidly. I am certain Lewis Corey told my father that Harriette Johnson helped him because she was concerned about me, Janet Scott. I know this because in the years that followed, my father was always glad when Harriette visited. He was glad when Harriette took me, and other girls, on visits to Asheville or Winston-Salem. When Sandy Smith and Harriette helped pay for my schooling, and Davey's schooling, my father felt a debt of gratitude he could never really repay. I do not think my father ever felt that Harriette was anything but a white woman, but he quickly came to trust her. That could only happen because of Lewis Corey and his honesty.

On the following day my father disappeared into the forest with his dogs. I think he was being thankful. I think he needed to find some place which felt as good as he did. He arrived home at sunset, arrived in peace; but the dogs did not return until the following morning. We heard them that night, running a fox across the lower reaches of the mountain.

On that following day, a white man, Harriette's sharecropper, seemed awfully bereaved by Lee's death. It would later develop that Lee had arranged for the man to frighten Harriette from the land. The cropper then planned to buy the land with Lee's help, if necessary. As it would turn out, the cropper went ahead with his scheme on the likely chance that he could get a bank loan. He reasoned that if Harriette was sufficiently frightened she would move quickly and the land would sell for less. The tire prints made by Lee's truck were made because the cropper used that truck instead of his own. His own was too well known around the place.

It was a small, sad affair. One thinks of Lee's bitterness, because one must. Perhaps Lee knew he was about to die. It is painful to think of any old man dying with petty revenge as his last act. Perhaps the Raven Mockers really were around, although people hear ravens all the time.

The situation kept breeding mysteries. Peter Lee had sold the land to Dan Johnson, although Peter Lee believed there was gold on the land. Peter Lee had been pursued by a witch. In addition, the main mystery which asked after Dan Johnson's motives seemed no nearer solution than ever. That mystery had always puzzled Corey, and it certainly puzzled Harriette. That is the way things stood two days before Warwick was to arrive.

Except for some minor unpleasantness which only Harriette knew: In the mail, when she went to the road to pick it from the box, was a cold and formal note from the minister of her mother's church. The note thanked her for her choir service in the past. It said that another choir director was performing ably. It remembered the godliness of her mother. The preacher looked forward to the joyous day when Harriette would once more come to Christ.

She turned while reading the note, and walked back up the lane. Johnny still slept. She felt dispossessed of the Indian world, and now dispossessed of the white world. When she returned to the house she phoned one of the members of the choir.

She should have known. Johnny had been living at her house for several nights. This was rural North Carolina. She was a painted and tainted woman, a woman living in sin with a man twice her age. She thanked the choir member, who had once nearly been a friend, but she told herself she would be doubly damned to every Presbyterian hell that ever existed before she would explain why Johnny stayed with her. Plus, she told herself, she would be triply damned before she would ever ask Blaine to clear the matter up. It occurred to her that, more and more, the only sensible place in the world seemed to be in that clearing on the mountain.

And then there was her school job. No one would hire a teacher who was immoral. She was frightened at the thought, not because she needed money but because she did not want to be through with teaching.

She crossed the living room and hesitated before the picture of the teaching Jesus. She reached, removed it from the wall. Behind the picture the old wallpaper was lighter, nearly clean. The roses stood out in bright relief, as if they were touched by sunlight. She held the picture, looked at it, really looked. She thought of Johnny. Maybe the picture made Johnny happy. If it did make Johnny happy, she had no heart for taking it away. Maybe the picture helped Johnny, if Johnny believed in witches.

"I think you were probably okay," she said quietly to the picture. "Maybe you were even as smart as Lewis Corey. So I guess you stay, and you can't help me, but you go ahead and help Johnny." She hung the picture back on the wall, straightened it. The room was the same as always, but life was not the same as always. She had never been known as a harlot before.

She figured she had two choices. She could feel awful and make an ugly fight, or she could laugh if not forgive. She told herself that maybe she did not have a man, but she had dear friends; and not a single one of them—she hesitated because her thoughts seemed like blasphemy—not a single one, was a damned Presbyterian. Then she smiled. If the picture made Johnny happy, her thoughts were making her happy.

Warwick was coming. That meant laundry, and fixing up her room for him. She had it planned. Johnny in her mother's room, Warwick in her room, and she would sleep in her grandmother's room. It would be cold up there, and in a way that would be nice. She loaded sheets into the old wringer washer, somehow comforted by its familiar creak creak and slap slap. She straightened the house, and for the first time since her mother died found herself looking at the familiar rooms and saying they belonged to *her* house.

Her mother, her father, her grandmother were still here; but now it seemed not disrespectful if she began imposing her own order and ideas on the house. The thought was quietly exciting. She could change things now, could make the house a reflection of herself. She looked at the familiar rooms. She was a little surprised because it seemed there was not much she wanted to change.

Lewis Corey called during the late morning.

"Frank is grateful," Corey said. "You would not know it if you talked with him, because Frank would just hide behind a frown. Frank will find his own way of thanking you. I wonder how he will do it?"

"Jan?"

"Teenagers," Corey said. "She is about as well off as teenagers ever are, which is to say she is enduring her life." He actually chuckled. "Were she three years older she would be talking about arresting the sheriff."

"I have a friend who will visit," Harriette said. "I want you to meet him."

"Warwick," Corey told her. "I know his name because Tom spoke with the old woman. Tom went to the mountain at dawn, then came back and got to work. Farmers never seem to have a free moment."

She smiled this time, remembering Tom Corey saying that the town was a rube town. She thought about the preacher's note. It was a rube county, maybe a rube state.

Still, it was where she chose to live. "Warwick is an old, old man," she told Corey. "He was a history teacher."

"I expect he is something more than that," Corey said. "A simple history teacher would not cause much of a stir in that clearing." He chuckled again. "What is fascinating is how old shapes take us over, no matter how ancient we become. Tom says the old woman has swept the floor and washed the window. It must have taken most of her energy for the day."

She was a little shocked, but only said she was surprised. She could not exactly imagine Molla doing things like that.

"Because we place people in slots," Corey said. "Then what does not fit the slot, we deny as possible."

"It still seems a little strange. Maybe the old ways and old medicines are dead, but Molla has power. Maybe religious." She thought she said that last part because she had been thinking of preachers.

"The Christian God," Corey said, "was reputed to walk across dusty country. Yet apparently he was not supposed to sweat or have dirty feet or relieve himself."

She looked at the picture of the teaching Jesus, clean-faced with combed beard. She suddenly felt more friendly toward the man in the picture, but not the picture. Any messiah ought to look at least a little bit scruffy.

"I understand," she told Corey. "I think you just gave me another present."

"Meanwhile," Corey said, "your attorney is in Winston-Salem. Frank Scott has no say in this, but I think he would be happier if a local attorney handled whatever arrangement you decide for that land."

"He's a good attorney."

"I have no doubt of that," Corey said, "but he is in Winston-Salem, and I think Frank is afraid of that. At least have a local man deal with your attorney."

The old Indian suspicion. Still, she told herself, it was not unwarranted. Every time an Indian ever got close to a white attorney, it seemed the Indian lost. That was not strictly speaking true, but it was pretty true.

"I'll take care of it," she told Corey. "As soon as Warwick's visit is over."

"Then I will tell Frank. It will erase any worry he has left. And I look forward to meeting Mr. Warwick." Corey hung up. Harriette found herself happy, and for no particular reason; or maybe for many reasons. She felt nearly domestic. The slap, slosh, and creak of the old washing machine made a housekeeping sort of music.

Chapter 29

So much has happened since those troubled days. People have died, others born, the face of Cherokee, North Carolina has changed and is not so pretty now. Yet, the streams and rivers still run, the hills roll away into the western land and still seem endless. I, Janet Scott, have known joy, mourning, hope, and peace. The Viet Nam war arrived, departed with a suctioning wake which surely draws forth another war. Change, rapidity, speed, quickness pant along the busy roads that run beneath this clearing in the forest; a clearing to which Harriette—and later, I—would finally remove.

But the rest of the story will arrive in its time. Harriette would soon be at peace with her father's murder, and with her father. It came about, and it began, with Warwick's visit in that long ago autumn.

On Saturday morning, when the pasture lay white with frost, Johnny and Harriette drove to Asheville to pick up Warwick. Tom Corey had promised to drop by the farm after his morning work. The car ran smoothly, and Harriette was glad Johnny drove. He had spent two days working on the car.

Along the roadside, frost covered the gravel, and frost even appeared on the pavement in shadowed spots where trees overhung the road. Winter, which should not arrive for another six or eight weeks, seemed threatening. Trees dropped leaves in patches along the road, and the leaves looked like small fingers of frost.

Harriette had little to say because she was happy and sad at the same time. She somehow felt guilty about Peter Lee's death. She was more discouraged than angry when she thought of Blaine. Blaine lived in a world she knew well enough, but never understood. He was probably the only man in the whole county who owned a new truck. He worried about the value of land, instead of a child's feelings. She had never understood Blaine's world because she found it offensive. In a way, that made her a bigot.

Blaine represented a certain kind of power. Always before she believed it was the power of the white world—dynamic and in its way constructive. Now she sat beside Johnny who was more or less white, traveling to meet the white man Warwick; while behind her Lewis Corey who was also white expressed power Blaine would never understand. When it came to power she had been taking too much for granted.

Yet, all of the power came from old people. She looked at Johnny. His face was weathered, his hands on the steering wheel every bit as weathered, yet his hands were strong. He was a lot like Lewis Corey. He moved like a young boy. He spoke his own language in his own way, and what might seem silly or clumsy in someone else's mouth, seemed just right for him. Both of the Coreys respected him, Blaine respected him.

She looked at Johnny, and he was a fine-looking man. Her friend. She felt happy being with Johnny, happy because Warwick would arrive. In a world that seemed awfully unsafe, she felt surrounded by safety. The combined power of Warwick and Corey and Johnny and the old woman was stronger than anything Blaine could imagine.

They arrived in Asheville a little early and waited at the bus station. An Indian couple sat silent at one end of the room. The woman was dark, the man tall and lighter. Two country women in floral printed housedresses chatted idly about someone's coming marriage. They made dire predictions, but the predictions were tranquil. Harriette decided that no one in their immediate families was getting married. A young white mother carried a baby, and the baby did not look healthy. The mother was sallow, tired-looking, and she did not seem healthy, either.

When he arrived Warwick looked the same as Harriette remembered. He dressed informally and carried a small suitcase; looking only a little incongruous in the old bus station with its chugging engines, its tired travelers, and its occasional loafers. Warwick's white ring of hair fluffed from beneath an old fishing hat. He looked more like a man on vacation than a man on a pilgrimage. The seedy waiting room of the bus station, the tired people sitting—worried or bored or sleepy—and Warwick appeared among them so unremarkably that he seemed one with the place and the people.

She was a little shy, thinking she really did not know him well.

Then she told herself, no. Warwick was so self-confident and open that one knew him well ten minutes after meeting him. At least that seemed so.

"The Cherokee," Warwick said, once he settled in the car, "did not have religion in the terms whites understand religion."

She smiled. It was like Warwick to begin this way. It was not that the man was all business. It was simply that he was absorbed, filled with wonderment, a man bent on information and thought.

"The Cherokee would have been confused by the idea of faith." Warwick chuckled. "In fact, they were confused by the whole notion when missionaries first came among them. I can just imagine the stir those old Puritans and Moravians made."

"Those Spanish fellas," Johnny said, "they done it first." Johnny had been silent during introductions. Harriette thought he might be shy, but would get over it.

"Exactly right," Warwick said. "The difference is that the Spanish were on their way to dreams of wealth and other dreaming matters. Perhaps they spoke of settling, but I think none of them ever coveted permanency."

They were all three in the front seat, Harriette in the middle. Johnny drove through light traffic, and seemed happy.

Harriette knew that she was happy. She was with two of the people she most cared for, and soon Lewis Corey would meet Warwick. It was exciting to think of Corey and Warwick in the same room.

"At any rate," Warwick said, "the Cherokee had rules and customs and beliefs. What they did not have was the necessity for faith. They simply accepted the obvious, which is to say they understood the completeness of what they saw and felt. A mystical people."

"You have been doing a lot of work," Harriette told him.

"I've been having a wonderful time," Warwick said. "And before I once more fall into error and pedantry, perhaps you will tell me all that has happened." Warwick did not look feeble, but he seemed frail. What was not frail was his engaged, excited look.

"It will take a while."

"We have a while. Go slowly, so that I may know everything."

Some of it even Johnny did not know. Johnny did not know about Corey's bird stone, and she had only told him in a general way of the encounter with the Nunnehi. She thought carefully as she told the story. Each time she told something that Johnny did not know, she prefaced it by saying so.

"The Nunnehi who spoke," she told Warwick, "the one who broke the knife looked exactly like Lewis Corey. Talked like him. The other one just stood there looking sleepy. The problem is that Lewis Corey was not anywhere near that mountain."

"The state of your mind was good?"

"I was afraid, had been afraid. No, I had been terrified."

"I fancy," said Warwick, "that Moses was a little more than frightened when he encountered a burning and talking bush."

Warwick's speech held overtones of amusement, but without disrespect. She told about the petty attacks, about Blaine, about Peter Lee. It was a lot to tell, and they were well on toward home before she finished. Warwick showed growing excitement.

"I'm afraid I have a burden for your Sheriff Blaine," he said, "although it may please him. We can get rid of small mysteries right away. Peter Lee's witch is doubtless your attorney Judge Alan."

It was shocking. Warwick looked at her, saw her distress. He slowed his speech, spoke kindly as though to a frightened child. "It is not so very important," Warwick said. "Although it was important to Mr. Lee. What is important is the power on that mountain. It is important to understand why your father was compelled to behave as he did."

"Naw," Johnny said. "You not been here. Got a crazy man lynching deer, got a sheriff act like a spoiled baby." Johnny looked straight ahead, occasionally checking his mirrors, the road narrow and now warm with autumn sunlight. When he approached the deep shadows cast by trees Johnny slowed until he could be certain no people or animals were concealed in the shadows.

"Fear is important," Warwick said. "It gets in the way. That is the main power of witchcraft. It can make people delusional. Judge Alan does not even think of himself as a witch, although in our context he is one."

"Why Judge Alan?"

"Alan was a young man after World War I. He sold that land to Peter Lee's grandfather. The history of the land is dark. There is even a legend of gold on the mountain, although in this particular area the geology shows there is none. When Alan told you that anyone who has owned the land has come to harm he was not exaggerating much."

"Alan hires somebody to lynch deer?" Johnny shook his head. "I don't know Alan," he said.

"Judge Alan is not hiring anyone," Warwick said. "A man of his experience and reputation would not get trapped into something silly like that. But Alan put pressure on Peter Lee. He would probably even admit as much."

"He doesn't lie," she said miserably, "he just will not tell the whole truth about anything."

"He will," Warwick told her, his voice not exactly unkind but certain. "Not that it makes much difference. With you the land does not suffer or give harm."

"I don't understand how you can be so sure." She did not doubt Warwick. She thought maybe she doubted her own ears.

"It will come clear," Warwick told her. "I'll go over it when the sheriff is present. Since it is lengthy there is no good reason to burden you twice."

"One thing you didn't say," Johnny told Harriette. "That old woman knew this man was coming. Magic woman."

Warwick was a lot more excited by that information than he had been about the Nunnehi. She thought that, knowing Warwick, he had taken the story of the Nunnehi as evidence, had taken Lewis Corey's acceptance of the Nunnehi as evidence. "Tell me," Warwick said to Harriette.

She explained what happened, that Molla had known of Warwick's visit although she had not known his name.

"I mentioned," said Warwick, "that I had made other pilgrimages which came to nothing. It appears this one will be otherwise." His excitement did not cover what she sensed was more than interest in new information.

"Couldn't a been trick," Johnny said. "Man, she knew."

"The capacity of the human spirit . . ." Warwick mused. He looked at Harriette, at Johnny. "Has it ever occurred to you that in the western world, we, who are so proud of our intellects, know nothing about our intellects?"

"Lot of smart people around," Johnny told him. "Lewis Corey is smart."

"We train our minds," Warwick said. "Oh, do we train them. We devise psychological systems to understand them. However, we never really attempt to experience them." He smiled. "There is an old story from Japan about two celibate monks who arrived at a swollen river. A woman stood helpless, but wishing to cross. One monk picked her up, walked on water across the river, and set her carefully on the other side.

"The second monk swam across and emerged sputtering. 'You have defiled yourself by touching a woman,' he said. 'I must tell our abbot.'

"The first monk replied, 'It is true that I picked up the woman, but I then set her down. You are still carrying her.'"

Molla would understand that story. Harriette knew it. She also knew that she almost understood, but not quite. She said so.

"The first monk was not sidetracked by a form that made no sense given the situation," Warwick said. "He saw what was there and not what the world had taught him to see."

She almost understood. She looked at Johnny. He grinned, understood, and to him it was a good joke. Of course, Johnny was a man who spent most of his life in the forest.

"Perhaps the old woman has learned a different way of seeing while we are still sidetracked by form," Warwick said. "There must be enormous energy on that mountain. She is part of that energy. Do not attempt to logic it out. Wonderful tool that it may be, logic will not help us with this."

When they arrived home, five head of scruffy-looking cattle grazed the stubble of the pasture. The cattle looked like an accumulation of bed slats. Tom Corey whistled with happy dissonance. He stretched beneath his truck, tinkering. The truck's hood was up. Tom rolled from beneath the truck, waved as they got from the car. One cheek was smudged with grease. He looked at his greasy hand when introduced to Warwick.

"You'll have to take my word for it," he told Warwick about the missing handshake. "Your cropper came by," he said to Harriette, and he nodded toward the pasture. "More dead than alive," he said about the cattle. His face showed disgust.

She did not need a bunch of sick cattle on the place, especially more stock than the cropper had asked to pasture. Not now, not with so many people around.

"I'll call him," she said. She was puzzled. A man as penurious as her cropper would not neglect his stock. Sick cows were worth nothing. She said so to Tom.

"He probably took them in trade for something," Tom said. "Aims to bring them back into shape."

Johnny looked at the cattle, looked sad, looked angry. He said nothing, turned to Warwick. "Long trip. We get you some rest."

Now she really *was* angry. Here she was, distracted by sick cattle, and Warwick, her guest, her friend, was being cared for by Johnny. How dare that sad little cropper do this? How could she possibly have allowed herself to get distracted? She took Warwick's arm. "Virulent coffee."

"You and your daddy," Johnny said to Tom, "come here this evening?"

"He wouldn't miss it," Tom said, and he began to crawl back under the truck. "Clutch," he explained.

"I change clothes," Johnny told him. "Be right out and help you tie job all back together."

Chapter 30

THE history of that land was dark as the wings of ravens. As a child I knew nothing of the history, but had a child's knowledge of forces that, as adults, we are trained to forget. When Warwick told Harriette that he had been having a wonderful time, he did not tell her the great number of hours spent understanding the history of that land.

The first treaty with the Cherokee—not counting those written before the Colonial period—was written in 1721. By the time of the definitive treaty of 1866, forty-seven treaties were written. These, and other matters, were documented by Charles Royce, who was one of the greatest white friends the Cherokee people ever knew. It was Royce, working in the late nineteenth century as James Mooney's contemporary, whose work would show legal basis for Cherokee claims in the mid-twentieth century. Royce had the mind of a bookkeeper, but his soul was just fine.

Warwick, being thorough, had gone through those old treaties. The land in question, as he would find out, did not really become a treaty matter except in the vaguest terms. For a while it must have seemed to Warwick that everyone and no one actually owned the land. It was not until just after the Civil War that land registrations came to amount to actual ownership.

In 1850 a man named Sanders MacDonough held the land, and he held it until 1868 when he was lynched. The men who lynched him, whoever they were, had been caught without rope. They hanged MacDonough by splicing the reins from his team of horses. They must have wanted to hang him pretty badly or they would never have ruined good harness. It may be that MacDonough had been a Union sympathizer. MacDonough, as we guess from surviving fragments of reports, was not otherwise a bad man for his time. He married a Catawba woman, and while he was not wealthy, he was sufficiently well-to-do. He had built a school for neighbor children as early as 1856.

In 1868 the land was purchased from the courts for fifty cents an acre by John Bascomb, a carpetbagger from Illinois. It was Bascomb who first acted on the old rumor that gold deposits lay in the land. He prospected until 1871 when he was shot in the back, then dismembered, by an unknown party, probably the negro Joe White. White was a former slave, one of the negro judges appointed by carpetbaggers to the bench during Reconstruction. White could not read, but he could sign his name to papers given him by white men. He was one of the many exploited blacks of that time. If he did shoot Bascomb, and then scatter the pieces of the corpse along a wagon track, he probably had other motives than ownership of land. Reconstruction in parts of the south was an expression of rapine and brutality which has escaped the attention of a good many northern historians.

From 1871 until 1880 Joe White held the land in consort with Albert Levy, another carpetbagger. The legend of gold continued. The two men formed a loose partnership for its discovery. In 1880 White's corpse was found trussed to a spit. He had been slowly roasted over a fire pit in the manner that the frontier people roasted deer, bear, cattle. It had also been a primitive form of torture hailing back to prehistory. It was not a common occurrence in those days, but it was not unique—the Ku Klux Klan was often vivid. Or, White's death may have come at Indian hands, although the form of torture is more Huron than Cherokee. Levy, for reasons unknown, but probably through fear, sold out to a man named Jeb Rich. Levy, with death in his lungs, returned to New York where he died of tuberculosis in 1894.

Some old people still remembered stories of Jeb Rich, although none ever admitted that they knew him. From 1880 until his death in '87 he walked that land, much as Peter Lee would later walk the land. Jeb may have dreamed of gold, but he was shiftless. He laid trap lines but did not often run them. An old story tells of a fawn trapped by one foot, then starved to death because the trap was left unvisited. Rich's skeleton was found not far from a main trail in '88. The skeleton was badly broken but intact, which was a mystery. Had bears or other scavengers chanced on the body, the skeleton would not have been intact. Rich died in a crushing fury, but no one ever knew what killed him.

In 1889 Homer Mathias bought the land from a second cousin of Rich who lived in Pennsylvania. Homer Mathias, according to old people, was one-fourth-blood. Of all owners of the land he seemed least cursed. Homer was a solitary man who tended a small place at the base of the mountain. He grew some corn and beans, hunted, did odd jobs to the extent of his strength. His luck was bad, or else he was a bad farmer. The place wore him down, was said to have made him obsessive about fertilizer. He never brought in a good crop, spending most of his time figuring different methods for processing manure. After twenty-three years on the land, and in his old age, he sold out to Jasper Alan. Jasper was Judge Alan's father. Homer Mathias then moved in with his daughter and she tended to him until he died of pneumonia in 1917.

By then, Jasper Alan had built a two-room cabin on a clearing and used it as a camp while he prospected. His wife and two sons lived on the Alan farm until Alan was forced to sell his land. Then, for two years, Jasper Alan, his wife and younger son lived in the cabin. The older son, Samuel, enlisted in the Army and was killed in World War I during the second battle of the Marne. That was 1918, the same year that Jasper Alan was killed.

Jasper Alan's death came about because of gold. He is said to have been an honorable kind of man before acquiring the land. Then he got struck with gold fever. His farm went into decline, he was no longer welcome at the church where he had been a deacon, and he rapidly lost his property through inattention. Other owners had hungered for gold, but only Jasper Alan fell into obsession. He acquired fancy machinery. He began to sluice hillsides. As his capital waned he brought in a logging crew with the intention of building a sawmill. He died in the forest when a small tree fell, thrusting him backward against the projecting limb of a dead tree. The limb, as effective as a spear, pushed all the way through the body. For some reason members of his logging crew would not touch the body. It was removed and buried by his son.

The younger son, Raymond Alan, had stayed beside his mother in order to protect her from Jasper Alan's increasing madness. After Jasper's burial the son moved his mother first to Chapel Hill while he studied law, then later to Winston-Salem. In order to finance the move and his education, he sold the land to Peter Lee's grandfather, Theodore Lee.

Sometime after the son moved away with his mother the cabin was inhabited by Molla. This probably occurred in 1919, although no one knows. Old people say that Molla moved to the clearing after the death of her last relative. Her youngest son was born in 1893. He died from influenza while serving with the army in France. Neither Theodore Lee, nor latterly, Peter Lee, ever disputed Molla's right to live in the cabin.

Theodore Lee was as different from his grandson Peter Lee as two humans can be. Theodore Lee was a hellion. Born in 1870, he managed to drink and womanize for most of his seventy years. When he died in 1940 it was said of him that the world did not owe him a thing, but that he had a fine and outstanding account with the devil. Some of that talk came from envy. Theodore Lee had a good time. He ran a small store where he worked hard. Women liked him, and he liked women. He never refused a drink in his life. He never refused a woman. He rarely visited the land, and then only for firewood. He outlived his children, thus left the land to his grandson, Peter Lee.

This was substantially the account Warwick gave to Harriette that evening. Warwick did not know all of the small details. He did have the main lines of the history.

"The enigma, of course, is Peter Lee," Warwick said as they sat in Harriette's living room that evening. "He would not sever relationships with Judge Alan who sold him the land. He would not take the evidence of a half a century of prospecting. He still searched for gold. There is also the question which asks why Alan told Harriette nothing of that legend.

"And gold," said Warwick, "was the principal problem of the Cherokee. Had it not been for the gold discovery of 1828 I have no doubt that a great many more people would have escaped the removal to Oklahoma."

"That follows," said Lewis Corey. "Except for timber the land is commercially worthless." He sat in Harriette's living room which to her suddenly seemed small because it was filled with people. Lewis Corey, Tom Corey, Warwick, Blaine and Johnny scattered about the room. She could not recall a time when there had been this many people in the house.

She watched the men, wondering at their seeming complacency since she was still angry from an earlier confrontation with her cropper. Even Johnny seemed settled down. Of course, she told herself, Johnny felt responsible to care for her and for Warwick, responsible to keep Blaine from ruining what might still be a nice evening. If Johnny had not been present during her confrontation with her cropper she might still be incoherent. She listened to the men. Blaine talked now, asking Warwick some irrelevant question about the Civil War. She paid little attention, while thinking that now she would have to get someone else to farm the place.

The cropper had driven up the lane near feeding time with an old watering tank in the back of his truck. He aimed to place the tank in the pasture. A block of salt sat in the truck. Harriette walked from the house and toward the pasture. He backed his truck to the gate and sat waiting. It was normal courtesy for her to open the gate. She stood, waiting him out.

Finally he shrugged, opened the door and stepped out to walk to the rear of the truck. He moved with impatience, maybe with a touch of contempt. He was not large, but he was muscular from work. He unlatched the gate.

"When you get it open, Mr. McAlpin, leave it open until you get your stock back on that truck." She was nervous. This was the first time she had ever confronted him. At all other times she had simply listened to him and more or less agreed to his demands.

He turned back. Abrupt. She wondered why he should be so angry. From the angle at which she stood, the oak tree at the bottom of the pasture seemed like a small tuft behind his shoulder. The sun already stood behind the hill. Maybe he was angry because he had work to do and was rapidly losing daylight.

"They look sick," she said. "I want no disease in that barn. There never was any in that barn."

Animals almost never got sick if they were well-treated. Her father never lost animals. She had heard old stories of people burning barns because they were infected. She did not know if the stories were true, but she wanted no sick cows in that barn.

His anger did not vanish but he managed some pretty good concealment. He was tow-headed, blue-eyed, thick-lipped. Now his lips seemed thinner. "We'll disinfect," he said. He reached onto the truck bed for a hand sledge and a spike to anchor the salt block.

"We will not disinfect," she told him. "You brought more head than you said you were going to bring. You brought sick cattle. I want them out. Now." She was not only nervous, she trembled. In spite of her control he saw it happening. He smiled. Turned. Pulled the salt block from the truck.

"Old wives' tales," he said. "Disinfectant handles it."

"Now," she told him. "Get them out now."

On the phone he had wheedled. He had nearly fawned. But that was on the phone. Now, face to face, he seemed like a man who was looking for a good fight and had found one.

"You'll get used to it, missy," he told her. He walked back to the cab of the truck so he could back into the pasture. She watched, unable to understand. He was pushing her around because she could not fight back. How could he possibly believe he could get away with this.

"I promise you," she told him, "that I will have the sheriff here before you get unloaded."

He climbed in the truck. "You take your share," he told her. "It's a damned good share, more than anybody else will earn for you. You don't do a lick of work." He started the engine.

She did not know how long Johnny had been standing behind her. Maybe from the time when the cropper looked like a man wanting a fight.

"Maybe we look at him this way," Johnny said quietly. "When Dan die, this woman did not come looking for you. This woman's momma did not come looking. You the man who came wanting shares." Johnny grinned, like the whole thing was a misunderstanding and somehow a good joke. "Go home, get loading chute. Johnny help you load."

The cropper began slowly backing into the pasture. Johnny waited. Once inside the fence the truck stopped. The cropper sat for a moment, then opened the door but did not climb from the truck.

"McAlpin," Johnny said, and his voice sounded sorrowful, "you acting bad. Don't make me have to do nothin'." Johnny managed to look genuinely sorry, as if he regretted that he would have to tear McAlpin's arms from their sockets. She nearly smiled, fooled by Johnny's ease, momentarily believing everyone was still civilized, that this was somehow a silly scene from a play. Then she gasped. This was not an act. This was the South. "Don't," she said.

"Toss that stuff on the bed," McAlpin said to Johnny. "I still got chores over t'other place." His voice was cool. He backed away from a fight with Johnny, looking for a graceful exit. He was at least twenty years younger than Johnny, but he backed down.

"Pull him up aways." Johnny walked to the salt block, but did not walk behind the truck until it was in gear and moving forward. It occurred to her that she would not have been so smart. The cropper might have thrown the truck in reverse.

Johnny set the salt block in the truck. "Bring chute tomorrow, my friend. I help load 'em up." He grinned as if nothing, absolutely nothing, had happened. "I'll water them tonight."

The cropper slowly drove away, like a man who had not a care in the world. She thought that were she the cropper, she would be trembling. Then she found that she did not need to be the cropper, she was trembling anyway.

She tried to thank Johnny, but made a bad job of it.

"I think," Johnny said, "you maybe will want somebody else on your land." He grinned. Happy. "Big night," he said. "Lot of folks comin'." He turned back to the house.

Now all those folks were here and gathered in her living room. Matters began quietly. Even Blaine seemed reticent, testing the mood and quality of the people around him. Only Warwick and Lewis Corey were completely at ease.

"In spite of what these folks believe," Blaine said to Warwick, "a murder is not a joking matter. Not even a seven-year-old murder."

Blaine made the assertion sound like a question. He tried to avoid argument, but was willing to argue if need be. "Lee is dead. Scott is no longer worried about the land."

Warwick smiled, glanced at Lewis Corey, almost seemed to wink. "You know this county well, do you not?"

"Lived here all my life."

"Know the land, the people?"

"It's my job," Blaine paused, caught by Warwick's manner of asking questions. "At least it was my job for years." Blaine began to look restless. A man who felt that a lot of talk leads nowhere.

"Your reputation preceded you, Sheriff. You are a man of great mercy." Warwick turned to the others. "Sheriff Blaine once took a man to the V.A. hospital. The man was armed and insane. Many sheriffs would have shot in self-defense."

Harriette had not known that. She wondered if the insane man was the same one Blaine told her about, and guessed that he was.

"There was a small account in an old newspaper," Warwick said. "I phoned a witness."

Blaine looked uncomfortable. He had been researched, investigated. At the same time he had been complimented.

"In your many years," Warwick said, "I suppose other matters besides the murder of Dan Johnson were necessarily left unsolved?" Warwick was not playing with Blaine. He respected Blaine.

"Lack of evidence," Blaine said. "Practically impossible to prove arson when a barn burns. Practically impossible to show foul play when there is a missing person. You think someone has found trouble, then find that for five years he's been working in Kentucky. Disappearances, mostly." Blaine paused. He seemed to be wondering if he should say what he was going to say. "Cherokee County was not my jurisdiction. This county was. Cherokees in both counties keep matters to themselves." He paused again. "In my opinion half the town of Cherokee knows who murdered Dan Johnson." He looked apologetic, then looked defiant.

"Perhaps," said Lewis Corey, "you are correct. However, our county has police."

"Cops with the same problem you have," Tom Corey said. "If they had the identity of the murderers they still could not find them back in those hills."

Harriette silently agreed. She could not figure out what Warwick had in mind, but she knew no one would find the men who killed her father.

"I only mean to suggest," Warwick said, "that sometimes there are larger dimensions to a problem than the ones we see. I will also add that if the killers could have been found you would have found them. Could we but know the motives of Dan Johnson, we might better understand the motives of the men who killed him."

Harriette sat feeling that Warwick was practically drawing a blueprint for Blaine.

"It's pretty hard to get anything out of a dead man," Blaine said. "Lee is gone, Dan is gone, Dan's wife is gone." He looked apologetically at Harriette. "They were good people, your folks." Then he caught Warwick's drift. "Alan is not gone," he said.

"Precisely," Warwick told him. "And while Judge Alan may have nothing to say about Dan Johnson's motives, he may have something to say of his own."

Blaine seemed nearly startled. "The land went from Alan to Lee's grandfather to Lee to Dan. Lee continued his association with Alan."

"I suggest," said Warwick, "that you will not find the killers but you will find the reason for the killing."

"I'll find both," Blaine said. He stood, reached his hand to Warwick. "Thank you, sir." To Harriette he said, "A history teacher was exactly what we needed."

To Blaine, Harriette said goodbye. She tried to be gracious but she was not sorry to see him leave.

Chapter 31

TAIL lights redly faded down the lane as Blaine's truck disappeared. Beyond her windows darkness seemed complete. When Harriette had opened the door for Blaine, autumn chill swirled in on a light wind while a glow above the hills signaled moonrise. Maybe dark shapes moved out there in the wind, maybe not. The deep power of night lay across the land, but at her back there seemed an equal power. Warwick and Corey were free to speak now. She turned back to the warm room, to the men sitting near or around the wood stove.

Johnny stretched, grinned. "We move to living room. I light the fireplace." He shooed the other men. They rose easily, drifted more than strode, and Johnny managed to steer Lewis Corey and Warwick to the most comfortable chairs.

With Blaine gone the men were less guarded. Tom Corey sat in the presence of older men and kept his mouth shut. She felt the force of Warwick and Corey and Johnny. A council of elders, and yet it was not that, either. Maybe a council of wise men.

"We may begin," Warwick said, "by giving our full appreciation to attorney Alan and Sheriff Blaine. They are deeply engaged in the work of the world." His voice was kind. There was no antagonism or contempt.

Silence. Harriette almost spoke. No one else was speaking. She felt the weight of the silence. The men sat comfortably. Tom Corey lit a cigarette and the smoke swirled in the firelight. Lewis Corey had once told her to sit in silence with Molla. Was this what he meant? She was curious, seemed to herself too impetuous; and as silence continued she tried to appreciate the silence. If wind touched the windows it was too light to make itself felt. The fire popped and cracked. A small stream of sap cooked in a piece of fir.

Silence. Warwick was relaxed. Corey was relaxed. Johnny was relaxed. Tom Corey was watchful. Harriette puzzled. What were they doing?

"Suppose you have good daddy," Johnny said. "Then he go crazy. You scared for your mother. Brother get killed in war. Turn around and your daddy is dead." His voice was calm, low but not whispered. His voice was firm.

When he began she momentarily thought Johnny talked about her own father. She quickly realized that he talked about Judge Alan. Alan had lost a father and a brother in the same year. He had, and maybe desperately, sold the land and moved out to a life of struggle. Back in 1918 that land probably did not bring much. Certainly not enough for Alan to support his mother and attend law school.

Silence had its place in music. Now she understood that it had its place in council. Maybe, she thought, silence was itself a power. She sat admiring the silence. In the midst of it she imagined that young man who had grown to become Judge Alan. She thought of him frightened, maybe desperate. She thought of how he must have sold his father's equipment, probably for little or nothing. How he had taken a mother who was probably shocked insensible by the loss of a son and a husband, taken her to a strange town. How alien it must have been. How terrified both of them must have been.

And this kind of understanding, she realized, was a key to Warwick. This was what history could be—was—at least ought to be. Warwick felt the great enigmas, the pain, the hope that lay behind facts. Facts did not make history. People did.

"When I was young," Lewis Corey said, "I made decisions. Then for years I did not examine those decisions. I continued to live in the way of decisions made when I was little more than a boy."

Seven years ago she had decided to go into seclusion. Seven years. Harriette realized that she was still living in a manner she had decided on when she was twenty-three. Maybe it had been a good decision at the time, but was it still a good decision?

Now silence seemed like a great friend. Silence had helpful power.

She really began to understand the power of silence.

Maybe Judge Alan had done the same with decisions. Maybe as a young man he had hated the land. Maybe he had never asked himself if he should still hate the land. She remembered Johnny once saying, "In this South revenge happens a lot." Maybe old decisions lay at the seat of revenge. She watched the men and saw that they were understanding at least as much as she was.

In the distance, but surely on one side of the hill behind her house, a hound called. The dog voice existed nearly as an echo in the silence. Dogs ran among the spirits and powers of the night. They seemed to thrive on those powers.

"Blaine, being of different temperament, will perform what we cannot." Warwick sat beside the fireplace, for all the world like a man who had pencils and a yellow legal pad beside him. She remembered Warwick's home, his chair, what she had once thought of as his small and well-loved and sunny place. "We may trust Blaine," he said.

She did not trust Blaine. She almost impulsively said so. Then, instead, she thought of Warwick's words, attempted to follow the drift of Warwick's thought.

She had taken her seat on the piano bench. Now, silently, she touched the well loved series of keys that would allow music to be heard were she to allow her hands to play. The piano seemed not an extension of her but a part of her. She thought that people formed themselves with their tools. Johnny with his enamels and chainsaw, Corey with his stoneworking tools, Warwick with his books. What kind of tools did a sheriff use? And to what purpose?

She suddenly understood Blaine. It was unfair for her to expect Blaine to understand the power of that mountain. It would be like asking her to understand how you could stand up to a man with a gun, how you could do all the necessary things which would disarm the man and then take him to safety.

Because there were maybe many levels of thought, but there were at least two big levels. There was the workaday world which asked you to pay attention to all kinds of details, although a lot of those details were only important because of other details. Blaine had spent his life in that world, taking care of cars, filling out forms, doing thousands of small tasks. He even had to pay attention to the way he looked because he had to *look* like a sheriff as well as be one.

It was no wonder he could not enter that other, luminous world, where sometimes things seemed timeless. She imagined him here and surrounded by silence. He would be unable to stand silence, would feel it a great waste.

The white world must make some kind of sense or it would not be so powerful. It occurred to her that it was a world of rules. One of Blaine's tools was a rule book. Warwick was a part of that world. Was it possible that he had a different set of rules? Then she understood that with this silence she followed one of Warwick's rules. Strange. Silence was also a rule the Indians knew, and that long before the whites. She felt herself engaged in an ancient practice, one that hailed back maybe twenty thousand years.

She felt herself sliding away from thought. Her mind felt open, receptive. It was not a mind consciously trying to think about anything. She had never experienced this before. Her mind was not passive. It was simply open and waiting to see what it would do.

Tom Corey shifted his position. He looked at Johnny, at Harriette. Then he settled again into silence. Tom trusted the silence. It was true that he would not speak before the older men had spoken, but the older men *had* spoken. She felt that Tom was learning nearly as much as she.

"I must explain myself," Warwick said with amusement. "Lest I seem a magpie moving into the nest of another bird." He paused, a man with his thoughts already framed, a man now wording his thoughts. "The history of religion is not altogether dismal, but it is fairly consistent, whether pagan or otherwise. Generally speaking, theology is used as a buffer to avoid a face-to-face look at that power which some call God. Dogma is a buffer that justifies theology. In other words, most religious people have erected at least two walls between themselves and what is real. Being who I am, I hope to encounter creative energy in its raw state." He chuckled. "Because, you understand, theology and dogma are stone walls. Perhaps there are no walls on that mountain."

The voice of the hound faded into the night. Beyond the windows normal night silence lay like a soft hand across the hills. Of course, out there small and dying screams of mice or rabbits sounded as owls made their kills. There was the high winding of automobile engines along the roads, the mist-smoking headlights, the machines that inevitably would kill a few possum, rabbits, an occasional deer. Harriette found herself hoping the hound had enough dog-sense to stay away from the roads. Then, thinking that the hound chased a fox, she felt a small relief. If you could not trust dog-sense you could surely trust fox-sense.

"When Tom's mother was alive," Lewis Corey said, "when Susy was alive, I spent most of my time just being happy. Now that she is gone I have thought about the mountain. I have done some reading." He lapsed back into silence, his old but boyish face was touched with grief. Harriette wondered how long Susy had been dead. Susy had had some power. The old woman said that Susy could call fish to her.

She looked at Johnny. He sat, silent, his face reflecting some of Lewis Corey's grief. She did not know if Johnny had known Susy, but Johnny knew Lewis Corey and he felt his friend's pain. She told herself that surely, here, in this room before this fire, dwelt more power and compassion than existed in the distinguished pulpits in every city in the country. She had never known men to be this way. Men were almost always like Blaine, or generally a lot worse. She thought of the cropper, pushed the thought from her mind. Thoughts of him had no place in this gathering.

It seemed that Tom Corey read her mind. He moved slightly, looked a bit cramped as he sat before the fire. Uncrossed his legs. "I think maybe religion does not make people kind," he said to Warwick. "I think maybe it can give naturally kind people a reason to be kind."

It was true. She knew it. Some of the meanest people she had ever met were educated people and religious people. She wondered why Tom had suddenly decided to speak, then she looked at Warwick and saw that he was quietly delighted.

Johnny reached to place a balk of wood in the fire. The back log was a huge piece of oak which squatted behind the fire, glowing in a red checkerboard as it reflected the fire.

"There are two separate powers on that mountain," Lewis Corey said. "The first is ancient Cherokee. The second is what some writers have called ineffable. It can be experienced, but not described in words." He looked at Harriette, at Tom. "I tell this to Mr. Warwick," he said to them. "I would not ordinarily tell this to you. It cannot be understood as a factual matter."

Tom grinned, and she thought Tom was being irrepressible again. When he spoke, though, it was with respect. "You are over my head," he said. "I don't know what ineffable means."

"The word goes back to Latin," Warwick said, "and the meaning is 'not utterable,' the root word is 'fari,' 'to speak.'" He looked at Harriette. "In churches you have heard the phrase, 'that peace which passeth all understanding.'"

"Yes."

"Such peace exists," Warwick said gently, "but I cannot tell you how to feel such peace, can only assure you it exists. My failure to describe in words comes not because I do not know the words. My failure comes because there are no combinations of words which allow your understanding. In that way, even my human knowledge is ineffable."

"Which means," said Lewis Corey, "that part of the power on the mountain may be experienced but never described."

That was the reason he had not told her about the Nunnehi. Some things had to be discovered. If Lewis Corey had told her that the Nunnehi killed her father, and even if she believed it, the knowledge would still not have been a part of her.

"In which case," Warwick said to Corey and Johnny, "I have a notion if not a theory. I would appreciate knowing what you think, but would first like to know what Mr. Whitcomb thinks."

Johnny looked at Corey, at Warwick, his voice serene. "That old woman," he said, "she make that mountain strong." He nodded toward Harriette. "This woman make that mountain strong. Maybe people living in old ways make him strong." Johnny looked at Harriette like a loving father. "The old woman say Dan Johnson did a bad thing so he could do a good thing. I think Dan make that mountain strong."

Silence. She sat numbly, her mind which had been so receptive was now shocked to silence. Somewhere in her emotions, her instincts, she knew Johnny was correct. She simply did not know why or how. She sat awed, her fingers dropping from the run of piano keys.

"I feel the truth of your understanding," Warwick said to Lewis Corey and to Johnny. "My notion is this: let us suppose that power which is ineffable is the source of that power which is ancient Cherokee. The ineffable will never die, but the Cherokee will die. Since men create their gods, the gods pass when men's beliefs pass. It has happened before in history." He smiled, his old face serene. "For you see," he said, "I think gods are not simply the desperate figments of confused imaginations."

Lewis Corey's old but boyish face was now more boyish than old. He turned to Johnny. Johnny grinned, like he had heard a good joke, a joke that explained something puzzling.

Corey stood. "I would like to think about this."

Johnny also stood. "I think I see him. I think I see what happen. Johnny will work this out."

She sat listening, watching, her mind still numb. She knew vaguely that what she saw was maybe Indian. There would either be consensus or there would be no decision. The other men were asking for time to study new information. There would be nothing further said tonight.

Johnny grinned at Harriette. "We gonna make coffee, hot chocolate." He reached for her hand.

Chapter 32

HARRIETTE, Johnny, and Warwick left home just as reddening light in the mist showed the sun about to break over the hill. Not many days began this way, and all of those days were in autumn. Mist covered the mountains. In the roadway mist was thin, retreating to ditches where it lay like small and tranquil rivers of gray. Across the fields mist hung thick only a few feet above the land. Birds rose from the stubble of cut hay and disappeared only to descend from mist like feathered phantoms as they moved to glean in a further part of the field. Trees overhanging the road stood in deep change. The oak at the bottom of the pasture tinged red in beginning change.

Her night of dreams had found her lonesome, hopeful, puzzled. For awhile she stood in some center of red, not outlined by a sunrise or fire or sunset, but as one with the red field of color that might come from sun or fire. Vague figures moved beyond the field. She had waked, thought of her former lover, and that made her feel even more lonesome. She told herself that if he were here, right now, they would have nothing to say to each other. Then she understood why they had parted. At twenty-three, even so young, she had somehow understood that, good as he was, he still represented Blaine's way of understanding. That way was closed to her now. She did not know if any paths were open, but she knew that one was closed.

Johnny concentrated on his driving. This early in the morning, with mist still clumping in spots, animals often jumped into the road. Warwick seemed absorbed in thought. On this day, going for what would be to him a strenuous and perhaps impossible walk along a mountainside, he dressed carefully. He wore a summer suit of light gray, a white shirt, a summer hat that was certainly southern but not Confederate. His walking stick glowed yellowly.

She thought Warwick took a pretty bold attitude. He might have a heart attack on that mountain. He surely put his life on the line. At the same time, she sensed eagerness behind his absorption. She told herself she had no right to caution or judge. This old, old man must not be questioned about anything he chose to do.

It was difficult to be young. She never really understood that before. It was probably difficult to be old, as well; and she found herself silently hoping that when she was old she would be as proud of herself as she was of the men beside her.

When they arrived at the mountain it was clear they would be walking the whole distance in mist. Mist lay above the clearing, and she noticed—as she had never noticed on other days like this—how primary colors shone through mist more distinctly than they ever shone at other times. Gray muted into gray, orange was muted although not as much; but where reds and greens and true yellows existed, they appeared from the mist with the certain clarity of spotlights.

"Our old friend," said Johnny, and he pointed through the windshield. "Our friend come to meet us." Beyond the clearing where blackberry had taken hold came movement. Then there was none as the bear faded back into the forest.

She reached to the back seat for a light jacket, felt in her pocket for the broken knife and the bird stone. For the last several days she had carried both wrapped in a handkerchief.

Warwick stepped from the car and she followed. Warwick moved carefully over uneven ground. She did not believe he could achieve the fifteen hundred foot level. For a moment she wanted to call all three of them back. Then she told herself, no, trust Warwick's judgment.

"A principle of history," said Warwick, "shows that men will pursue power while never defining the nature of power."

She thought he sounded like a teacher introducing a proposition to a class. He must have thought the same, because he chuckled. "Old fool," he said. "Still, the men who least understand the nature of power are generally the men who enter politics."

They walked slowly across the clumpy ground. As they approached the trail the silence of mist deepened, became the silence of crystal. The trail seemed closed against them, as if silence were itself a barrier.

Power descended. Unthreatening. Indifferent. Impossibly calm. Power beyond any requirement of faith. Beyond belief. Power.

Power that—if there were such a thing as eternity—would regard eternity as indifferently as she would regard a small scratch while picking blackberries. Power that, were it to speak in the slightest whisper would fell these giant trees, would raise winds to blow storms like chaff about the sky.

Warwick stood. Unabashed. Head unbowed. Then, still unabashed and without her help, he knelt on knees that seemed not old man's knees. He knelt untrembling. The silence of the forest seemed to wrap around him. Calm. Indifferent, but containing.

"I have asked only to serve," Warwick said. "That was a lot to ask." He knelt in the cool dust of the trail, head still unbowed. "Each time I taught I walked away hoping and believing there was that much less ignorance left in the world, especially my own. I did not forsake you. I hope I have never forsaken you.

"Yet," he said, "I had a lot. A long life. A wife. The books. Recognition from my peers. I had a lot."

Drums. Somewhere high along the ridge, and invisible to the ears, but somehow not to her fingertips, her sense of music, the drums spoke with the authority of ritual music. They were not spirit drums, but they existed in the distance as spirits.

"And yet," Warwick said, "that is not true. Sometimes when the classroom was empty I wanted to call all of them back, wanted to say what I meant and not what I had just said. It is not so easy to tell everything about the truth."

Johnny crossed himself. Knelt easily beside Warwick. He did not look like a man praying. He was a man listening. Harriette wondered if she should kneel, then thought maybe she was too young and had not earned the right. She stood quietly behind the men. Maybe the two men were unafraid and untrembling, but she was not. On this mountain she was safe, protected. Yet the power which surrounded her was now greater than any power which could weave day and night or cause seasons to tumble.

"Because," said Warwick, "among the complications and often foolish intellectual assumptions of a man of my time, I have sought the truth. I come here seeking." He stood easily, rising back to his feet in the midst of the power. He stood as serene as a tree although he stood amid power as ancient as the stars. He turned to Harriette, and his old eyes held tears. "Life has given me so much. Now this." He turned back to the mountain and stepped forward onto the trail.

A crow called, winging above the trees somewhere out in the mist, on its way to scavenge a drying creek bed, a barnyard. Light breeze moved in the mist. Here and there a leaf dropped, whirled, as though whirling through smoke. The distant stream was an echo of water. The drums ceased, but a chipmunk seemed trying to take over the world with its scolding. It sat high on a branch. If a chipmunk could orate, this one orated. Johnny stood to follow her as she followed Warwick. The power still surrounded them, was still indifferent. If it was not asking their passage at least it was allowing passage.

She followed Warwick and thought the mountain was actually helping him. He moved at an old man's pace, but he no longer moved with an old man's caution. The walking stick touched the ground lightly. Perhaps it assured his balance, for he did not use it to bear his weight.

She first sensed, then felt completely relieved of responsibility. She was in the hands of forces she had not the least chance of comprehending, forces so profound no act of her will could alter events. All she was called on to do was follow Warwick.

Mist deepened as they ascended. Movement in the forest began certain and unafraid, but she could not tell who or what moved. A doe suddenly appeared walking parallel to them for a dozen yards, the deer as placid as cattle. The trail somehow seemed easier, broader, more welcoming. In the deeper forest, mist lay like paint around the columns of trees, and trees disappeared into gray. It seemed that men and animals moved as though they were in concerted escort. She found herself making a prayer which said her heart was good and she was here to help her friends.

As they ascended, time and muted colors moved back and forth before her, but she could not exactly explain what she saw. The trail remained easy. Ancient trees were great columns glistening redly with mist. Totemic. The red did not come from the sun, or at least she could not see how it could come from the sun. Red clustered at the base of trees, growing upward, and through the mist, flashes of white seemed a backdrop for ochres framing yellow and green figures in the mist. Sometimes she thought the figures were men, sometimes figures of animals; but when she looked at them they moved or changed. The forest still seemed as familiar as the forest had ever seemed, but now the trees seemed so ancient they might be the parent trees of the ancient ones she knew. It occurred to her that she could not absolutely say, not absolutely, that she remained in the same century. She felt that they did not walk backward in time, but that ancient times advanced to meet them.

In places they walked in near darkness. When the first faint light of the clearing showed ahead, Warwick stopped and leaned on his stick. He did not breathe heavily. He pointed with the stick. "She is there?"

"She is," Johnny said. "Maybe Harriette and me should stay here?"

"Not at all necessary," Warwick said, "but let us pause for a moment to prepare our thoughts." He leaned on the stick, eyes closed, and she felt he struck some sort of bargain with his eagerness. Johnny stood in repose. She felt the repose of the entire forest, thinking that her grandmother was buried among such repose. She did not understand why she thought of the dead, but she now wished her parents were buried in the forest and not in the white and regulated rows of a cemetery.

When they arrived in the clearing the mist was pink. In some places where the upper layers of mist had thinned it was red, and drying yellow grasses were moist with mist. High above, and invisible in the mist, the dark ridge stood, and the sound of drums was now unmistakable. She did not need her fingertips, her trained musician's sensibilities. The drums were measured, certain, and, although far away, were real drums. She heard the primitive mind of the drums and felt that her own music in this clearing had been little more than the performance of a child. The drums were pagan, controlled, physical.

The dark ridge stood above them blanketed in mist. The corn patch had been harvested. Pumpkins now nested almost completely orange among the dying vines. Molla stood in the center of the clearing, and she seemed different although not exactly changed. She was still small and old, but she stood as erect as had Indians in the romantic paintings of the nineteenth century. Her hair seemed thicker, shining white in the mist, and she wore a deerskin skirt which reached to her knees. She wore moccasins and a deerskin matchcoat which passed under her right arm and crossed her chest to be tied above her left shoulder. Molla stood without ornamentation, no head covering made from the skins of birds, no totemic signs of power or office. Behind her the dead cornstalks and the new pumpkins glowed like luminescent symbols. At one time Harriette had thought of her as some ancient goddess. Now, here in this clearing, with the broad sound of the drums talking like the voice of the mountain, the feeling was true.

"Warwick," Molla said.

Warwick removed his hat, held it against his chest.

"It is good that you are here."

"I am honored to sit before your fire," Warwick told her.

"The man who makes pictures," Molla said to Johnny. "Maybe somebody is coming who you know about."

"The trail was wide and easy," Johnny said.

"Some men are coming pretty soon," Molla said to Johnny. "You will bring them to the fire."

She looked at Harriette. "The men will say what you will do." She looked at Warwick, turned toward the cabin, and Warwick followed. Harriette and Johnny watched them go.

Chapter 33

THE two Nunnehi appeared at the edge of the clearing, stepping from mist-shrouded forest with all the calm of the forest. They were not much taller than men but seemed larger. One of them was old. He wore breechclout and moccasins. On his head he wore a cap of vulture feathers, and his bare chest and strong shoulders were unwrinkled. The middle-aged man was a warrior. He dressed like the older man, except for the cap of feathers. At his waist he wore a steel knife, and, like the older man, carried a pouch. The pouch, she knew, would contain tobacco, flint or matches, a pipe. The Nunnehi moved methodically, and they seemed an incarnation of the drums. As they approached she saw the curiously twined and tied handle of the stone knife the older wore. Then she saw the old and ugly scars of wounds on the warrior's arms and chest.

She did not know how long she and Johnny stood in the clearing, and she did not even know if Johnny had been there all the time. The world seemed liquid, like a mixture of colors and shapes that kept blending and changing. It had been that way since Warwick and Molla disappeared into the cabin.

The world carried the quality of a dream. Rather, it was like being awake while dreaming. Improbable scenes appeared, impossible things happened; but she did not think about that because they *were* happening. Figures came before her as though carried on the voices of the drums—her grandmother, her father. They walked toward her, faced her. They had not spoken.

Her father stood tranquil. He seemed pleased to see her. Then he moved upward through the air, as if he rode the vortex of a circling wind. Owls, ravens, deer appeared from the mist, faded back into the mist. Beams of sunlight cut the clearing and then faded.

Her grandmother stepped backward into the mist, but before she left her grandmother looked at Harriette with pride.

And even the clearing changed. Maybe the cabin was over there shrouded in mist, maybe not. She smelled no smoke from the fireplace. In this mist surely the smoke would hang low and she would know it was there.

The Nunnehi walked across the clearing and suddenly Johnny was at her side. Johnny seemed to be speaking to her but she could not hear him. He stood slightly in advance of her, between her and the Nunnehi. As the two came close she could see them perfectly, the hard-muscled arms, the long and ugly scars, the dark braided hair. She saw them in sunlight, but that was impossible because it seemed that stars were overhead and the moon placed a broad band of light across the tops of trees, illuminating the mountainside and the clearing. Then mist returned, and day returned, the dark night prowling off like the flight of ravens. The Nunnehi spoke to Johnny. Johnny talked back. The three of them seemed wise, worried about her. The elder pointed toward the trail which led downward from the clearing, the trail that would take her back to her car. She understood that she was to walk that trail. Was she being dismissed? Too young? Not allowed to be here in this council? She felt ashamed, like a child who has behaved badly and is sent to her room.

Johnny turned to her, frowned, explained, reassured; and she could not hear a word he said. Johnny looked unhappy. He touched her arm, said something further, then turned in the direction of the cabin. The Nunnehi followed him.

Drums accompanied her to the edge of the forest. Drums entered the forest with her. Drums were the very foundation of mist as she descended first in shame, then resentment. Then good sense returned— if, she thought, you could have such a thing as good sense in the middle of all this—and she slowed her pace. There had to be a good reason for her to be here. She understood that because she understood Johnny. Nunnehi or no Nunnehi, Johnny would not allow her to be insulted. He would not allow her to walk into danger. Not alone. If she were in danger Johnny would be here right now.

The mist thinned as she descended. The drums were constant, ancient trees the same. She recognized many of them. Nothing about the trail seemed remarkable, yet she had the sense that it was a little different. Here and there a bit of moss, a vine, a tangle of brush lodged in a different place from the trail she remembered.

She wondered if she were dreaming, if she were being made to dream. She wondered about visions. Among the Cherokee, men had often endured great hardship and had experienced visions. Women had not been tested as had the men. If she was given a vision, she could not understand why since it did not follow after a great ordeal. Then she thought maybe the vision, itself, might be the ordeal.

As she descended further, not far from the place where she first met Peter Lee, she saw a spot of yellow through the thin mist. It was downhill and in the clearing. Then the trail dipped and the spot of color was hidden. She almost felt lonely without it. It had been as strong and certain as electric light.

The trail was definitely different now. Here at the low elevation it ran at least one summer overgrown. She pressed back branches, walked slowly amid the beat of drums, then found her way blocked.

Small and fading blossoms of a tulip poplar were like stars in dying foliage as the felled tree covered the trail. The huge umbrella of branches which had stood a hundred and fifty feet above the forest floor now lay shattered and broken on the forest floor. The downed umbrella stood high above her head, tattered, still expressing fading flowers. It was freshly cut and she was shocked. Angry. Then frightened. She could not remember a tulip poplar in this area, and certainly not a giant tree. She could not see into the clearing because the foliage of the dead tree was so thick. The tree covered the trail, spread beyond the trail where smaller trees lay crushed in its fall. Around her the sound of drums ran steady, but lowering. Their beat changed. It was an interrupted beat now, angry and puzzling to itself.

She looked about. Mist retreated, nearly rushing up the mountainside. Sunlight reached into dying leaves and now dead branches. The world was no longer a world of shades and shadows, a world of mist. Her eyes picked up details more clearly, it seemed, than ever before. Fresh white wounds of shattered branches seemed vivid as bones. A small beetle glistened green and black. It ran, its nest torn away when roots of trees were ripped from the soil. She tried parting the foliage, peering through; breathed the smell of the freshly broken wood. Sight could not penetrate that thick umbrella.

She touched her pocket. Felt the knife and the bird stone. If this was a vision it was a strange one, because it now held none of the surreal quality of a vision. The scent of the newly twisted wood, the scent of sap, was like the very scent of pain. She reached forward. Touched bark. Leaves. Not surreal. This was real wood, real leaves.

She searched the forest looking for the most likely way around the tree. Downhill was blackberry. Uphill seemed possible. She stepped from the trail, parting brush, pressing through leggy stands of rhododendron which stood high above her head. It was slow going. She was forced to concentrate, to maneuver, to plan the next step and the next. It was like being in a maze, except that she could establish the directions of uphill and downhill. She did not know how long she worked her way up the hill and around the tree, but figured it was probably a half hour.

When far enough up the hill and to one side of the tree, she turned to descend into the clearing. She wanted to rest, knowing she could not rest, wondering why great power would be so capricious as to bring her to a mountain and then send her away. She could see the trunk of the felled tree through the forest. She gasped. It was immense. It lay like a collapsed tower. Were she to stand beside it the log would loom above her head. The stump, torn at, in places hacked at with the chainsaw, had a hollow so large she could have slept in it. The stump looked as much like the foundation for a small house as it did a stump.

She stepped forward, sideways, planning her movements into the clearing. She parted brush, stepped into a small clear space in the forest; found herself looking into the clearing, almost as if she sat in the center row of an enormous theater. She gasped. She wrapped one arm around a small tree, holding tightly so she would not fall.

Her father stood in the clearing, head bared, eyes closed. He stood motionless as any tree, his logging shirt a checker of red against the red clay soil.

He stood in the midst of desolation such as she had never seen. No doubt war caused this kind of devastation, but she had never seen war. A yellow bulldozer—the yellow spot which had seemed almost friendly from a distance—stood in the center of tangled roots, churned soil, splintered and broken rock. The blade of the bulldozer was polished, scratched, hammered by rocks as it had hammered rocks. The blade seemed independent of the machine. It stood taller than a man, like some obscene tool of an awful inquisition. Trees lay felled and unstripped of branches. She could see no stack of logs. In the clearing lay only meaningless destruction. Large trees were shoved and shattered. She did not know much about lumbering, but it was clear that some of those trees would have made good sawlogs. Now they lay broken by the bulldozer. Piled helter-skelter. Even a bomb would not throw large trees about this way. Her father was destroying without motive. He was not even making a profit.

Slabs of slate and limestone stood upended, tilted, jagged. They stood in the churned soil just as the bulldozer had left them. Her father was taking out rock, had torn at the very base of the mountain. In places, soil glistened with the sheen of oil; the smell of diesel, and the smoke of diesel, lay like a violent afterthought above twisted and shattered limbs of seedling trees, rhododendron, runners of blackberry that lay beaten into the churned soil.

It looked like an enormous and vulgar graveyard, the broken slabs of slate and yellowed limestone like obscene grave markers tilted before the winds of hell or heaven. Nothing moved. No little snake. No insects. The smell of sulphur from the broken limestone seemed like powder in the air.

Her father moved. He stepped toward the bulldozer, behind the bulldozer, and he leaned down like a man who was tired, discouraged, maybe a man tying his shoes or doing some other innocuous but necessary task. She held tightly to the tree, watched, gasped as she saw black wires leading from the stump, across the clearing, and behind the bulldozer. Her father leaned over a detonator.

The explosion bellied upward, outward; the flash of dynamite in faded sunlight was like a red and yellow ball of violence. The explosion cracked, efficient as thunder, sharp and brilliant. The force of the blow, even from great distance, hit her, shoved, smashed at her and she fell before it, falling to the warm forest floor, but not before she saw the stump as big as a house rise almost as if tired—slowly—shattering and tumbling upward.

She lay on the forest floor on a cover of newly fallen leaves. The stink of explosive soured the air. All around her dust, dirt, small rocks, bits of wood clattered through the leaves of trees and fell like flakes of ice.

War. Her father was at war. Her father who knew about war had not departed from war. The smell of the dynamite seemed even more obscene than sharp. She pushed herself up, kneeling on all fours, and vomited into the cover of leaves. The sour taste of the vomit was almost a good taste because it was only a little violent and not at all senseless.

She rested on her hands and knees, and as she rested love for her father, and fear, and hatred, feelings of doom, feelings of transgression, sin, shook her. She began to weep and did not know which feeling had the most power, but of all the feelings she thought betrayal held the most. How could he? When she had loved him so much. Believed him such a good man. Her quiet, quiet father given to disappearing into the forest, seeking the forest calm. How could he?

She wiped her mouth. Struggled to her feet, and the struggle seemed long and tired. She felt like an old, old person willing an exhausted body into movement. She helped herself up by holding onto the young tree.

The Nunnehi appeared from the forest. They walked single file. The older man with the cap of vulture feathers moved slowly. His movements carried great sadness. The stump now lay in two burned and twisted pieces; the stench of explosives rose from burned ground and the great hole where the stump had been seemed a tangle of broken snakes as smaller roots were white and reddish and sap-bleeding; torn, charred. The older man stepped past the stump and he avoided the stump as a man might seek to avoid a corpse. The middle-aged man followed, the two men moving steadily to the slow cadence of the distant drums.

Her father stood erect. There was no pride on his face. There was happiness. Then she told herself, no, no, that was not simple happiness. Her father was filled with joy.

The Nunnehi approached. Her father waited. The older man said something. Her father replied. The conversation seemed friendly, yet filled with sadness, and it seemed filled with joy; and she could not tell how the men could be feeling both such feelings at the same time. The three men seemed like old comrades. As they spoke they raised their hands in friendly motions. Her father nodded yes, seemed to be explaining something. The other men listened, were sad; yet somehow the men showed great respect for her father. They looked at him as if he had pleased them.

Her father drew a pack of cigarettes from his pocket. Offered them around. The men smoked, but not ritually. They smoked as men might when gathered together at a cattle auction, or standing before a church after morning services. Unhurried. Successful men whose place in the world was established and unthreatened. Her father's face continued to carry his great feelings of joy, of gratitude.

She wanted to scream. Then she did scream, and her screams were soundless even in her ears. She attempted to move forward, downhill, attempted to run across the torn ground and through the stench of explosives. She was unable to move.

The older man finished his cigarette. He crumbled the small bits of remaining tobacco and, raising his hand, cast them westward. He took the stone knife from its thong. The middle-aged man passed his knife to the old man. The old man stood holding both knives. He seemed to be talking to the knives, or maybe he was making a prayer.

The old man turned to Dan Johnson. He held out the knives. Her father touched them, and it seemed to her that his touch was professional. He was like a man examining tools. He accepted the steel knife and seemed to thank the older man. He flipped the knife. It made a quick, short, sun-flashing arc in the air and the hilt settled back into his hand. He stepped back a half dozen paces.

The warrior accepted the stone knife. He stood looking at the knife, speaking to it. The knife in her father's hand reflected sunlight. It cast small flashes into the forest as the blade moved in a slow sideways motion, the knife like a flag of war. The stone knife gleamed black, like wet slate beneath the sun.

Now they were enemies. The men began to circle. She had never seen men behave this way. Once in a street in Charlotte she had seen men fight, and she had left that street as quickly as she could. But that fight had been with fists, with rolling around on the ground; and besides the men had been drunk and clumsy.

These men moved as quickly as the flashing shadows of birds. Their movements were controlled, as accurate as the movements of dancers. They circled like dancers. Their knives pointed toward each other, and sometimes the sun-flashing knife arced through the air, sometimes it jabbed. The stone knife kept pointing, pointing, darting like the flight of a hummingbird. The left arms of the two men became bloody as they fended knife strokes. Blood soaked the sleeve of her father's shirt. Blood covered the brown arm of the warrior. It seemed an immeasurable amount of blood, blood dripping from fingers. The two men kept their knife hands away from the blood so that the knives would not become slick. The knife hands remained browned, unblooded.

It seemed so short and yet it seemed forever. Neither man fell. Neither man gave ground beyond his circle. And then it was over. An upward feint by the warrior, the knife then dropping and flying downward like wings as he stepped inside her father's knife, a thrust with the stone knife into her father's side. The steel knife dropping, her father staggering, and then falling forward into the arms of his enemy. The stone knife dropping as the warrior held her father, speaking to him, easing him to the ground, kneeling above him as the warrior's upper body was painted red with blood. Blood flowed onto her father's chest, colored his shirt red, the two men's blood mixing and mixing. Her father spoke. His enemy spoke, but now his enemy seemed not his enemy. He seemed sad. Blood mixed on the ground. It welled from her father's side. The warrior spoke, reassuring, and her father's shirt turned black, as the warrior picked up the steel knife, felt the rib cage and carefully, quickly, thrust the knife into her father's heart.

Chapter 34

So many years have passed. So many of the people who lived in this old history have themselves passed into history. Warwick, Molla, Johnny, Lewis Corey, Blaine, Alan, my father Frank Scott. Only Harriette, and I, and Tom Corey remain. The mountains still roll away to the westward. Ancient trees are guardians of the trail. Some old people still say these things that happened are true, but the old people say their thoughts to each other because the young do not hear very much. Cherokee looks like a richer town but is really a spirit town. I think maybe it will not last so much longer.

But, the clearing is still alive with grasses, and the stream still liquidly walks down the mountain. The corn grows, the pumpkins, the tobacco. Mist still caps the ridge, and still there are the voices of drums.

In that old past, when she witnessed her father's death, Harriette dreamed for two nights and days in the cabin. Some say she walked back to the cabin, some say she was carried there by a vulture, and some say she never left the clearing in the first place. I say what she has told me, that she was awake while dreaming, that she walked, and that she lay in the isolated bedroom of the cabin. Molla did not even allow Johnny in the same room. Molla did not allow Warwick there, and Molla did not go there herself.

They could not see her, because Molla insisted that only she, Harriette, must do the dreaming. She must have no help. Even as she dreamed, and even though they could not see her, she could see them.

Warwick dozed, woke, dozed. While awake he sat mostly silent.

Molla slept by the fire. Woke. Sat by the fire. Johnny tended the fire. Tom Corey, down in the town, figured on coming to the clearing. Lewis Corey told him it was not his business.

And Blaine, who finally paid attention to Lewis Corey's question about the burning haystack, figured out who had been harassing Harriette. A man trying to buy a property was not going to burn a barn on that property. Blaine went in search of McAlpin.

Blaine found McAlpin in the clearing, and Blaine was shocked. McAlpin was an experienced man. No experienced man ever got mauled by a black bear, yet it happened to McAlpin. He lay on the trail, and he was near death. He mumbled, shrieked, cursed Blaine and Harriette and Peter Lee. In his great pain he was nearly mad—or maybe he was mad—and his insanity rang into the forest, swallowed by the forest. He had been clawed, flesh laid open, and one side of his head was bone-shattered by teeth. His left arm dangled. Even his rifle stock was broken, although the rifle had been fired three times. Blaine took him to the hospital and McAlpin lived, but he afterward walked in a halting, skewed manner. He still walks that way after so many years, although he is very rich. Old people say the mountain sent the bear to him, and maybe so, but I think sometimes if the old people were right McAlpin would not have survived. He had come to the mountain with the intention of firing a shot to frighten Harriette. He had no stomach for murder.

And then Blaine left for Winston-Salem. He went to see the attorney Alan.

With Harriette the dreams came and went, came and went. They were red dreams, of fire and the east and war. They were dreams of blood. In the dreams blood flowed from the sky. Blood ran in the streams. Red for luck. Red for war. Blood was like a bright talisman of war in the forest, of war across those distant battlefields where her father had suffered miracles.

When a people usurp the power of their gods then that people is doomed. Warwick had said that. Now, as she lay awake while dreaming, she heard Warwick's voice, Johnny's voice, Molla's. She could not speak to them. For awhile she did not even hear them because she was interested in the way that blood edged the clouds and lay like a bright ornament across the ridge.

"A tragedy," Warwick said from some great distance, and she heard it but it made no sense. It made no sense even when he repeated it while musing. But when he repeated it she listened while watching the bright edges of blood.

"In ancient tragedy the hero put himself before the gods." Warwick seemed talking to himself. Molla grunted. "That did not happen here," Warwick said, "but it is tragedy nonetheless."

"How long she sleep?" Johnny's voice sounded far away, his voice sounding as if he were crying.

"When the sun is straight up two times, three times," Molla said. "If the sun is west she will go there."

"Wake her?"

"You cannot."

She did not mind the blood after awhile. Blood glistened along the edges of leaves. It spread across the tips of grass so each blade was a tiny knife. Blood dripped from the beaks of birds, seemed a film of certainty on the steady beat of drums. When the blood began to alter form she did not even know it was happening at first.

"Because tragedy," said Warwick, "is a great definer. We humans have explained who we are with drama."

"Why you talk this way?" Johnny's voice filled with fear, with sorrow, but his voice was also annoyed. "Talk like a teacher, but man, this is real."

"Tragedy is real," Warwick said, "and I apologize for musing aloud. Mr. Whitcomb, you already know the answer. You gave it to us three nights ago. You and Mr. Corey. Do not deny tragedy."

The red kept changing shape, and now she realized it was no longer blood. Red for luck, maybe. Not red for miracles. Miracles were not red. She dreamed that she chuckled. Red lay like a pale wash across the fields, the pasture, around her house. She dreamed of pale red fencerows, of cattle walking chest deep in a pale sea of red grass. The white bones of the tree her father had destroyed were now touched with red.

"Because," said Warwick, "you conjectured that Dan Johnson made this mountain strong. That Harriette Johnson made this mountain strong. That Molla made this mountain strong."

Molla grunted. Her voice was a whisper like wind in dry grass. She seemed to be wandering in her mind. "Plenty of years now. Too many years. Winters."

"Because," said Warwick, "the Cherokee gods will die when there is no one left to believe." He looked at Molla's old face, then at his old hands. "Too many years." He smiled, and he was only a little sad. "And the Cherokee will die when their gods pass. They will still have their blood, but not their persons."

Now the red was not so pale, and it flowed, gathering together in a stream, and she floated not on the stream or in it, but with it and of it. The red had direction but she did not know what the direction was.

"So Dan try to beat mountain, so mountain can beat him." Johnny's voice held only a little puzzlement.

"Not quite," Warwick said. "Dan Johnson suffered miracles."

In her dream she understood, and the great love for her father made her want to leave the dream. The red flowed and she could not wake. Now the red deepened, not so bright.

"Dan Johnson," said Warwick simply, "was not in a battle with his gods. He gave his life in order to find out if his gods were real. In that discovery he has assured us that they are real."

"It's a damn hard way to do the job," Johnny said. "Why they kill? How come they don't go scare him off?"

"We are talking about a man's soul," Warwick said. "Perhaps we should sit quietly for a few moments. I think the answer is obvious."

The silence was not passive, existing as a vibrant, forward-thrusting form. There was nothing urgent about the silence. She did not know how long it lasted but it seemed to last a long time, and silence somehow explained the reason for blood.

Finally Johnny spoke. This time he was not indignant. "Suppose Indian man see miracles. Suppose he want proof of what he knows, that don't have nothing to do with miracles. Can't find the power of the mountain. . . ." Johnny's voice reflected his love for his lost friend. More than that his voice held his admiration for Dan Johnson. "So he buy saws, bulldozer, and he do worst thing he can think. He force them men to show themselves."

"Knowing he would die," Warwick said. "Knowing that." Warwick's voice held great sadness, but also admiration. "Because he had to die. Were it not inexorable, inevitable, then what he knew would have seemed a sham. Dan Johnson forced his gods to prove that they are real."

Her quiet father. Her father who had been given to disappearing into the forest. Her father who had been driven by luck and chance and white ways. Her father who had loved her, and who she could now love always. Now she understood his joy as that warrior stepped from the forest. The red flowed, and through the dreaming she felt warm movement in her pocket; dreaming that the bird stone was a small and living creature, the very embodiment of life.

And then the red began to take shape, the firm bark and trunk and limbs and leaves, the oak standing in an autumn flame of leaves. The tree red, but not for war or luck or the east; for the tree had its nature. Red meant the tree of her childhood, flaming, passive, powerful; and she first understood that it was happening and then it did happen. She became the tree. One with the tranquillity and power. Tree's Friend no longer. Tree.

So it would be this way, for this was her nature. And now Molla could die, as Molla must have wanted to die for so many years. Because now her father had brought her not to belief but understanding. Now Molla could go because she, Harriette, would remain.

She woke in Johnny's arms. He cradled her as a father cradles a child, and in his eyes was desperate concern; but his eyes held tears greater than concern. She watched him, heard him murmur that all was okay.

More than he knew, all things were just fine. The power of tranquillity lived in her mind. Knowledge that was easy and simple and obvious existed in his presence. Unutterable knowledge. She could not speak at first, but she knew something that she was not going to be able to say very well, anyway. Better not to speak.

She wanted him. She did not want a man, just any man. She wanted him. He was old and he would get older and he would die. But better a few happy years with Johnny than many years with someone else. She did not know how she was going to tell him all this, and she expected an argument—in fact she could almost hear the argument—"Naw, naw think about him. I am twice of you. I get old, maybe break down"—and so maybe it was just as well that she could not speak right away.

Chapter 35

THEY came from the mountain a little before the sun slid behind the dark shoulders of the ridge. Harriette and Johnny and Warwick walked in silence; and when Lewis Corey met them in the clearing they at first greeted him with silence. They did not wonder if Corey had waited for them a long time, or if he had known of their coming. His patient waiting, or his foreknowledge, was his own affair.

When they met, Warwick and Corey walked together, and they held hands as though they were children, like small brothers, or like patriarchs brotherly aiding each other along some familiar street. They walked through the clearing as though through well-loved rooms of silence lit by the echo of the day's vanishing sun. Shadows in the clearing reached toward them. Warwick gestured to the shadows, and the great serenity of Warwick's knowledge changed Corey's air of calm to an air of complete peace. "It is only one more adventure, Mr. Corey," Warwick said, "but by all that is wonderful it is a great adventure."

When they arrived at her car, and Corey's truck, the four turned back to the mountain and waited, as though they expected something would happen. When nothing did, and when the great indifference of the mountain was finally cloaked in the blue and deepening light of nightfall, they turned to the vehicles.

"Sheriff Blaine has been having adventures of another kind," Corey said with amusement. "I expect he will want to speak with you."

"Not this night," Johnny said.

"Tomorrow night," Harriette said. "You come to my house? And Tom?"

"We will," Lewis Corey told her. His peace was one with the peace of Warwick. "I wondered once—when I gave you the bird stone—what you would pay. I think you have paid a lot and very well." He climbed in his truck and departed.

The next evening found them as they had gathered before, but among them dwelt a variety of knowledges they had never known before. Blaine seemed more relaxed, a man who had succeeded, or a man persuaded that the problem he faced was not to be solved. At any rate, a man relieved of responsibility.

Harriette watched him and thought that Blaine had a great deal of which to be proud. It occurred to her that Sheriff Blaine had carried a gun for over thirty years. She had never heard a single story that said he ever took it from the holster. Maybe Blaine did not represent the power of the white world, but surely he represented some of its power. Earlier Harriette had disliked Blaine. Now she thought she had been pretty silly.

She was even glad Blaine sat in this warm house among friends. In fact, she thought, the house was even a little too warm. A cold front pushed down from the north. Normal cold of the season skidded lower, and Johnny had a fire in the woodstove as well as in the fireplace. The oak back log burned smaller now, but it still reflected heat from its red and yellow glowing checkerboard. It cast faint light upon the roses of the wallpaper, toward the picture she had left hanging in case it helped Johnny.

"Your attorney Alan," Blaine said to Harriette, "is ashamed. In a way that I will explain, he has managed to conspire against you. He will petition the court asking that another executor be appointed." Blaine looked at Warwick. "You were correct, sir. I don't much like the word 'witch,' but Peter Lee was so skillfully manipulated that the word might apply. Judge Alan manipulated Lee."

"Tell about McAlpin first," Johnny said. "What happen there?"

"He'll live," Blaine said, "and I doubt if the world will be better for it." He told of McAlpin, of the man's plans and ambitions. His voice held no contempt when he spoke of McAlpin. It seemed to Harriette that Blaine had seen too much pettiness. Blaine's voice did not really carry contempt until he returned to the subject of Judge Alan.

"In the South," Blaine said, "I can vouch that men are not simply average in the way they behave. They are either honorable or they are not. Southern men either do not compromise their principles, or like McAlpin they have no principles to begin with." His smile was sour. "I would have sworn it was that simple. Then up pops the case of Alan."

"Ambition?" Lewis Corey asked. "The man must be too old and well established for bad ambitions."

Harriette nearly spoke. She felt somehow compelled to defend Alan. He had been nice to her, even kind. Of course he had dealt sparingly with the truth. She looked at Tom. Tom did not shush her, exactly, but moved one hand in the way of asking silence.

"He did what no honorable man would ever do," Blaine said, "and he did it with some aforethought. He used his friend Dan Johnson to effect greater revenge on Peter Lee." Blaine looked at Harriette. "The situation got out of hand. Alan never dreamed that his action would cause your father's death. Alan admitted all this after I did some leg work. He's a skilled attorney, but a tired one. I think after I checked the conditions on that deed, he was relieved to have the whole matter known."

"Gold," Warwick said. "Revenge. In the history of our race I do not know which has been valued most, nor which has been valued longest." He sat staring at the red checkerboard of fire. Warwick, a man who, together with Corey, walked in peace with eternity. To Harriette it seemed strange to see him seriously considering ugly matters.

"He try to cheat Lee out of gold that never was there in first place." Johnny stared at the fire. "Naw, naw. That can't be. What is?"

"Samuel Alan was Judge Alan's brother. Peter Lee and Samuel Alan were best friends as well as being related. Remember that Samuel Alan was killed in World War I, while Peter Lee was only hospitalized from mustard gas. Jasper Alan, the father, did not really start slipping hard until after Samuel's death. It was then that he bought the equipment to sluice the mountainside. In the enormous grief over

Samuel Alan's death, Jasper Alan actually seems to have thought that, if the gold was found, then he would be so powerful that he could even defeat death."

"I understand," said Corey. "For some reason Judge Alan came to blame Peter Lee for the deaths of Jasper and Samuel Alan."

"He also blamed Lee for transgression against his mother," Blaine said. "Her shock at the deaths of her son and husband was so great that she never really recovered. She lived for only three years more."

"Judge Alan must have been insane," Harriette said. "He was brave too." She had not meant to speak, but here she was speaking. She defended the man who had in some way betrayed her father. "Think of him," she said. "He lost a father and a brother. His mother was helpless with sorrow. Would any of you have been sane?"

Silence. She felt defensive. Yet she knew no one was critical of her.

"He became sane later on," Blaine said, his voice kind. "Sane enough to get through a law degree, build a good practice, and be a judge." He turned this time to Lewis Corey. "There are lots of old tales. Maybe you've heard some of them. Back in World War I it seems like the whole country went crazy with patriotism. Men who did not want to go to the Army were held in contempt. Alan swears that Peter Lee shamed Samuel Alan into joining the Army."

Harriette could not remember Lewis Corey ever losing his composure except for once. He had lost it when he told of Indian children being swallowed by the cities. Booze. No work.

"The Indians do it," Lewis Corey said. "I watched it happen in World War II, saw it happen in Korea." He looked at Harriette. "Your father was an exception. He was in the infantry. Since the development of parachutes, you will find most Indians trying for two places in the service. They either become parachute troops, or they go for underwater demolition. Warriors. Warriors." He seemed ready to weep. "At any rate," he said apologetically, "I am quite sure that Peter Lee shamed Samuel Alan into going to war. It happens so often that it's a law unto itself."

"It's not just Indian," Blaine said, and now he was also sad. "It's southern. Every blamed one of them carries a rebel yell in his shirt pocket." He looked toward Warwick. "But that is beside the point. It may well be that Alan was insane for awhile, but he was clever in his insanity. He made provisions when he sold that land to Peter Lee's grandfather."

"Then I see it clearly," Warwick said. "It was not Peter Lee who held back mineral rights on the land. It was attorney Alan."

"The deed reads 'precious metals,'" Blaine said. "There is no reason to believe that Peter Lee's grandfather, Theodore, ever knew that the clause was in that deed. If stories of Theodore are true, he was too busy drinking or womanizing to pay much attention."

"White lawyer business," Tom Corey said, and he was startled. "When I talked to Frank Scott, Frank said that Lee claimed white lawyer business. Claimed his grandfather was cheated. Claimed he was cheated."

"Alan was awfully young to be so clever," Lewis Corey said. "Alan was little more than a boy. Of course, at the time he may still have believed there was gold on that land. So he had an attorney draw the deed that way."

"That is probably true," Blaine told them. "The whole method of revenge came to him after Peter Lee recovered from tuberculosis." Blaine looked at each of them. "In a pretty long career I've seen revenge. I've even seen feuds. But they have always been violent. I've never seen anything so carefully drawn and executed as this.

"Because Peter Lee never knew that Alan sought revenge. Alan pretended to be Lee's friend. He made a written deal with Lee. If Lee discovered the gold he received a ten thousand dollar finder's fee. After that he received fifty percent of all income from the mine."

"That," said Warwick, "is simply incredible. The fires of the old Puritan hell could not compete with that." He turned to Harriette, saw that she was puzzled. "Because, you see, Lee was doomed either way. If, on some one-in-a-million chance he discovered gold—and being who he was—the gold would destroy him. But, the great revenge was that Lee walked that mountain for over thirty-five years in search of an illusion. I am sure that attorney Alan continually fed the illusion."

"To the extent," Blaine said, "that he wrote letters to Lee, extended hospitality on Lee's visits to Winston-Salem, and on two occasions hired phony consultants to make Lee feel optimistic." Blaine grinned and that seemed inappropriate to the situation. "Alan does not see this part," he said. "Sooner or later he will. If he arranged for Peter Lee to waste a life in a hopeless search, and die a failure, he also set himself up. He wasted an awful lot of his own life in seeing that Lee kept walking that mountain." Then Blaine stopped grinning. "What a waste of two lives. What a godawful waste."

It was horrible. It was a different kind of violence, but it was still violence. She sat thinking of the long, long years, and the hundreds of thousands, maybe millions of footsteps that Peter Lee had taken along the sides of the mountain. She thought of him growing older, more desperate. She thought of his lungs entering a final stage of decay, and how his footsteps became slower and slower. How each morning he must have struggled from bed, literally struggled to open the door of his truck. She thought of his slow footsteps and awful breathing on that day when she met him on the mountain. Could such things happen? It had happened.

"Dan," said Johnny, "what about Dan? What about Dan Johnson?"

"He had money," Blaine said. "Lee needed money. Dan came to Alan. Alan had Lee sell the land to Dan so that Lee could continue to live and walk." Blaine shook his head. "Lots of lies have been flying around. I made a fool assumption. I always thought Lee had money. Everybody thought that."

"He was going to lend McAlpin money," Tom said.

"Lee knew that he was dying. He didn't care what he told McAlpin, as long as he revenged himself on Dan by revenging himself on Harriette. Lee blamed Dan. I don't know why."

"It's Indian," Lewis Corey said. "If Lee had not sold the land to Dan, then Dan could not have torn up the land. Lee brought shame on himself. Blamed it on Dan."

"Makes no sense," Blaine said. "Anyway, what we forgot was that Lee never did a day's work for pay in his life. His work was to walk that mountain. He did not know enough to invest. He just lived off of capital."

"Alan tell him that," Johnny said. "Sure, Alan tell him that."

"So Alan used Dan," Blaine said. "He swears that he had no notion of Dan's motives in connection with the land. Swears it. I almost believe him."

"Why did he try to get me to sell the land?" She wanted to cry at the waste, the motives, the awful misunderstandings.

"He gets a little credit for that," Blaine told her. "He did it to protect you. Alan is absolutely convinced that the land is cursed."

It was terrible. Nothing that Alan did would have changed what her father did. Her father would have found some way. At the same time Alan had deliberately used her father to further his revenge. She found that she was weeping. Not for her father. For Alan. "He has helped men coming back from war," she said. "He has done that."

Silence. The men did not judge her. They were waiting for her to think it through. She looked at Blaine. "Of course," she said, "other men have done that, haven't they? And they didn't hurt anybody doing it."

Blaine seemed shy, and that was a silly way for him to seem. "Lots of people have helped. Lots." He turned to Lewis Corey, and was deferential. "As for Dan. I trust you, Lewis. Who killed Dan Johnson?"

Lewis Corey answered easily. "Two men living in the old ways. Old people call them Nunnehi. To some people they are a myth. To me they have ceased to be a myth. For your purposes, two men living in the old ways. You will never find them."

"I don't even pretend to understand that."

"Two men living in the old ways," Tom Corey said. "We all understand that. *You* understand that."

"I'm not sure I do," Blaine said, "but I'm sure you're not lying. I just never believed anything about old ways."

"I think you may believe them, Sheriff." Warwick's voice carried the authority of his years. "Those mountains are vast. I venture that there are still places in those mountains where no white foot has ever stepped." His voice was friendly, even sympathetic. "Which is why you will never find them, no matter how good your equipment and intent."

"In a way it's a relief. I'm closing my books on it." Blaine turned to Johnny. "McAlpin's cows are still in the pasture. McAlpin has a date with a judge when he finally gets out of hospital. I'll tack anything on him that will stick."

Harriette was shocked. It was incredible. Blaine had been talking about life and death. He had been talking about motives and revenge.

He showed sympathy. He showed sorrow for the wasting of lives. Now he talked about five sick cows and his own revenge on a petty little man.

"I'll take the stock," Tom Corey said. "Feed them up. Charge him for feed when he gets well."

"Blaine," said Johnny, "what in the world you thinkin' about? That man never gonna do nothing again. Man, half his head is busted."

"It's not the way it works," Blaine said. "If he doesn't get the word he may burn a barn next time." He looked at Harriette, at her disbelief. "There is law and there is law. I'll let Mr. Warwick explain the laws of God. Maybe he will also explain that without the laws of men we have no civilization."

She watched him and her disbelief changed to belief. He was sincere. In some white way he did what he knew was right. For Blaine there was no luminous world, and she supposed there was no magic. She reminded herself that he had showed compassion. She reminded herself how he spent his life. He probably could not help being the way he was.

"You went to a lot of trouble," she said. "Sheriff Blaine, I've been caught up in this. I almost forgot to thank you."

Chapter 36

THE end, it is written, is in the beginning. Maybe that is true. Or maybe, as Warwick knew, there is no beginning or end. Or maybe things just start up and stop, start up and stop.

Anyway, when Blaine departed, and after Warwick returned to Winston-Salem, the next of many winters arrived. When she visited the mountain, or Tom Corey visited, they walked on a carpet of wet and skeletal leaves. Streams rose with light rains, then dwindled, then rose again.

In the chill nights sound seemed like crystal, and moisture settled to film the roof of Molla's cabin. Moisture pocketed in the hands of leaves; a preparation for morning that would be a burst of white, a cloud of heavy frost lying over the retiring forest.

Silence seemed an articulation of cold. To the trained ear of dwellers in cities the silence would be vast and horrifying, for to dwellers in cities there is no experience and no time of day that lacks sounds the trained ear discards. It is not that way in the forest.

At times there is no sound. The city dweller will not understand the responsibility of that. The politician does not know of it, and it would terrify the general. The artist with her paint, the writer's words, the black-laughing, thick-lipped man with his horn will search gravely; and in the silences between words and notes and lines there will be sounds to surround the responsibility of silence; even that final silence of death with its death song, strokes to be blanked by the practiced ears of dwellers in cities.

I tell of the sleep of the flowers
I live as a flower
I dream as a flower

I depart as a flower
Unremembered but as a flower
It is good that I have been here

As white frost forms on the grass, life is slain under the indifference of cold. The uneaten moth completes his cycle. The beetle tumbles in his hard shell. A death song sounds on the low wind that searches the grasses, that pushes a fist of cold into the hollows of rocks and trees, that picks at the matting of leaves and the carpet of needles and twigs. Late seedlings sprouted with the autumn rains crumple in the disruption of their intricate chemistry. In the woodpile mice huddle. Squirrels and rabbits seek sanctuary. Bears hibernate and deer find lowland cover. The remaining birds with high body temperatures and frozen feet shun altitude, and domesticated farm cats, summer-running and now wild in the forest, snarl to corners of unfamiliar barns.

Molla died among the small sounds and communications of winter. Mice chewing on the frozen sap of the firewood, the subdued sound of the iced stream, the movement of melt on the roof. Harriette and Tom Corey found her when the fireplace had not yet given up its small knot poppings, its minuscule sizzlings of pitch. The fire was still strong, and fire is the first sacredness. Fire was the focal point that first brought our people to ceremony.

"An old woman," Tom said. "The ground is not frozen too deep."

It seemed wrong to Harriette, somehow. She stood beside Molla. Touched Molla's hand, looked at Tom.

"Take up the floor," she told him. "I am not being silly. We will bury her here, where she has lived."

"Then burn the cabin?" Tom's question was honest. "No one will live in this cabin if she is buried beneath the floor. No Cherokee will do that."

In the clearing, snow lay beneath the cold sun as a slate of thin, refreezing ice. At night, freeze crusted the light drifts. Where daytime melt ran from the roof, the cabin was circled by a thin line of ice ringing the hard crust of snow.

"Then the Cherokee will have to build a new cabin," Harriette said. "My grandmother is buried in a clearing. A small stone marks her grave. This cabin will be a marker." She knew she was not confused. She also knew she must seem dreamy or romantic.

"The dead are dead," she told Tom, "and the part that is worth something is gone. We mark the dead not to make them happy. We do it to tell ourselves that we understand respect. I don't want to be a woman who has no history. I don't want to be of a people who have no history."

It was more complicated than that and she knew it. At the same time it was the best she could do. She knew she would understand it later. For weeks now her mind had been working on levels she had never known before.

Even with a lot of help the burial took two days. Johnny and Tom dug the grave and put the cabin in order. Harriette dressed Molla in the old way, as Molla had been dressed when Warwick came to the clearing. Harriette went home, took the red blanket from her grandmother's bed, took the broken knife and the bird stone. Then Harriette went to see Lewis Corey. Lewis went calling on people. He returned with vulture feathers and a cap of birdskin. Harriette did not know if the burial went exactly according to old ways, but she knew that what she did was right. She robed Molla in the red blanket, stitched feathers to the blanket, and tucked knife and bird stone, pipe and tobacco into the folds. The men held the burial and replaced the boards of the floor. The mountain stood silent and the clearing was silent when they left.

In spring Lewis Corey closed his store and moved to the mountain. He was Inagehi for thirteen years, and I think—and I, Janet Scott, am plenty well not a romantic—maybe Susy came to him in some of those years. Maybe she only came in dreams. Lewis Corey did not build a new cabin. Lewis spoke mostly with silence. He spoke even less than Molla had spoken.

Warwick died in March, 1959. His was a quiet passage. A neighbor found him sitting in his favorite spot. He left a final book, a history of the Moravians in North Carolina. He left no journals. Fragments of his journals were found in the fireplace. Warwick was a private man, but I think maybe with those journals he was too private.

My father Frank Scott died of exposure in 1979. He went to the forest with his dogs. Snow had been followed by rain, and then by more snow. Then, when even more snow arrived, tracks began to cover the balds and clearings as animals were forced to forage. The dogs were trained to fox. They ranged a long way off. My father broke his ankle sliding from a rock fault. He didn't have any matches with him. By the time the dogs returned and a search party went out he was dead. He was getting to be a pretty old man.

Blaine died in 1963. He was seventy-one. He had a heart attack while pulling an injured boy from a wrecked car.

Judge Alan died in 1961. He also had a heart attack. Maybe he made peace with himself. His will gave his estate to a negro college, but his relatives contested the will. Lawyers ended up getting a lot of the money.

Lewis Corey died in April of 1971, but I was not around. I was on the west coast. Tom Corey did the burial by himself. Harriette stayed at Tom's house with Tom's wife, Mary Ford Corey, because by then the two women were like sisters. Lewis died the same way Molla died. He just stopped.

Tom Corey went a little crazy. He ripped up the floor, buried Lewis beside Molla, and then spent a week going back and forth to town. He carried lumber, tools, nails. He put in a new floor. He reshingled the roof. He spent another week repairing the chimney and recaulking the cabin. Then he disappeared into the springtime forest. Nobody knows what happened—or maybe Mary Ford Corey knows—but Tom does not talk very much these days. He came back out of the forest. He is happy. Mary is happy. He just doesn't talk too much.

Sandy Smith went back to Boston. She intended to change the world. She has not changed it, but she anyway changed part of it. It was mostly her help that sent David and me to college. For all these years she has used her money and time to work in the schools of Boston. They don't like integration in Boston. Sandy gets discouraged sometimes. I go down the trail and into town about once a month. Go to the post office. We still send letters to each other.

Harriette and Johnny had a little over thirteen and a half good years together, and they both learned about what is sacred. Custom and ritual grew between them. They had friendly names for each other, like children imagining in games. It's the small things Harriette remembers. The little courtesies. The light touch on her shoulder as he walked past when others were around. The old coffee pot in Johnny's bus, dented, and each dent polished. They lived in both places, at the bus and at the farm. Sometimes they lived apart for a few weeks.

Lots of people said they had fights like everybody who is married. It was the only way to account for them going off by themselves. That wasn't true. They knew about silence. About solitude.

The little things. Johnny's rosary in a buttoned shirt pocket, a small pressure against her sometimes when he put his arm around her. Grease like a cartoonist's paint on his face when he repaired his old truck. His face framed by new leaves as they rested in the forest. The way, as he got older, that he paced himself at work so she would not think he was so old.

The little things. Dusting the picture of the teaching Jesus because it might make Johnny happy. Music in the evenings. Because Harriette now played music only for Johnny and for Lewis Corey and the mountain. She taught off and on, but her music became as private as Warwick's journals. She remembers sunlight on Johnny's white hair or on his tanned hands as he cleared fencerows. She remembers a chipped cup, his favorite, a grin at his own smartness when he worked a complicated rigging to replace a main timber in the old barn. All the little things. A blue checkered tablecloth, a funny sketch of a rabbit dressed like a preacher, or Johnny's shadow crossing the door sill ahead of him and before the westering sun.

And then Johnny made a mistake. Or maybe because he was seventy-three he got forgetful. He was splitting wood in that last August, getting ahead of the winter woodpile. He got to dreaming, maybe. Anyway, he forgot to keep a clear area behind him. Balks of wood lay around. He stepped backward, tripped, hit his head against a log and was dead.

She went crazy for awhile. She thought sometimes that she would never not be crazy. Her world stopped. In the deep heat of August the valley seemed frozen.

Johnny was too well known, and he died in the wrong county. She had to buy his body to keep him from being buried in a cemetery. Tom Corey and Mary Ford helped her. She gave them a thousand dollars and they gave it to an undertaker. The undertaker buried an empty coffin. Tom and Mary buried Johnny on the mountain. They thought Harriette was not there. By then she had disappeared into the forest. She watched the burial from a cover of blackberry, and her arms and face ran red from unfelt cuts.

She remembers stumbling through ditches or across fields. She remembers finding herself in the middle of roads, and remembers the loud sounds of automobile horns. She remembers her grandmother's grave, remembers herself kneeling, cursing, praying. Her long hair tangled in brush. She chopped it short, hank at a time, chopping at it with a knife. She was forty-three. That was not old enough. She was not old enough to die.

Except during storms the August breeze was light and warm, but it felt like the winds of the arctic. She wandered, freezing, and sometimes she wandered naked so that the great cold would kill her and give her peace. On an evening when madness pressed her homeward she found herself kneeling beside the tree of her childhood. She felt the rough bark, felt some hopeful glimmer that the tree would say what she should do. The tree had its nature. It stood silent, almost alien. The tree gave no threat, but it gave no peace. Peace was on the mountain. The tree allowed her to understand that. She actually went to her house and actually slept. It was the next day when the stories began.

She wanted to die. So great was her madness that she went to the one place in the world where she was safe. She went to the ridge. Most of the stories are lies. All of the stories are wrong. Maybe some of the stories are made up for tourists.

August storms walked through the mountains. Whickers of heat lightning flashed pale on every horizon as great salvos of storm boomed through that August. Trees buckled before winds. Trees died with the howl of torn wood as bolt lightning walked here, there, set fires in the forest. Lightning walked across Thunder Ridge like the forked legs of ancient gods, and it was to Thunder Ridge she went. No one sane would go there. No one without great power could even get there. All Harriette remembers is that there was a trail.

She walked the bare rock ridge in the heart of storm, a bowed silhouette dwarfed in flashes of electricity. Wind poured around her, tore at her clothes, and so she threw them away. High-driving clouds of storm wrapped her away from the cold. The winds of storm, the clouds of storm were like the comforting warmth of Johnny's arms, and she walked, walked, her short hair pulled by wind.

Rain washed her, rain ran from the rock, and the rock turned black and glowing with rain. Mist boiled in slow-turning waves below the crest so that it seemed she walked among clouds. She moved through blue and white light, breathless in the stench of ozone; the heavy smell of burning ores; and the mountain made her safe. She was a small figure six thousand feet on the ridge of a mountain filled with iron, and as she walked lightning walked beside her, striking with velvet hands.

Cold rain warmed her like the memory of her grandmother's voice, her father's silence and respect; the lightning turned the water, the very rain, to steam. She does not know how long she was on the mountain, but when she came into the clearing she was sane. She sold everything except the land which held her grandmother's grave and the pasture where stands the tree. She moved to the cabin.

Davey and I went to college, and here my pain begins so I'll tell it quick. We went to a small college near home for the first year. Then Sandy Smith and Harriette gave us some money. We went to U. C. Berkeley. We had always talked about it, dreamed about it. Be careful what you dream.

Everybody was crazy then. Nobody was getting married, but Davey and I thought we should so we did. I studied anthropology and history. Davey started to study law. Davey did not become more white, he just became more Davey. He wanted power.

I thought maybe we should have a baby. Then I thought a baby would make me go home. You couldn't have a baby there. I studied hard. Davey studied hard. Everybody liked us because we were Indians, but after awhile they found out we were not peyote Indians and then they left us alone. Before they left us alone, though, we got sick enough of people liking us because we were Indians.

I loved Davey. When we loved each other I don't think anybody ever did better. Nothing about loving Davey or him loving me was ever wrong.

But Davey started fighting that white world, and he didn't even know what he was fighting. Crazy people were running around throwing rocks and having riots. Policemen were sneaking up on everybody. People were talking about how the war was all wrong.

Davey knew the war was wrong just like any war. But what did that have to do with anything? The question just drove him and drove him.

He was a door gunner on a helicopter in Viet Nam. The helicopter exploded and everybody burned up.

So I got my degree and then I got another. Then I worked at some jobs. Jobs were easy to get. I knew all the right things to say. I thought maybe I should get a man. The men were all like Blaine. Mostly they were not even that good. I worked in California; but I did not have the thunder, the streams, the forest.

So I came back here, and Harriette and I live in this clearing. In spring we plant corn and beans and squash. Sometimes I think of going away, but then I think that I already know the difference between a road and a trail. Then I think I don't want any more to do with roads. Sometimes I think there might still be a man besides Davey, but it better happen pretty quick or there won't be a baby.

And the streams still run. The mountains still walk away to the west, and they still seem to go on forever even if I know better. Down in Cherokee the people drive back and forth in new pickups. They sell things. They sell their history. They sell stories, sometimes, even when they do not believe the stories.

But Tom and Mary have a grandchild, and that child is happy visiting this place. Each August Harriette walks the ridge. Lightning still strikes about her like the soft hands of respect.

Maybe someday the mountain will claim her. If that happens I will be Inagehi. I will live plenty long. The grandchild is growing strong. Drums still pulse through the autumn mist. It all continues. It's okay.

About the Author

Jack Cady has worked as a truck driver, tree high-climber, and auctioneer. He has taught at the University of Washington, the University of Alaska, Knox College, Clarion College, and he is currently Adjunct Professor at Pacific Lutheran University. He has published nine books, and his stories have appeared in *Omni* and *The Atlantic Monthly*, among other magazines. He is a recent recipient of a major National Endowment for the Arts Fellowship, and in 1993 he won the World Fantasy Award for *The Sons Of Noah and Other Stories* (Broken Moon Press, 1992). He makes his home in Port Townsend, Washington.

Design by Laura Joyce Shaw.

Text set in Sabon with Albertus Light
by Blue Fescue Typography and Design,
Seattle, Washington.